Sheep's Eyes and Hogwash

Joe stood aside and as Polly passed, he peeped shyly at her like a member of an endangered species. *Oh God*, she thought, hastily stepping back into her Bond Street shoes, *Please don't let this rustic hunk get a crush on me. That would be altogether too tedious.*

'Well, I'm off, then,' she said, looking firmly at Mrs Swain and not her steaming son. 'Thanks ever so much for everything. See you tomorrow.'

And she stepped out into the night, which was, rather inconveniently, as black as the deepest pits of hell.

Sue Limb is the author of *Up the Garden Path*, *Love's Labours* and *Love Forty*. She is also the alter ego of Dulcie Domum, harrassed heroine of the *Guardian*'s 'Bad Housekeeping,' and scriptwriter of a number of successful TV and radio series including *Up the Garden Path* and the very popular *Wordsmiths at Gorsemere*. She lives in a remote part of rural Gloucestershire with her young daughter, some splendid hens and several free-range toads.

SUE LIMB

Sheep's Eyes

and Hogwash

Mandarin

A Mandarin Paperback
SHEEP'S EYES AND HOGWASH

First published in Great Britain 1992
by William Heinemann Ltd
This edition published 1993
by Mandarin Paperbacks
an imprint of Reed Consumer Books Ltd
Michelin House, 81 Fulham Road, London SW3 6RB
and Auckland, Melbourne, Singapore and Toronto

A CIP catalogue record for this title
is available from the British Library
ISBN 0 7493 1089 8

Printed and bound in Great Britain
by Cox & Wyman Ltd, Reading, Berkshire

For Eve

Chapter  One

'You're a high flyer, Polly. You've got class. And there's a nice little project taking shape that I think might be right up your street.' Tony Lewis paused in his pacing up and down the room, and beamed uncertainly at Polly. She waited, nodded, smiled to hide her irritation. Why did he always have to present work to her as if it were a frilly feminine treat, all done up with pink ribbon? What a pill this guy was.

Look at him now. Furtively fiddling with his underpants behind his back: hoicking them out of his majestic bum, then pretending afterwards he'd only been scratching the back of his thigh. He couldn't even keep his clothes in order. What must his kids be like? Polly hated to think.

Tony waddled back towards the window, fiddling with his armpits inside his jacket. He was like a sort of uncomfortable bald bear prowling about in a glass cage. Polly suppressed a shudder, and surreptitiously sniffed her left wrist, where there was quite a generous dash of Guerlain's *L'Heure Bleu*. She needed it. The smell of bear-grease on grey nylon shirt was beginning to permeate the room.

Poor Tony! His wife had left him five years ago and he had dripped dry ever since. But Polly tried not to feel sorry for him. She sensed, by the nervous way he played with his belt as he peered through the venetian blind and out across the city, that he was up to something. Even fat, bald, out-of-condition bears could be cunning.

'How does this grab you? A comedy series based on *Cold Comfort Farm*. And we want you to do the adaptation. Eight episodes. Nice little earner, eh Polly?'

He leaned forward on his desk. Both his plump wrists, with their deltas of veins, bulged towards her under the weight of him. His bright blue eyes, horribly vulnerable as usual, swivelled over her, magnetised for an instant by her gleaming knees, before dropping modestly onto the grey carpet tiles beneath her feet.

Polly recalled that awful moment in the lift last year, but hastily banished it from her mind.

Cold Comfort Farm. Nice little earner. Lots to recommend it. No need to invent characters: there they all were in the book, obligingly larger than life. No need to wrestle with storylines, local colour, texture: it had all been done for her, most skilfully, by Stella Gibbons, bless her. One of Polly's greatest literary heroines, as it happened. All Polly had to do was sit at her word processor and lift the dialogue gently out of the pool of prose with her skilful net. Add bits here and there, no doubt: round it out. But not all that much. TV was such a very considerate medium. A few words went a long way.

Polly cheered up enough to give Tony a genuinely appreciative smile. So what if he had groped her in the lift? The poor chap must be desperate. She hoped that somewhere in the world—probably somewhere in Manchester, perhaps here in the offices of Granada TV—there was an obliging little woman, a widow perhaps or a rapidly fading spinster, somebody fond of animals and the fresh air, who would in due course drop a pile of documents just as Tony was waddling past in the corridor.

In a split second Polly had envisaged an entire comedy series based around their courtship. The Wally and the Frump. The nation, itself composed largely of Wallies and Frumps, would be mesmerised by it. She'd have to change the setting, of course. Granada TV was much too glamorous. It'd have to be—oh, the head office of one of the big building societies. A Tale of Possession—and Repossession. The Frump would be one of those dim clerks who look for files all day, but within her she would have the spark of Venus. Wally would light her blue touch paper and stand well back.

Polly had an affection for the idea of the Frump transformed, as she was a secret Frump herself and knew how much careful rinsing and tinting and cutting and dieting and tailoring was necessary to make the transition from Frump to Vamp. Not that Polly desired to go so far, on a daily basis. She was content merely to look wonderful in a modest kind of way. Admiration was welcome in her chosen circle, but absolute abasement was not necessary. And it was not particularly male admiration she enjoyed. She dressed as much for other women and for herself. She did not like being naked.

So. The Wally and the Frump. That would do nicely. She liked to have her own projects, stacked up and waiting to land, like aircraft circling over Heathrow. Something for next year, after *Cold Comfort Farm*. Would it be too wicked to offer it as a project to Tony? People never recognised themselves, but still . . . perhaps it would be kinder to take it elsewhere: Marcia Harriss at Visions, for example. She was a bit of a frump. Or Fred at Three Five One.

But no, she was sure it would appeal to Tony. And he had an excellent script editor in Fiona Hirst. Polly loved to work with Fiona, who would certainly recognise Tony and think it a wizard wheeze to provide her poor perspiring boss with the good woman he needed—in fiction, at least.

'The thing is,' Tony said, slumping gratefully into his chair now the idea of *Cold Comfort Farm* was delivered and Polly had not frightened him with one of her frigid frowns, but instead encouraged him with a real smile, 'the thing is, Pol, it's got to be genuine. I mean, it mustn't be cardboard.

The sets mustn't look like a TV set of a farmhouse kitchen. It's got to be for real.'

'Not actually saturated with pigshit, though, one hopes?' enquired Polly with a distaste that was not entirely mock. Tony laughed uneasily.

'No, but, you know—genuine. In fact we were thinking about doing it all on film. No studios. All on location.'

'No studios?'

Polly tried to hide her dismay as the prospect of several delicious stays in five-star Manchester hotels vanished from her eager gaze. The mini-bar, the en suite bathroom with its huge snowy piles of towels . . . lazing in bed watching an in-house TV movie whilst an obliging girl from Room Service brought her her muesli and yoghurt. And then perhaps a morning in the Jacuzzi and a gentle swim before work started in earnest. Other people's work, that is. The actors, the technicians, the director. Her bit was over and she could lounge about and admire the production team doing their stuff. The studio VT recording sessions were the writer's little treat. She reckoned she'd earned them. How dared Tony even think of doing it all on film?

'You can't do it all on film, surely?'

'Well, apparently we can afford it. Amazingly enough. I think there's been some cock-up with the budgets, to tell you the truth. But anyway—while the going's good, let's do it! Now, what I'd like you to do is go away and find me the perfect farm.'

'Find you a farm?'

'Yeah. A proper working farm with animals and stuff. Not East Anglia, that's no good. All arable stuff there, prairies, you know. Devon or Somerset more like.'

'And you'd shoot it all on this farm?'

'Yes. So it's got to be bloody picturesque. And not too many fertiliser bags hanging about. Mustn't upset people.'

'But you'll never get a farmer to agree to all that.'

'Won't we? Wait till he sees his fee. Times couldn't be

worse for farmers, you know. I think he'll jump at it. If he's the right kind of farmer. And I know you'll find the right kind of farmer, Polly.'

'You want *me* to find this place?' Polly could barely speak with incredulity. She had got used to the idea of how and where she worked, and this was a complete outrage.

'Yeah. Well . . .' Tony undid his top button, pulled down his tie and massaged his thick neck. 'You go off and reread the book, right? Immerse yourself in it. You'll be the best person to suss it all out. And I think you should go down there for a while.'

'Go down . . . where?'

'Down on the farm. Live there for a few weeks. Work there. They all do B & B nowadays. Times are hard. They'll be thrilled. And so, as you write the scripts you can sort of plan them around the locations, see? It'll be great. A month in the country. Wish I could come with you.'

'Two months, more like. Do I get remission for good conduct?' Tony laughed. Polly got to her feet. The thought of Tony not coming with her was her only comfort. She had to get out now, though—to think. Her first reaction was to scream aloud, but that might not be the best plan in the long run. There was a lot of money involved. She mustn't do anything rash. She had to have time to think.

'Excuse me, Tony. I've got to go. It's Daniel's dress run now and I promised to drop in.'

'Fine. Fine. And get Monica to call me.'

'Sure.'

Monica was going to have something to say about this. Her clients tended to swan off to Venice or Barbados on writing jobs, sure. But not Pigswill-on-the-Mire.

Chapter  Two

Polly marched down to the studios, seething. How dare Tony do this to her? She was bursting to talk to Dan, but as usual he was on the phone in the little room across from the control box. She went into the control box where the director, Anna MacDermot, was wrestling with a technical problem. Polly installed herself at the back of the room, where there was a cosy dark little corner with a monitor and chairs for the producer, executive producer, producer's girlfriend, miscellaneous passers-by and droppers-in.

'There's that shadow again, Mark.' Anna was lamenting into her mike, whilst fathoms below, on the studio floor, the mighty Mark Graham, floor manager and company beefcake, wrestled with microphones and booms and God knows what.

Polly looked idly at the monitor. The actress Zara Prynne, who played the lead in the series—based on the hurly burly of life in a contract cleaning company—was sprawling on a sofa looking bored whilst around her the bums and stray disembodied shoulders of the technicians wrestled with the rogue shadow.

'Is that better? Is that better? Is that OK?' Mark's voice boomed anxiously from the speakers. He was always so anxious to please, Polly remembered . . . He spared no exertions, did Mark, to give a lady satisfaction.

'No,' sighed Anna. 'It's still there.'

Poor Mark was having a hard time pleasing Anna. Did

6

they, Polly wondered, ever . . . These speculations distracted her, but not for long. After she had decided there
was not the shadow of even half-remembered lust in Mark's
or Anna's voice, she returned to her private anguish. Two
months in the country! *What, exiled, my good lord?*

'I want to start this run at four thirty,' Anna was saying.
'Time's getting on. For God's sake—can't we put in an
extra light or something?'

Polly got up and went out. She had sat through enough
dress runs of *Clean and Decent*. This one was obviously
going to be a dog, with Anna suffering from pre-menstrual
tension and the persistent shadow hanging over them, like
the Angel of Death. For once she didn't want to relax and
be amused, even though it was a good show and written
by that Scots bloke whose name she could never quite
remember. He was a riot, but what the hell was his name?
Macsomething. MucSpreader came into Polly's mind, like a
malicious bottle-top thrown by a poltergeist.

Thanks very much, brain, she observed tartly, making for
Dan's little cubby hole with his desk and telephone. *No
more country jokes if you don't mind. You're going to hate it there
too, you know: even more than the other bits of us. You'll probably
atrophy. Hah! Serve you right.*

Dan was still on the phone. He looked up and held out
his arm towards her. She went up and stood by him. He
picked up a pencil and wrote *It's that asshole Goldberg in New
York again*. Polly sighed. She often wished Dan would not
use vile American slang to underline his sophistication.

Dan's hand dropped the pencil and crept up her skirt,
satisfied itself that she was wearing stockings, and then
busied itself amongst the black intricacies of her camiknickers. Polly wasn't really in the mood for this sort of thing.

'Yeah . . . Yeah . . . Well, I'm afraid my hands are tied.'
Sometimes, thought Polly, I wish they were.

She wrote, *I am pissed off—not with you! So I'm going back
to the hotel. Can't face sitting through the show tonight. Hope it*

goes well. See you later. Dan looked up at her with a puzzled expression.

'No . . . no . . . well, I'm really sorry, Paul, but until they take the decision I can't do a thing . . .'

Polly disentangled herself from his hand, bent and kissed him on his rather fine nose, and was gone.

It was raining outside, and getting dark. In her bottled-up rage Polly forgot to call a taxi from reception, but just flung out of the building, down the steps and up the road towards the city centre. The rain, gentle at first, intensified once she was was outside the hospital. Her elegant French mac wasn't designed to keep actual rain out, of course. Dammit, not a taxi in sight.

A tall figure lurched out of the drizzling dark: bearded, his face scarred and spotty, his teeth black, his hair lank and greasy. He smelt of spirits and the damp trampy stink of clothes that have never been washed.

'Hey, love!' He barred her way, swaying slightly. 'Got any change?'

'No I bloody well haven't!' snapped Polly, and dodged sideways to escape him.

'Fockin' slag!' he roared, behind her, as she sped away. What the hell was happening to Manchester? And it was even worse in London. The police themselves had warned that they were losing control of the streets. Polly felt a sudden surge of panic. She glanced behind her—the beggar was leaning against the wall of the skin hospital, apparently having a coughing fit. She could have given him 50p. Why not? By his standards, she was rich. A rich bitch. Polly's heart smote her for her lack of generosity.

She walked on, though, fast. She mustn't have one of her attacks. Her heart was beginning to thunder. Above her the buildings loomed, impossibly tall and dark. Cars' headlamps dazzled in the winter twilight. A passing truck swished through a puddle and hurled a tidal wave of water

8

at her, wetting her through to the silk camiknickers. Any minute now she would scream, or be sick, or both.

Ah! God sent a taxi. Just at the very minute she needed it. Suddenly safe and snug, she leaned back and breathed deeply. She'd be all right now. She closed her eyes until she felt the cab arrive at the hotel, then she ransacked her bag, gave the driver a large tip to compensate for her earlier meanness, and passed, with a silent groan of relief, through the glass doors of the Queen's Hotel.

Ah! Soft carpets, low lights, flowers everywhere, discreet music—it was a bit like a church. She collected her key and summoned the lift. Later perhaps she'd go down and have a sauna and a Jacuzzi in the spa. Right now she wanted solitude. The lift surged upwards to the twelfth floor like a spaceship conveying her to another planet.

And it was like another planet, after life on the streets. Quiet, luxurious, the crisp white sheets turned back, the windows giving a stunning view of Manchester, glittering in the dark, the traffic far below translated into trickling jewellery, the city's life-systems offering only a faint and discreet cosmic hum. It was grand, it was handsome, it soothed her.

She bathed, dozed, ordered Duck and Salad from room service, and ate it sprawled on her bed in her oyster satin dressing-gown, watching a naughty movie called *Night Romps in Stockholm*. Polly had a friend who had lived in Stockholm for a while, and had informed her that there was very little in the way of Night Romps there, and in fact everyone went home early, ate herring and cream cakes and went to bed at about nine thirty in order to able to get up at five the next day.

The screen suggested otherwise. A bevy of blonde beauties turned their terrible tits relentlessly on a couple of hapless blokes who had apparently just turned up for a bit of innocent rewiring. *Göran and Bengt were certainly in for a shock*, droned the laborious subtitles. Polly wondered, as

9

she stuffed down her duck, how many tired businessmen in other rooms in the hotel were watching the same movie. No wonder they were tired. The relentless writhing on the screen was enough to exhaust anybody. It was worse than Polly's dim memories of house hockey.

Even now Bengt's head had disappeared, Polly feared for ever, and she could not for the life of her work out how many girls were feasting off him at once. It reminded her of a wildlife film she had seen once of a dying wildebeest being devoured by hyenas. Polly got the giggles and nearly choked. She ran into the bathroom and sipped a glass of water in an attempt to fend off death for another few minutes.

WRITER CHOKES ON DUCK WHILE WATCHING PORNO MOVIE. FOWL PLAY NOT SUSPECTED. Polly cringed at the thought of dying in a way that would embarrass her parents—or offer opportunities for puns. Grief is bad enough without burdening them with humiliation as well. She changed channels to watch the news, but it was the usual murder, pollution and starvation, with only the statutory brief glimpse of the Princess of Wales at the end to save the population from utter despair.

Just as Polly was enduring the weather forecast (Cold, and rain, but colder and rainier later) Dan burst in, threw his briefcase aside and flung himself on the bed beside her.

'Now what's your problem, darling?'

Polly told him.

Daniel listened. He was a good listener. He picked at the last of the duck salad, his head cocked on one side, and waited until Polly had blown herself out, like a storm. Then he turned and gave her a compassionate little grin.

'It might not be so bad,' he whispered playfully. 'It might be quite nice. Real ale. Trees and stuff. Real people.'

'Listen, I won't have any of that real people crap!' cried Polly, finding new reserves of outrage. 'People who live in cities are just as bloody real. For goodness sake!—there aren't any cinemas in the country! Let alone theatres. Let alone restaurants. In some villages there probably isn't even a shop. Imagine having to drive six miles just because you've run out of Camembert.'

'Camembert? Do they have Camembert in the country?' Daniel was teasing her now. But Polly wasn't in the mood.

'That's right! They probably don't! It's probably Cheddar or nothing, mate. And that's another thing—suppose I'm stuck in some Godawful farm at the Back of Beyond, having bed and breakfast. That'll mean loads of greasy fried stuff, won't it? Where am I going to get some decent food? Where am I going to go for lunch and supper and everything?'

'I'll send you food parcels,' promised Dan. 'All your favourite little urban delicacies. You can curl up in your room and nibble at Halva and Pesto and Lollo Rosso and all the other things the yokels won't have heard of.'

'But it's not funny, Daniel!' Polly closed her eyes in horror. 'Imagine the dullness, the dreadful dullness of it. Nothing going on at night except horrible owls letting out these blood-curdling shrieks. Nowhere to go. No one to talk to. Nothing ever happens in the country, does it? All they do is bottle bloody plums and arrange jumble sales.'

She leaned back with a deep groan, and her nightdress parted with the kind of silken style that would be wasted on a country swain. A hedger and ditcher would have been left gawping, his hedging tool hanging limp in his nerveless hand. Dan, however, moved expertly into gear. He hung above her navel like a buzzard surveying its favourite landscape.

'And I bet it'll be freezing!' Polly went on. 'I bet there are lots of places that don't even have central heating. I'm not going back to bloody electric fires at my age, Daniel. I tell you. And walking down a corridor to share a bathroom with strangers? No thanks! And I bet the bathroom floor will have bloody vinyl on it and I bet there'll be icicles hanging from the ceiling. I'm just not going to bloody do it.

11

If Tony thinks he can make me do it, he's got another think coming. What a cheek! It was spite, that's what it was. I'm going to see him tomorrow and tell him where he can stuff his *Cold Comfort Farm*.'

'Think of the money,' said Dan softly, and slid his tongue over her hills, and thickets, her banks and braes. Polly was silenced.

Afterwards she gave a great sigh, turned her head and admired the stunning panorama of Manchester by night. There was no doubt, Daniel knew how to present an argument.

'That's another thing about the country, though,' she murmured, reluctant to abandon her outrage altogether, as there was something perversely delicious about it. 'Nobody ever has sex in the country. Except sheep. And they only have it once a year. And then only for a split second.'

But Daniel was asleep.

Chapter  Three

'It's very good of you to make time to see me,' said Lynn Smythe, unpacking her reporter's notebook. 'I know you must be very busy.'

'It's all right,' said Polly, making coffee. 'You just caught me at the right moment actually. I'm going to be out of London for the next few weeks.'

'Oh really? Work or holiday?'

'Oh, work. We're planning a TV series out of *Cold Comfort Farm*. I'm going to install myself in the depths of the country and absorb a bit of rural background.'

'Oh, how nice.'

'Yes.'

Lynn Smythe looked as if she would be at home in the country. Her legs, for example, were spectacularly hairy—in Polly's view, long overdue for harvesting. Lynn produced a banana out of her big leather bag, which lay slumped and scuffed at her feet like an old dosser.

'Do you mind if I eat bananas? Only I'm pregnant and I get these desperate attacks of hunger and if I don't eat, I faint.'

'Please!' cried Polly, desperate that Lynn should not keel over in mid-interview, all pregnant and hairy with her half-dead bag. 'Are you feeling OK?'

Polly had not had any first-hand experience of pregnancy. Most of her friends had not got around to it yet, and she had avoided too much contact with those who had.

'Oh yes. I feel wonderful.' Lynn smiled in a complacent way Polly found rather irritating. 'It's just this terrible hunger. I feel I've been taken over, sort of, by a kind of invisible monster. I could eat anything.'

She looked around Polly's flat, paying particular attention to the chocolate-brown carpet. Perhaps any minute she was going to fall to her knees and start grazing. Polly hoped not. None of her visitors had ever eaten her carpet before and she was grateful for their restraint.

'Well,' she brought the coffee and set it on the low glass table, which pleased her as usual by its immaculate shine, and the way it reflected the vase of narcissi placed on it, 'as far as I'm concerned, you can munch away all morning. White or black?'

Once coffee was served, and Lynn had demolished her first banana, she wiped her hands—on her dress, Polly noticed, but it was one of those multicoloured ethnic jobs, designed to hide stains and rumples. The interviewer cleared her throat.

'Well, it's part of a series about working women in their thirties. We thought our readers would be interested in you because of your TV series, er, *Skyscrapers*, wasn't it? I loved it.'

'Thank you,' said Polly with a modest smile. 'I'm glad.'

'Are you enjoying your thirties?'

The question sounded inane, but Polly willingly engaged with it. Poor Lynn was only doing her job. Polly had done a bit of interviewing people herself, years ago, and had found it extraordinarily difficult. She never dared to ask the dangerous questions, so her efforts had always been terribly dull. She had escaped with relief to the world of fiction, where one could bestow the most ghastly personal problems upon one's characters without a moment's hesitation. The fiction writer could also tip-toe into their bathrooms and bedrooms undetected and observe their most private rituals with a pitiless eye. Above all, there was no need to be polite.

Whereas in real life, politeness was one of the cornerstones of Polly's life. She was eager now to give polite answers to polite questions, to do her best without giving anything away.

'Yes. I am enjoying my thirties. Tremendously.' Polly lay back on the sofa and crossed her smooth successful legs. 'I think it's to do with not being desperate about things any more. When I was in my twenties, I didn't know what sort of work I wanted to do, where I wanted to be—who I wanted to be. I was lost. But now . . . it all seems much clearer.'

'So you are where you want to be?'

Wait a minute. Was Lynn Smythe one of those subversive interviewers? Polly never trusted pregnant women. They looked so helpless and fecund: she must remember they could also be cunning. Now, mustn't be tricked into sounding complacent.

'I'm not so much where I want to be exactly, but I am lucky enough to be doing work I like, for a start.'

There, thought Polly, make that into a startling zippy quote if you can, you poor sod. Then her kind heart provoked her into a little helpfulness.

'I love writing for TV. The actors are so funny, and talented: if what you've written is a bit mediocre, a brilliant actor can transform it into something amazing. And the make-up girls are a great laugh. Gossip in the Granada canteen . . . I love all that. A writer's life can be a lonely one, you know.'

'And you live alone,' pondered Lynn, looking round the flat for tell-tale signs of male company. As if an inconvenient lover might have been crammed into a cupboard somewhere, to be taken out and shaken into shape again if the need arose.

'Yes,' said Polly firmly. 'I like living alone. You can spoil yourself a bit. Have things exactly the way you like them. I'm a bit particular, I suppose: too particular, probably. I couldn't bear a man leaving his cheesy socks all over the bedroom floor. It's good to come home here at the end of the day, make myself a cup of tea, put my feet up, listen to people walking past in the street, their voices . . . not have to talk to anyone. And the order of it all: it's soothing.'

Lynn looked around again.

'You're very tidy,' she sighed. 'I'm hopelessly untidy, I'm afraid.'

Polly smiled.

'It takes all sorts.'

Lynn had indeed made a mess of her little corner of Polly's flat, already, with her dosser bag and her wilderness legs and her banana skin sprawled on the glass table, going slightly brown at the edges and with sticky strands hanging off it.

'But you have got . . . a relationship, haven't you?'

'Oh yes.' Polly paused for a moment. She had a horror of confessional interviews, of intrusions into what should be private. But she had agreed to this interview, after all. It was up to her to keep it tidy. 'I've had a boyfriend, let's call him that, stupid word for somebody my age, but never mind. We've been together for about four years now.'

'It's Dan Birnbaum, isn't it? The independent producer? I read about it somewhere.'

'Yes.'

'But you've never lived together?'

'No. He lives just down the road. In Belsize Park. We're almost neighbours. It's a good arrangement. Convenient. We go on holidays together, of course. Things like that. But because we each have our own place, we don't get on each other's nerves, you know. We can each retreat to our private territory. Have some time to ourselves.'

'And this is a good relationship? Easier now because you're in your thirties?'

'Oh yes. When I was in my twenties I specialised in unrequited love. Ate my heart out for people who were impossibly out of reach. This is much better. I feel more in control.'

'You like to be in control?'

Polly hesitated.

'Of my emotions, yes. I can't stand all those passions. Jealousy and all that. Awful, awful. They eat you alive.'

Lynn's eyes lit up.

'So you're not jealous?'

'No. For goodness' sake, I mean—Dan travels a lot, he goes to New York, he goes to San Francisco, there's no use my sitting at home wringing my hands and wondering who he's having supper with and tormenting myself with horrible fantasies. I don't own him.'

'But isn't this the era of monogamy? Are you saying you don't mind if he has affairs on the side? I mean, love's a dangerous game, these days, surely?'

'I'm monogamous,' said Polly firmly. 'I just like things to be quiet and cool and civilised. And at the moment, thank goodness, they are.' She recrossed her legs, to hint that a change of subject was due. But Lynn Smythe wilfully ignored the body language for an impolite split second.

'You're not madly in love, then?'

'No, thank God. Who wants to be mad? I had enough of that in my twenties. Staying by the phone all night in case some arrogant bastard might ring me up. And they never did, of course.'

'So you were badly hurt in your twenties and you've decided to switch off and stay cool in your thirties to guard against getting hurt?'

'Not at all. I don't mind getting hurt. That's what life's about, after all. We never learn except by getting hurt.' Polly hoped Lynn would accept this at face value, though she herself suspected that it was poor camouflage for a whacking lie. *I don't mind getting hurt?* She hoped the gods hadn't heard that one, or they'd be sharpening their thunderbolts like nobody's business.

'Why do you live in Hampstead?'

Polly's hackles rose.

'Where do *you* live?' she retorted sharply.

'Hackney.'

'Well, why do you live there?'

'Because it's cheap.'

'Well . . .' Polly pondered. 'I came here by accident, really. This flat came on the market at the right moment. It was near Dan. And I don't care what anyone says, I like Hampstead.'

'What do you like about it?'

'You can still sense the original village, you know . . . those twisty little streets, the hill, the Georgian houses, they're so pretty . . . and it's saturated with history, of course, poor old Keats just down the road, madly in love with the girl next door, madly in love and dying . . .' Polly paused, and Lynn Smythe waited, her pencil poised above her shorthand pad. She was turning it all into Sanskrit. Polly wondered what was the shorthand for *madly in love and dying*.

'I love the shops, too, even the preposterous little expensive ones where they sell hand-painted shirts that cost a fortune—I wouldn't ever buy any, of course, couldn't afford it, and wouldn't want to if I could. I just like looking in the windows. And the bookshops, and the print shops, and the smell of croissants coming out of the coffee shops, and the hum of traffic, and people milling about and shouting to each other across the street, and that lovely little cinema, and the sense of things happening, of being part of a city but not in the monstrous centre of it, but high up and sort of floating above it, and the lovely Heath . . . walking there on a Sunday morning, and hearing the faint sound of church bells, and people flying kites . . . I'm not being very coherent, I'm sorry.'

'No, no,' said Lynn Smythe, scribbling frantically, 'that was all wonderful . . . You've obviously worked out what you need in life. And what you like. And you've got it. I envy you.' She shut her notebook with a snap.

'Yes,' murmured Polly, rather touched by the music of her own contentment as it had poured out of her, 'I'm very lucky really, I suppose.'

'You know where you're going, then?'

'Oh no,' Polly paused. 'I don't think anybody knows that, do they?'

This was quite a satisfying last thought. It added a dash of bitter to what might otherwise have been too sweet. The fiction writer in her was pleased with the note of modesty and uncertainty with which she had completed her self-portrait. She smiled uncertainly at Lynn. She could not help hoping that this strange subversive hairy-legged woman liked her.

'I'm really sorry,' said Lynn, suddenly awkward and stumbling, 'only I think I'm going to be sick.'

Chapter  Four

After Lynn Smythe's metabolism had stabilised, Polly declared she must be leaving.

'I've got an appointment in town—I'm awfully sorry.'

'No, that's fine—you'd given me masses in any case.' They travelled down on the Northern Line together.

'Travelling by tube is one of the worst things about London,' sighed Lynn Smythe, as they rocketed and swayed southwards, crammed together, standing up because the seats were all occupied, mostly by sturdy young men. 'I didn't really register how awful it was till I got pregnant.'

'Shall I ask one of them to give you his seat?' asked Polly. 'You look a bit pale.'

'No, no. Please don't. I'm all right. My fault for getting pregnant.' She smiled grimly. 'Are you thinking of having children?'

'To be honest,' said Polly, 'that's the last thing I'm thinking of. I've never felt the slightest urge. I know people sometimes do suddenly go all broody in their mid-thirties, but it hasn't happened to me.'

'What about Daniel? Does he feel the same?'

'Oh well, it's different for men, isn't it? He could marry some fertile young thing in twenty-five years' time and have kids. But they just wouldn't fit into the lifestyle we've developed for ourselves at the moment. And frankly, I enjoy my freedom too much to want to chuck it away.'

'What's the meeting you're going to today?'

'Oh, just a general chat with the girl who's going to be my editor for this new series.'

'Do you like working with women?'

'Are you still interviewing me?' Polly smiled.

'People often do say the most revealing things after I've put my notebook away or switched off the cassette recorder.'

'Have I said anything revealing yet?'

'No.' Lynn Smythe grinned ruefully. 'In fact, you haven't said anything revealing at all.'

Polly felt pleased.

'I'm so sorry. That's rotten for you, isn't it. I used to interview people and I know how hard it is.'

'Oh, I'll cobble something together. But do you? Like working with women?'

'Oh, very much.'

'Would you call yourself a feminist, then?'

'Not really—I mean, it's not the chief focus of my work or anything. But men certainly suppressed women for years in a state of domestic slavery. And it was all cleverly justified with all those myths.'

'What myths?'

'Fairy stories,' said Polly. 'Romantic love. *He swept her into his manly arms and carried her off into the sunset.* Bullshit! It never said anything about the piles of washing up that were waiting for her when the sun came up again.'

Lynn Smythe smiled.

A small girl got onto the train, clutching her mother's hand. The train lurched off: the child stumbled: a young woman wearing hornrimmed glasses got up and offered the grateful mother a seat.

'Mummy?' said the child.

'What, love?'

'What does "smouldering" mean?'

'It means sort of on fire, but only gently. Not crackling flames and stuff. Just a little bit of smoke, and a gentle glow.' Polly admired the patience of the educated mother, and sighed with relief that she would never have to define 'smouldering' for the very young.

'Mummy . . . in the song it says John Brown's body lies a smouldering in the grave. So does that mean Grandma's on fire?'

'No, love,' the woman dropped her voice. 'It's mouldering, not smouldering.'

'What does mouldering mean, then?'

'It just means lying quietly and sort of turning into earth. But what's happening to Grandma's body doesn't matter. It's what's happened to her soul that matters.'

'Her spirit!' cried the child with animation. 'In heaven! With Jesus!'

Her mother hastily got out a book decorated with baroque drawings of witches, and began to read, whispering into her daughter's ear.

'More fairy tales,' sighed Polly quietly. 'And nothing but fairy tales.'

'You wouldn't tell a child that sort of thing, then?'

'What I remember about all that,' said Polly, 'was how betrayed I felt when I grew up and found out it was a pack of lies. No Santa, no Holy Ghost, no Tooth Fairy. I thought, what on earth were the grown ups playing at? We've invented a sort of bogus world for children to live in. I'd like to see a child that was brought up with lots of love, but was told the truth about things, from the start.'

'No comforting little myths?'

'Well, what good do they do?' asked Polly. 'In the end. Look, I'm sorry, but I've got to change at King's Cross. Thanks for a painless interview.'

'Thank you. It's been very interesting.'

'Good luck with your . . .' Polly's eyes dropped to Lynn Smythe's burgeoning belly, 'your little stranger. I hope you get what you want.'

'Oh, I don't want anything special,' said Lynn Smythe.

'I'll just wait and see what Fate sends me.' The sliding doors closed across her, and Polly set off, deliciously alone at last, for Covent Garden.

The meeting with Fiona Hirst was at The Sanctuary, where Polly was a member. They often met there to swim, sauna, and offer themselves up to the tickling bubbles of the Jacuzzi and occasionally the pummelling of the masseuses. At the same time they discussed work, if absolutely necessary. As Polly arrived, Fiona was walking up Floral Street from the other direction and they met by the door. Polly was struck, as usual, by a twinge of envy at Fiona's long curling red hair, statuesque beauty, and freckles. And once they were inside, and naked, showering, she admired Fiona's long white legs and abundant bosom.

'You look marvellous, as usual, you beast,' she grinned. Fiona smiled primly. She was a self-contained Scottish girl whose only apparent vice was swimming.

They plunged together into the pool and floated on their backs, looking up at the tropical tangle of hanging plants and the scuds of reflected light dancing on the white pillars.

'Isn't this bliss?' murmured Polly. 'I had this woman interviewing me all morning. I hate talking about myself.'

'I expect you were convincing, though.'

'Well . . . I almost convinced myself!' laughed Polly.

'I'm glad I'm not the sort of person who gets interviewed. I'd just clam up, you know.'

Fiona set off on several lengths of the little pool, which she completed with a lazy, effortless crawl. Polly sculled about a bit with a timid breast stroke. They discussed Polly's new project.

'A month in the country! Polly! You lucky thing!'

'At this time of year? You've got to be kidding. I'm dreading it. This place is the nearest I want to get to nature.' Polly cast an affectionate glance around at the palms and parrots and tropical fish.

'But this place is just a magnificent bathroom really, you know. Nothing to do with nature, Polly.'

'I know. Well, precisely.'

'Will Dan go down there with you? You could have a little rustic love nest. Roses round the door.'

'What, in February? You're joking. Anyway, he's got to go to New York, I think. Or San Francisco. I lose track of it all.'

'I couldn't bear that, you know.' Fiona was married to a very obedient and well-trained publisher called Ian who was never even late home from the office without getting written permission from her first. 'I think it's wonderful the way you and Daniel manage to keep a relationship going when he travels such a lot. It must be awful.'

'Oh, no, it's rather nice,' smiled Polly. 'I'd hate it if he was in my hair all the time.'

'You're still happy together, then?'

'Oh, he's not a bad old stick. Come on, let's have some salad. I'm starving.'

They settled themselves at the salad bar, wrapped in snowy towels and feeling pampered.

'The great thing about Daniel, you see,' Polly continued with her thought, 'is that he doesn't expect me to cook for him or darn his socks or anything. He's a New Man.'

'It's easy to be a New Man in London,' Fiona pointed out. 'With all these take-aways and dry cleaner's. I don't suppose you'll find any New Men in darkest Somerset or Devon or wherever you go.'

'God knows what I'll find down there,' Polly shuddered. 'Stone Age man, I should think. *OO-ar on yer back, wench!'*

'Well, at least it'll make you appreciate Dan even more,' said Fiona. 'You'll probably come hurtling back and frog-march him to the altar before he can escape. You'll say, "Make an honest woman of me, darling! I see it all now: you're the best thing I ever had and we must never leave Hampstead again."'

'But no bloody darning, or ironing, or mending, thank you very much!' laughed Polly. 'With my body I thee worship, but keep your mitts off my worldly goods.'

'Especially my new CD player,' agreed Fiona.

'I could never promise to care for someone in sickness and in health, though,' said Polly. 'I mean, what if he went senile? He wouldn't even know it was you, then. I heard this heart-rending story the other day about a woman whose husband went senile in his forties and she's looked after him ever since—twenty years, feeding him and wiping his bum and everything, and every morning he greets her in the same way: "Who the hell are you? Why must they send me these new people all the time? What's happened to what's her name?" God, it makes me shudder to think about it. I couldn't nurse anyone, ever.'

'But she's looked after him for twenty years? Och, I think that's inspiring,' murmured Fiona, sipping her mango juice with a particularly Calvinist sense of forbidden fruit. 'That's marvellous, really.'

'It's not marvellous, it's disgraceful,' said Polly severely. 'The state should look after people like that. Just think— she's wasted the last twenty years of her life.'

'Perhaps she enjoys it in a weird sort of way,' pondered Fiona.

'Well, I'm not having any of it,' said Polly firmly. 'If Daniel so much as gets a verruca, he's out on his ear.'

Their salads arrived, and Polly and Fiona settled to girl talk: an analysis of recent events in Eastern Europe, a pitiless anatomising of the Government's failures here at home, and the Italian Foreign Minister's desperate need for a haircut. Polly revelled in it. This was not the sort of conversation she'd be able to indulge in in the country, she was sure. She tried not to think about what that might be like, but bottled plums loomed horribly in the back of her mind. Polly could not bear the thought of small-town small talk. To keep her sane she needed conversation that was witty, crisp and above all, urbane. She drank deep of it, now, like a camel who knows she is about to set forth across an endless desert.

Chapter  Five

'Polly, love! Hello! You look *marvellous!*'

Mum's arms were open, as usual, her brown eyes shining and every white curl was in place. She was beautifully dressed in grey silk, and smelling of English Lavender. The whole house smelt of lavender. Mrs Partridge didn't just anoint herself with it. She rubbed it in the furniture, the bits of parquet floor . . . even the window frames. She'd have massaged it into her husband's knees if he'd stayed still for long enough.

'Hello, Mum! Hi, Dad!'

Her mother got a fervent hug but Dad preferred a discreet peck. Polly had learned to read the signs. Her dad wouldn't know what to do with a fervent hug. Even the discreet peck was something he was keen to put behind him as soon as possible. A moment of danger, of exposure. You shouldn't have too much of that sort of thing in Finchley.

'Why did it take you so long to unlock the door? What were you up to?'

'Daddy's new bolts.' Mum ignored Polly's coarse innuendo and directed her daughter's attention to the bottom of the door.

Her dad dropped to his knees to worship at the shrine of high-tech security. His hands, getting a bit stiff nowadays, were still strong. He wriggled the bolt to and fro.

'Look at that, Polly,' he beamed, admiring the sturdy

whoosh and thump of it. 'You wouldn't get through that with a Chieftain Tank.'

'Polly doesn't want to be bothered with your blasted locks, Gordon! Come into the sitting-room, dear.' Polly hesitated by the door for a few seconds. Putting down men in general was a sport she deeply enjoyed, but not her dear old dad. She smiled, bent down, gave the bolt an admiring little pat, and whispered, 'I like it. I like it. British workmanship.'

'It's German, actually,' admitted her Dad with a hint of sadness, clambering laboriously to his feet. He had to haul himself up holding onto the banisters. Polly walked quickly into the sitting-room but even so she could not completely banish the faint crack of ancestral sinew behind her.

'Oh Mum—what beautiful flowers!'

'Aren't they! Silk, you know, Polly.' Her mother caressed the heavy blooms. *Cream damask roses*, you would have thought, *in England, in February? A miracle.* 'I can vacuum them, isn't it wonderful?'

Polly flopped down in her favourite chair: the one her mother had re-covered in chintz with a pattern of strawberries. She traced the outline of a strawberry leaf with her finger and noticed that her nail polish was chipped. Ah well. Better chipped polish than a broken nail. Polly had an unfortunate habit of picking, picking away at little imperfections, which only rendered them, in time, great glaring imperfections. She was aware of the futility of the operation, but could not help it. One day, she feared she would pluck irritably at a stray thread defiling the hem of a knitted dress, and end up naked, holding a ball of wool.

'Well, Polly, how are you? You look a bit thin, love.'

'No I'm not. It's this new haircut.' Polly slumped in her chair, to make the most of her meagre endowment of flesh. She thrust the root of her tongue downwards to suggest a double chin, and surreptitiously plumped up her lean cheeks with air.

'Don't you think she looks thin, Daddy?' Polly's father drummed nervously on the arm of his chair. There was a little patch of grease among the strawberry leaves, where he did his drumming.

'I think she looks—well, all right really. Yes! Very nice!' He shot her his shy schoolboy smile. Any minute now he would get up. Yes! There he went—hauling himself up and strolling over to the window. He peered out through the net curtains, lighting his pipe.

Polly's mother ignored this. She was busy getting an album out of a small cupboard at her side.

'Look, Polly! There was this about Jeanette—in The *Mail*.' Polly scanned the article: a routine young-actress-on-her-way-up interview.

'It mentioned *Skyscrapers*, see? Didn't say you wrote it, though.'

'It doesn't matter. Nobody's interested in the writers.'

'Well, they jolly well ought to be! Where would all these actresses be without girls like you, I'd like to know? It's all very well for her prancing about in her nightie – ' Jeanette was wearing a mini skirt in the picture. Mrs Partridge had thought mini skirts a great error of taste in the 1960s, when Polly had been a young teenager trying them out, and was appalled to find them returning now.

'Mum! I don't *want* to be in The *Daily Mail*! For goodness' sake! That's what's so great about being a writer! If I'd wanted the limelight I'd have been an actress.'

'Yes. You could have, too,' Mrs Partridge turned emphatically to her husband. 'She could easily have been an actress, you know, Gordon. Easily.'

'Oh yes,' he grinned quietly. 'Or a postman.'

'Dad is hopeless!' Mrs Partridge shrugged irritably, but not entirely without affection. Her husband looked out through the bare twigs of suburban trees, at the sky.

'Tidal waves can travel huge distances, you know,' he said. 'There was that earthquake in Chile in 1960, and do you know, the tidal wave from that reached Sydney Harbour. If only we could predict earthquakes . . .'

'So how was your trip to Manchester?' asked Mrs Partridge, pouring the tea.

'Oh . . . well, I'm a bit fed up, actually.'

'Oh. Why?' Her mother looked up sharply. It wasn't like Polly to admit to a problem. Success was what her mother liked to hear about.

'Well, I've got involved in this project, you see. Adapting *Cold Comfort Farm* as an eight-part series.'

'Oh! But that's lovely! I adore Stella Gibbons! She's an absolute scream!'

'Yes, but . . . the problem is, Tony wants me to go off into the country and write it there. Find a place where we can shoot it all on location. A farm.'

Her mother's face fell. She had picked up a plate of shortbread to offer to Polly, but the plate stalled in mid-air.

'Does that mean you'll be going away?'

'Oh, not for long.' Polly reassured her mother with a bright smile. 'Only for a few weeks. I expect I'll come back to town at weekends. You know.'

'Where are you going to go, then?'

'I haven't decided yet. Not really. It's got to be a really remote, old-fashioned sort of farm. I don't know where to start. I thought you might have some ideas.'

'What, me?' Mrs Partridge's voice rose to a shrill top C. 'I haven't a clue, darling. You won't be stuck out in the country for long, surely? Couldn't you do the research in a weekend? A weekend would be lovely. Somewhere civilised. Berkshire perhaps. Or Suffolk. Suffolk's lovely. You could take Dan. Get some fresh air into him. He's got a sallow look, sometimes.'

'I don't know,' sighed Polly, dutifully chewing the short-bread. 'It's got to be wilder than Suffolk, I think. And Tony wants me to write it there. To saturate myself in it. You can't pick up the ins and outs of farming in a weekend, Mum.'

Her mother sighed, and sipped her tea. Her eyes, too, wandered to the window, and Polly felt her mother's mind recoiling from the project.

'It'll be awful, love, that's the problem. February! All that mud. You'll catch your death of cold.'

'Oh, I don't know. Sometimes it's quite warm in February.' Polly's attempt at cheerfulness was not very convincing.

'In Madeira, maybe. We were thinking of going there for a fortnight in April. After my concert. I was going to ask you if you'd like to join us. And bring Dan too, if he could manage it.'

'I don't think so, Mum. Sorry! But I'll be up to my armpits in cowmuck.'

Mrs Partridge shuddered.

'They've got these volcanic bombs in Madeira,' said Polly's dad, knocking out his pipe in a gleaming glass ashtray. 'Bit of lava, you know, thrown through the air, spinning, and then they land, and cool and harden and turn into these rocks that look like bombs.'

'I know!' cried Mrs Partridge suddenly, making Polly jump. 'What about that friend of yours, Gloria? Didn't she go off and live in the wilds? She must know some farmers. Somerset, wasn't it?'

'Gloria! That's brilliant, Mum! I knew you'd deliver the goods. The Broomstock Hills. Perfect. I'll ring Gloria tonight.'

Mrs Partridge looked pleased, and got up.

'I think I'll just make a pot of fresh tea. Yes, Gloria. She'll organise it for you.'

And she bustled out.

Polly smiled wanly. Gloria couldn't organise a couple of apples to stay in a paper bag. Nevertheless it was a good idea to ring her. As long as Polly didn't have to submit to Gloria's disastrous hospitality. She closed her eyes in horror at the memory of the weekend she and Daniel had spent there. Small children, too many cats, ghastly soups made out of rotten cauliflower. Cat hairs in the butter and dirty nappies on the breakfast table.

'If we could only harness the power of nature, you see,' her father, encouraged by his wife's brief absence, launched himself for the thousandth time into his longing lament, 'if we could predict these disasters, and intercept—not prevent, just be there to harness the power and make sure nobody got hurt. Minimise the damage . . . the trouble is . . .' His words dwindled away in the implacable face of nature, history, the stars, the rocks, the infinite spaces and mysteries palpable even in Finchley to a sensitive soul such as he.

'Have some shortbread, Dad,' Polly advised. 'It's a triumph of science over nature.'

'Ah.' Mr Partridge smiled proudly. 'If your mother was in charge of the universe, we wouldn't have all this trouble, of course.'

Chapter  Six

'Sky, get off the table!' Sky was Gloria's eldest child, a girl with hair like storm-tossed hawthorn and a pale-green moustache of snot. She was standing on the table pelting her younger siblings with walnuts. Polly was not a violent woman, but her palms itched with the desire to smack.

'She's so imperious,' sighed Gloria proudly. Imperious was not what Polly would have called it.

A walnut hit Aqua on the head, and she screamed. Aqua was the middle child.

'She's a water sign, you see,' Gloria had confided, *vis-à-vis* the child's name. 'In fact, she's on the cusp of Aquarius and Pisces and you can't get more watery than that.'

Aqua was indeed watery. She spent most of her time crying or peeing in her pants. Perhaps, thought Polly, because her elder sister is so very imperious.

Terry, the toddler, had hid under the table. Polly experienced a brief desire to join him. Terry wasn't short for Terence. It was Terra.

'Sky, Aqua, Terra,' mused Gloria. 'That's three of the four elements under my belt. Air, water and earth. All I need now is a fiery little baby and it'll be complete.' She smiled complacently.

Polly reckoned the last thing in the world Gloria needed was a fiery little baby. Still, her husband Chris was understandably absent most of the time, these days, so there were grounds for hope.

33

'I expect I'll get pregnant anyway,' sighed Gloria in an irritatingly self-satisfied way. 'I'm so damned fertile. I'd probably get pregnant just from watching the local village boys play football.'

A walnut hit Polly quite hard on the tenderest part of her brow.

'For God's sake cut that out!' she shouted. She was not one to interfere with Gloria's Rousseauean principles of childcare, but she was not just going to sit and soak up an artillery attack either. It was all right for Gloria. Three inches of subcutaneous fat protected her from all the slings and arrows, the walnuts and the flying xylophones, that flesh is heir to.

Sky ignored Polly's shout, hurled the last two walnuts at Aqua, wiped her nose on her sleeve, and climbed down off the table.

'There's a good girl!' smiled Gloria.

There was a split second of peace.

'Tell me about this farm, then,' said Polly quickly.

Sky picked up the cat and tried to strangle it. Aqua celebrated the brief respite in hostilities by wetting her knickers. Under the table, Terry picked up an environmentally friendly wooden hammer, bashed himself on the head with it, and burst out bawling.

Sky plucked a handful of hairs out of the cat, who howled, scratched, and spat. She threw the hairs into the air. They pirouetted in the slanting light and came to rest on the butter. A child's shoe, covered in what Polly hoped was only mud, lay next to the butter, exquisitely lit by the low afternoon sun, as in a Vermeer painting. It was like a Dutch seventeenth-century still life. Without the stillness.

'Ah, the farm.' Gloria heaved herself out of her chair, flung the cat out of the catflap, sank down again and clasped Aqua and Terry to her heaving chest. Terry burrowed under his mother's stained Greenpeace sweatshirt and began to suckle. Aqua, not to be outdone, joined him.

Their two heads, vibrating beneath the Greenpeace logo, suggested an even bigger bosom than Gloria actually possessed—the pneumatic breasts of a fertility goddess about to burst and drown the world in milk.

'There, there,' crooned Gloria. She pulled off Aqua's knickers and tossed them in the direction of the laundry basket. They landed in the cat's bowl. 'There, there.'

'Still nursing?' Polly tried hard to keep the aversion out of her voice.

'Oh God no. Not yer actual milk. Fuck me, Pol, what d'ye think I am? A Friesian? It's comfort, that's all. But I'm not having my kids sucking dummies. Nasty plastic rubbish. Some of them go straight from dummies to fags. Here, Sky! Pass me a clean pair of knicks for Aqua, there's a darling.'

Aqua's knickers were lined up in a wan little row on the radiator. Sky ran her finger along it, knocking all the pants onto the floor, then gave a short, sadistic laugh and disappeared upstairs.

Polly retrieved a pair of pants and handed them to Gloria. She was determined not to be enlisted as a Mother's Help, but mere etiquette required a certain minimum degree of co-operation.

'Cheers, Polly. You know, Sky sometimes makes me think of that line from Blake—what is it? *Like a Fiend hid in a cloud.*'

'Yes. Er . . . the farm?'

'Oh yeah—Look, Aqua, why don't you and Terry make something with those pine cones?'

'Not pine cones!' whinged Aqua. 'Flour an' water!'

'Oh all right.'

Polly cringed as Aqua climbed up on a stool and turned on the taps. Terry emerged from Gloria's sweatshirt and announced solemnly, 'Wanna bikkit!'

'Here's half a flapjack, Terr. A flap! Or a jack . . . Ha ha! Wit's wasted on the under-fives, I'm afraid, Polly.'

'Er . . . the farm?'

'Ah. The Swains'—watch out, Aqua! Turn it off now, there's a good girl . . . *Turn the bleeding tap off!*'

Aqua was holding a big spoon under the stream. Water shot out sideways in a huge arc.

'Can't! Stuck!'

Gloria lumbered to the sink, turned off the tap, and settled Aqua and Terry at the table with a bowl of water and a bag of flour.

'I'll have to be off in a minute,' said Polly hastily, picking up her handbag to shield her Jacques LeFroque oyster crêpe suit, 'if I'm going to get a look at this place before dark. I suppose it's guarded by savage dogs and everything?' Polly was afraid of dogs. But nothing could be worse than Gloria's children.

'Oh, dogs, yeah. But the geese are the real killers.'

'Well, where exactly is it?'

'Look, Polly, why don't you forget this staying on the farm bit? I mean, you can go up there every day and watch the divine Joe Swain flexing his lovely young muscles, but for God's sake stay here with us. I mean, for God's sake, you'll want some intelligent conversation in the evenings, won't you?'

'Oh no.' Polly got up hastily. Aqua and Terry were preparing what her dad would have described as lava bombs, and she could hear the terrible pounding of Sky coming downstairs. 'I couldn't possible impose on you for all that time.'

'Nonsense! Nonsense! It's open house here. You know me. The more the merrier. I mean, you can't be stuck up that godforsaken track with the bloody Swains for two months. You'll go barking mad, Polly.'

'Sorry.' Polly grimaced in apology. 'Producer's orders. I've got to live there. Got to be on the spot, night and day. I can still drop in and see you. All the time. Er—where exactly did you say the farm was?'

'But you will stay tonight at least, won't you?' urged Gloria in dismay.

'Oh yes. Tonight. Fine. Where . . .?'

'Ah. Turn right, then through the village and out the other side, you'll pass the pub on your left. Then turn up a little lane opposite the phone box. The road goes up and up for about a mile, then the farm track is a turn off to the left in a sort of beechwood thing.'

Polly hastened to the door. Sky burst in carrying a wooden skittle and looking murderous.

'Hello, darling!' Gloria greeted the child with rapture. 'How about some of Mummy's lovely lentil soup?'

'Lentil soup stinks of farty poo-poos!' roared Sky, and hurled the skittle into Aqua's bowl of flour and water.

Polly fled.

Chapter  Seven

Polly drove through the village, found the telephone box, and followed the deep lane up to the beechwood. Then she parked the car in a layby and set off along the farm track. She felt like a breath of fresh air: she would walk the last few hundred yards. All too soon, however, she was cringing at the effect of the mud and stones on her Bond Street shoes. She picked her way painfully along, like the moorhens she had seen in London parks, on the verges of lakes. They had seemed hesitant, out of their element. Polly knew just how they felt.

Suddenly, round the corner came a sheepdog, in that curious sideways shimmy that sheepdogs have, simultaneously wagging its tail and barking in a kind of harsh carnivorous way. God, it stank. Wet dog was not one of Polly's favourite scents. She sniffed her wrist, where the last faint traces of *L'Heure Bleu* reminded her unbearably of Knightsbridge.

'Goo back, Scott!' bawled a rough voice, and the farmer appeared: a tall cadaverous man in his late fifties, a tweed cap on his head and a stick in his hand.

'Good afternoon!' beamed Polly, with the urgent friendliness of one who wishes to be protected from dogs. Scott slunk back behind his master. 'That's a fine dog you've got there,' Polly suggested, without complete conviction.

''E's a bugger,' replied the farmer gruffly.

'Mr Swain, isn't it?'

'Ar.'

'I heard in the village,'—Polly thought it would perhaps be more politic not to mention her friendship with Gloria—'that you do bed and breakfast.'

'Ar. The missus'll see to it.'

'Er—where . . .?'

'Yo' on foot?' Mr Swain enquired sternly, and Polly realised this was her first mistake.

'Er, no—I've got a car—but I left it in the lane—felt like a bit of fresh air. I've driven all the way from London.'

'London, eh?' Mr Swain spat accurately into the hedge. 'On yer holidays are you?'

'Well, sort of.' Polly smiled determinedly into his creased and weatherbeaten visage. It was like trying to get a smile out of the North Face of the Eiger. 'London's horrible. A madhouse.' Polly hoped that, given the lateness of the afternoon, no cock would crow to mark the betrayal of her beloved metropolis.

'Ar. Right. Well, follow the road on up: you'll come to the house in about half a mile. Her's in.'

Polly hesitated: should she go back for her car? Half a mile sounded rather a long way on foot, with the landscape darkening by the minute, and the possibility of savage cows and sheep waiting to waylay her.

''Snot far,' Mr Swain encouraged her. 'Go on up! She'll give you a cup of tea. Yo' look perished.' And—miracle! A grudging smile broke across his sour face.

'Oh thank you!' cried Polly, and set out with new vigour. Once round the bend and out of sight of Mr Swain, however, she broke herself a stout stick from the hedgerow. One should not go unarmed on safari.

A gleam of light beckoned her through the twilight; soon she was in the yard, the looming presences of barns and trees threatening her from the darkness. From a shed nearby there was the sudden honking of geese—shut in for the night, thank goodness. Feeling curiously sheepish, she knocked on the door.

A gloriously cosy-looking woman opened the door: all squashy cardigan and soft slippers.

'Mrs Swain? I just met your husband in the lane. I believe you do bed and breakfast.'

'Oooooh yes dear—come in, now, do.' Mrs Swain didn't so much speak, as croon like a hen. Polly took off her befouled Bond Street shoes and entered the parlour, where a log fire was crackling in the range, and horse brasses glinting in the lamplight. *Bloody picturesque*, thought Polly, gratefully sinking into the chair nearest the fire. She felt curiously vulnerable and rather stupid without her shoes, but she stretched her stockinged feet towards the warmth.

'How about some tea, dear?'

'Oh yes please! That would be lovely.'

Whilst Mrs Swain waddled about, putting the kettle on and ladling out rather a frighteningly large amount of tea into a pretty old china pot, Polly sketched out her supposed reasons for needing a place to stay.

'I'm a writer, and I need to be in the country for a while, you see, to do a bit of research for a project.'

'A writer is it? Ooooo I do like readin'. Readin's my only pleasure, dear. I love that Mary Stewart. I read all her books twice over.'

'Really? My mother loves her too. Anyway . . . I need somewhere to stay, well, for a few weeks. So I'm, well, I'm making enquiries really, in this area . . . I've got a friend down in the village and I'm staying with her tonight, but I really need to find somewhere for, well—a couple of months, at least.'

'Well, dear, that'd be no trouble. No trouble at all. I've got this one little room you might like, looking east it is, gets the morning sun. Or perhaps you'd prefer the double, that's got an en suite bathroom, but I'd have to charge you the double rate, see? Otherwise what with the spring bank holidays coming I'd be out of pocket.'

'Oh, no, of course, I'll pay the double rate!' insisted Polly, the thought of her very own en suite bathroom cheering her up by about twenty fathoms. In fact it was hard not to feel thoroughly cheerful here, with the friendly fire, the sweet brick-red tea steaming at her elbow, a fat ginger cat asleep on the hearthrug, and Mrs Swain lowering herself into a rumpled nest of an armchair, as if to lay a whole clutch of warm speckled eggs. The whole thing was too much of a ghastly country cliché for words.

'Ooooh, well, dear, that'll be lovely. It's always nice to have someone stay for a while. We did have an architect here once, he was working on Mrs Lillicrap's extension. Nice boy too. What was his name, now? Oh yes. Julian. Julian Beale, dear. Do you know him? He lives in London.'

'Er, no. I'm afraid not. There are . . . rather a lot of us there.' Polly hoped she had not been patronising. But Mrs Swain probably wouldn't have noticed or minded if she had.

'Who's this friend of yours, then? In the village? Local, are they?'

'Not really.' Polly blushed. 'It's Gloria.'

Mrs Swain frowned.

'Gloria? I don't . . .'

'They live in Hawthorn Cottage. The other side of the village. She's got three children. And her husband's in publishing. Chris. Chris Harcourt.'

'Ah, Mrs Harcourt.' Mrs Swain smiled enigmatically. 'She's got her hands full, hasn't she, eh? She's a friendly girl, though. Ooooh yes. I've not spoken to her above once or twice, mind. In the shop.'

'Well . . .' Polly hesitated. 'Her ideas about bringing up children are pretty strange. I mean, they're a bit wild. To tell you the truth, I don't think I could have stayed there longer than one night.'

'Never mind.' Mrs Swain smiled, shook her head and gazed into the flames. 'We all make mistakes, don't we now? I know I've made plenty in my time. Marrying Swain for a start!' She smiled, rather satirically for a hen.

'Me too!' affirmed Polly vigorously. The fierce heat was creeping very pleasantly into her toes. She did not want to move.

The door opened and Mr Swain came in. He hung up his coat and hat, sat in a ladderback chair with a grandstand view of the huge fire, and unlaced his boots. Mrs Swain brought him a cup of tea, took his boots away, and brought his slippers. *My God*, thought Polly, *how appallingly sexist. This dear woman is completely subjugated. Maybe I should lend her* The Female Eunuch. But Mrs Swain exhibited no outward signs of discontent.

It was established that Polly had come to stay for a few weeks, and then Mr Swain got talking about farming, and especially sheep.

'I've had some rotten rams in my time, mind.' He shook his head. 'Remember that one we had off old Harry Cook, Queenie?'

'Oh yes. Dear oh dear!'

'What was wrong with him?'

'Well . . .' Mr Swain launched into his tale with an epic air. He was not dour, despite his thin face. He liked to talk. 'We got him from old Harry Cook over at Langston Mill, see? And he looked very good, everything in place, well up together he was, wasn't he, Queenie?'

'Oh yes.' Mrs Swain had picked up some knitting.

'Big chap he was too, had some trouble getting him into the trailer. Awkward bastard he was. Nearly knocked my boy over, my boy Joe, and he's a big enough chap, God knows. Anyway we put him in the Lower Field with the ewes, and they were just about coming into season, they were ripe, see? They'd had good feedin' in September, there was a lot of grass that year, we'd had a wet August, hadn't we, Queenie?'

'Oh, yes. Yes. Very wet.'

'Anyway, they'd had good feedin', these ewes, and they were prime. So we put him in with them and left him to it. Went back there the next day, didn't we, Queenie? And what do you think? Ewes down one end of the field, ram down the other. Just bloody grazin', he was. Not workin' at all. Just not interested. Not a flicker of interest. And Queenie said to me, she said, you know what, Arthur, I think he's a poofter! And you know what? He bloody was!'

Mrs Swain shook her head and tut-tutted. Mr Swain glared at the fire. Polly dared not laugh, here and now. The deep tragedy of it was too palpable. She would save it up to laugh about later, on her own.

'How dreadful!'

'Dreadful's the word, too right. I took him back to Harry Cook and I said, "This bloody ram you gave me, he's no good, he's a shirtlifter, Cook, and I want my bloody money back." And I got it back, too.' Polly didn't dare ask what had become of the poor gay ram. Shepherd's Pie, perhaps.

'Well,' she said, reluctantly stirring from this fascinating catalogue of rural depravity, 'I suppose I'd better be going. Back to Gloria's.'

'Her husband there at the moment, is he?'

'No. Chris is in America. At a book fair.'

Mr Swain shook his head disapprovingly. Polly felt uncomfortable discussing Gloria's domestic arrangements, and stood up. Just as Mr Swain was about to volunteer some earthy judgement about the necessity of fathers being on the spot with their huge hands ready to hand out hidings, the door burst open and in came the younger Mr Swain.

'This is our Joe,' said Mrs Swain, as if showing off a prize dog. And he was a prize dog. He was tall and slim, with hair like brambles, and shoulders like a barn door. He was also covered with dungy straw from head to foot.

'What a shame,' said Polly. 'I'm just going.'

'Ah well,' replied Joe, and shrugged.

'But she's coming back,' said Mrs Swain, with a rather naughty tempting emphasis.

Joe stood aside and as Polly passed, he peeped shyly at her like a member of an endangered species. *Oh God*, she thought, hastily stepping back into her Bond Street shoes, *Please don't let this rustic hunk get a crush on me. That would be altogether too tedious.*

'Well, I'm off, then,' she said, looking firmly at Mrs Swain and not her steaming son. 'Thanks ever so much for everything. See you tomorrow.'

And she stepped out into the night, which was, rather inconveniently, as black as the deepest pits of hell.

Chapter  Eight

A day later Polly moved in to Harrow Hill Farm. She sank into the soft bed, drunk with sleep, at ten thirty. This country air was worse than claret. In the middle of the night she was roused by dogs barking, geese honking, and men shouting.

'You want to get your bloody head examinin'!' came the voice of Swain the Father.

'Too bloody right!' came the lighter tones of Swain the Son. 'I should have left long ago. Left you to stew in your own bloody juice.'

'Don't, you two! Behavin' like a couple o' schoolboys!' clucked the voice of Swain the Holy Hen.

A tractor was started up and driven off, apparently in a temper. Later Polly realised that tractors always sounded like that.

'You shouldn't talk to the boy like that, Arthur.'

'You don't know the half of it, woman. You've bloody spoiled him, that's what. That's the truth and you know it!'

A door was slammed. Huge boots tramped primally across the yard. Rural latches were unhasped, hinges squealed, and oildrums or similar resonant objects were dragged about. Then a machine was switched on and a high-pitched hum filled the air.

Ah, thought Polly, the peace and quiet of the country. The illuminated figures on her digital bedside clock-radio (brought with her from Hampstead) informed her it was six-thirty. She had asked for breakfast at eight, feeling that was quite courageously early. And here were the Swains up and bawling at each other in the pre-dawn dark. Polly had only previously witnessed six thirty a.m. from the other end—after a particularly wild night out. Six thirty was the latest possible time to fall into bed, dammit, not to prise one's eyelids open and attempt to face the horrors of a new day.

She pulled the covers over her head, reached out desperately for more sleep, and was eventually rewarded with a frightful nightmare in which she inhabited a landscape which might have been painted by Hieronymus Bosch. People were living in the huge empty shells of eggs: a strange mediaeval-looking youth pulled down his breeches to show her a flower which was growing out of his bum: two old people were asleep in a giant sardine-tin . . . Polly became aware that she wanted to go to the loo. She was searching desperately for a private corner among some derelict sheds, when a pair of cream printed curtains attracted her attention. They glowed with light; Polly awoke. They were the curtains of her room; dawn was breaking almost audibly through them. The central heating had come on.

She lay there for a moment savouring the warmth, and the pleasure of being restored to the real world, before going to her own bathroom. Above her head was an enormous beam, like a mighty arm protecting her. The room smelt of lavender. Outside, a cock was crowing. Polly thought for a moment of her elegant little flat in Hampstead, where she always awoke to the faint and friendly buzz of people walking in the street, and the hum of traffic. Here she seemed to lie in a huge alert silence, into which strange individual noises leapt, flourished and died. It was raining steadily, and one could somehow hear every drop.

Washed and dressed—in sensible jeans and the Guernsey sweater she had occasionally worn on holidays—Polly went down to breakfast, and assured Mrs Swain she had slept well.

'Ah,' Mrs Swain smiled. 'It's the country air. Full English breakfast, dear?'

Polly hadn't had a cooked breakfast since she and Daniel had gone to Aldeburgh for a few days last year. But she supposed that it was going to be necessary here: a rite of passage. They would never take her seriously if she asked for muesli and yoghurt. And where would they get it from, anyway? The nearest muesli was probably in Taunton or Exeter.

'Yes please,' she said, rather faintly.

All too soon a plate was placed before her. Three enormous rashers of bacon dominated it, gleaming obscenely like slices of a fat Yorkshireman's thigh: the sort of Yorkshireman who gets carbonadoed on the beaches of Tenerife. Two eggs glared balefully at her, still clucking from the pan, and a heap of mushrooms steamed like a mediaeval dunghill.

'How lovely,' she said faintly. 'Though it's rather a lot.'

'Got to feed you up, dear,' smiled Mrs Swain. 'You look a bit peaky if you don't mind my saying so.'

A bit peaky! Polly was affronted. She'd managed, by strict dieting and yoga, to get herself down to eight stone for the first time for years, and here was this old hen waddling about, planning to fatten her up along with the pigs.

'Arthur cured that bacon himself,' observed the dame proudly. What, thought Polly satirically, without sending for the vet? The bacon had certainly suffered severely from something. BO for a start. It didn't smell like city bacon, at all. It wasn't the sort of crisp salty stuff you get in avocado sandwiches from Gino's Sarnies To Go in the West End. This country bacon somehow conjured up a navvy's groin—not that Polly had ever been near one, thank God.

'How marvellous!' Polly picked faintly at a small fragment

of mushroom, and hoped Mrs Swain was not going to stand over and watch her as she ate. Luckily the phone rang.

With Mrs Swain safely out in the hall, Polly acted fast. She seized her wonderful Pucci handbag—the one Daniel had bought her in Florence—and slipped two of the bacon rashers and one egg deftly into it, coughing to hide the sound of the operation, which she completed with a firm snap of the clasp. Nothing, surely, would be worse than rising graciously from the breakfast table, complimenting your hostess on her delicious meal, and having your bag suddenly yawn open and a fried egg flop out onto the carpet.

Polly punctured the remaining egg and spread yolk everywhere to hide the sudden emptiness on her plate. She scattered the mushrooms about, and discovered a small piece of fried bread. Strangely enough, it was rather pleasant. Polly ate another piece. It crunched and exploded in her mouth, reminding her of her childhood. Why does one stop eating fried bread when one grows up? She finished up the fried bread with something approaching gusto.

'In future,' she smiled apologetically when Mrs Swain returned for her plate, 'one egg and one rasher will be fine, really.'

Back in her room, she opened her bag and sighed. The lining was ruined for ever. Some of the grease stains had even crept right through to the leather. There wouldn't be a specialist leather cleaner's round here, would there? Exeter or Taunton again. Polly tipped the bacon and eggs down the loo, flushed and urgently bade her breakfast farewell.

One rasher of bacon hung about with the rather forlorn air of a lover who cannot believe it is all over.

'C'mon, push off!' urged Polly, poking it out of sight with the loo-brush. 'Think of it as getting rid of the middle man.'

She emptied her handbag, washed it and left it inside out

to dry on a towel on the radiator. It lay there a thing murdered and flayed.

Polly sighed, recalling its original Florentine splendour. She and Daniel had bought it at a little place next to Santa Croce. Soon she would have to start work. But first she would just dash off a note to Dan.

> Harrow Hill Farm,
> Long Dangley,
> Somerset.
>
> cold and filthy Feb 17th
>
> *(not that you'd*
> *notice that*
> *kind of detail*
> *tucked up in cosy*
> *old London)*

My God, Dan,

You wouldn't *believe* this place! I mean, *vis-à-vis* yer rural idyll, it's completely over the top. The view from my humble attic is a complete knockout, though I have to admit the absence of skyscrapers was a bit of a shock to the system at first. Basically one looks down a valley that could have been painted by Claude or that other landscape artist you like. What's his name?

Anyway. You can't even see the village from here. In fact you can't see a single other dwelling. It's *relentlessly* remote. For about two hours a day, if the sun shines, you can kid yourself you're in the Ardèche, but once twilight is imposed—shortly after lunch, on dull days—you've had it.

The Swains have a little sitting-room for guests to watch TV, but the reception is ghastly owing to too many hills, trees and barn owls, so on the TV everyone looks as if

49

they're wilting slightly to the left and shaking with fear. A bit like the Tories before an election.

I haven't had the nerve yet to inform the Swains of their doom: that they've been singled out for televisual greatness by the goddess Granada. I thought I'd better settle in and get to know them first. Gloria has been sworn to secrecy. It would be hopeless if everybody knew what I was up to. So I shall maintain a Garbo-like inscrutability as I drift, apparently aimlessly, around the fields and woods. Except Garbo wouldn't have been seen dead here. And I shan't be going out today, I think. The rain's *horizontal*.

But behind my shades I shall watch everybody and everything like a hawk. I think I've actually seen a hawk for the first time since I came here, by the way, but I can't be sure. It might have been a buzzard. Well, it might have been a spotty-bottomed flyswatter for all I know.

Could you be ever so kind and get the *Duffer's Guide to British Birds* and post it to me here forthwith? It's not far from your office to Dillon's. But aaargh! No! I must not think of Dillon's. Dear Dillon's. How I long to browse for hours along its ambrosial shelves, and force my fivers into the hands of its suave and streetwise employees! The village shop does sell books, but only the she-fell-panting-into-his-arms-and-beneath-the-surging-velvet-of-his-frock-coat-she-sensed-that-his-Cavalier-heart-was-pounding-with-unusual-force type.

Mrs Swain (mine hostess) used to be a hen in a previous existence. Sometimes I get scared that she's going to wait till I'm asleep and sit on me till I hatch into something a little more fluffy.

Mr Swain has just stepped out of a niche on some Flemish cathedral. A fourteenth-century saint who suffered martyrdom by some kind of long-drawn-out deprivation. Agriculture, perhaps.

Mr Swain has a tragic view of life, but perhaps all farmers are like that. He explained to me yesterday that his income has shrunk by twenty-two per cent in real terms over the past few years. I have a feeling that, were the Minister for Agriculture to unwisely venture a toe into the farmyard, Mr Swain would personally thrash him to death with the nearest goose.

So: when are you coming down? And where are you, if I may make so bold as to ask? I've rung every day at different times but all I get is that asinine message on your answering machine. It really isn't funny any more, Dan. You should change it.

In general I'd rather you didn't ring me here, because the phone's right by the kitchen door and I wouldn't be able to vilify my surroundings with quite the necessary degree of freedom. Normally I'd like to ring you from the public callbox and get you to ring me back. But you're never bloody *there*. Do at least give me a quick ring here at the farm, whenever you have a minute, to let me know when I can ring you for a proper talk. I bet you're in New York. You swine!

Miss you dreadfully. My venerable double bed here is guaranteed to give you appalling backache, but I've got my own little bathroom and everything. What's keeping you?

> Much love,
>
> Polly.

Polly folded the letter up, put it in an envelope and addressed it. *Belsize Park Gardens*. It rose up magnificently in her memory: those huge pale mansions in their lofty tree-lined streets, the little row of shops only a quick walk away along helpful pavements. The taramosalata! The Aqua Libra! The French films, the croissants, the whiff of Marlboro mixing poignantly with carbon monoxide . . . Polly's eyes almost filled with tears for a moment, and Nature reciprocated by hurling a handful of raindrops against the windowpane.

Perhaps she'd miss London less if Dan came down for a weekend. But the odd thing was, she couldn't imagine her urbane lover here, at all. However, her task was not to think of lovers, urbane or otherwise, but get stuck in to her work. Her egg and bacon breakfast carried her through several chapters of *Cold Comfort Farm*, with copious notes, until she looked up at three p.m. and saw the rain had stopped. She was peckish, so she got up and struggled into her coat. She needed a walk. She'd go into the village to post the letter, plus a postcard to Tony to report herself safely installed. And maybe she'd treat herself to a little cake from the village shop to keep her going till suppertime.

Sod Daniel! He hadn't rung all day. She suspected he was up to something. And if he maintained radio silence, she'd have her revenge. In triplicate.

At the farmhouse door she met Joe. His dark curls were freckled with rain. He was taking his wellies off, and he gave her another of his endangered glances.

'Good morning!' smiled Polly briskly and set off down the lane. A purposeful manner would keep him in his place, she felt sure. She couldn't bear the thought of his going all spongy and spanielly and casting sheep's eyes at her. How many animal metaphors one uses, thought Polly. She had never really noticed, before.

The sun suddenly came out and flooded the valley with light. Her heart gave a strange surprising lurch which she realised must be relief that the weather had improved. The sun seemed to matter a lot more in the country than in town. Just her luck to be here in February.

Chapter  Nine

Ting a ling a ling a ling! Stepping into the village shop, Polly heard the sort of ancient tinkle, and smelt the smell of damp cardboard, soap and biscuits past their sell-by date, that is no longer experienced in Hampstead. Smiling behind the counter was the woman she'd met yesterday—a plump creature in her fifties with pink cheeks and a curiously sleepy manner.

'Hello, dear,' she smiled at Polly. 'Did you manage to track down that yoghurt you was after?'

'Er, no, it doesn't matter,' Polly said hastily. 'I didn't really want it all that much. Do me good to go without it for a while. I wouldn't mind a packet of those cup cakes, though.' Her stomach would have to subdue its demands for croissants and Camembert and see how the other half lived.

'On holiday are you, then?'

'Well, sort of. I'm staying at Harrow Hill Farm for a week or two.'

The woman laughed. 'Lovely spot,' she nodded. 'Mind you, bit wild up there.' She laughed again, at some private thought or memory. 'Well, what can I do for you?'

'Oh, I'd like ten first-class stamps, please.'

'I'll do that for you, Maisie,' came a sudden voice, and a little man popped up from behind the counter at her side. He had a whiskery moustache and a look that was ferrety but mild, as of a tame but eager rat.

'Ta, Fred,' smiled Maisie, and yawned. 'Walker are you, then?' she enquired of Polly, as Fred dived among the Post Office books, found the right stamps and expertly tore them off with his small, quick claws.

'Yes,' lied Polly. 'I've always loved walking.' *If a taxi wasn't available*, she added silently, with a wry grin.

'Can't bear it meself.' Maisie shook her head and perched her ample bum on a stool behind the counter. 'Lazy old trollop, I am. Do you know—I ent even been up Harrow Hill since I was courtin'.'

'Well, that's always the way, isn't it?' agreed Polly. 'You never explore what's on your doorstep. I think everybody's the same.'

A door opened behind the counter, and a large man with a solid red face like a boiled ham entered from an inner room, carrying a tray with two teacups on it. He set it down on the counter, placed one cup ceremonially before Maisie, and the other at a little distance, towards the Post Office department, evidently for Fred.

'England's collapsed,' he said majestically, and withdrew.

'He's a cricket fan, my Bert,' confided Maisie. 'Listens to it from all over the world. It's in the West Indies now, look. Still, 'sworse when it's Australia. He's up all night then.'

Having served Polly with her stamps, Fred emerged from his cage, ducked under the counter and brought out a biscuit tin, and offered them with a kind of desperate eagerness to Maisie.

'Have a biscuit, Maisie. Go on. You know how you love them Bourbons. Or them wafery ones. They're your favourites.'

Maisie hesitated, laughed helplessly, and took one of each. Fred looked triumphant. He turned to Polly.

'Would you like a biscuit too, Miss?'

'No thanks!' Polly smiled. 'I'm not a biscuit sort of person, really. These will keep the wolf from the door.' She brandished her cup cakes.

'He spoils me.' Maisie threw an indulgent sideways glance at Fred. 'He spoils me rotten, all day long.' She sank her teeth into the pink wafery biscuit, and a little shower of crumbs exploded from her lips, and besprinkled her ample bosom. She brushed them off. Instantly Fred fell to his knees—to lick Maisie's crumbs off the floor? No. He had seized a little dustpan and brush and was joyfully being useful again.

'What a treasure!' observed Polly.

'Ar. I'm lucky, ent I?' Maisie laughed, shaking pleasantly, and started on the Bourbon biscuit. 'So what brings you round these parts, eh?'

'Oh, accident, really. I've got a friend who lives in the village.'

'Oh? Who's that then?'

'Er . . .' Polly blushed. 'Gloria. Gloria Harcourt, you know. Hawthorn Cottage.'

'Oh, I do like Gloria,' said Maisie, licking her pink trotters. ''Er's a laugh, ent she, Fred?'

Fred produced a Wet One for Gloria to wipe her fingers on, and a dainty little towel to dry them. He nodded.

'Mind you, I don't let them kiddies of hers come in. Not all together. Bert told her once she'd got to tie 'em up outside like dogs. He's a one, ent he, Fred?' The ghost of a smile played across Fred's thin face.

'Ar,' he affirmed. 'He's a right comedian when he's had a few.'

'You'd never think it to look at him now,' Maisie gazed fondly at the door through which her solemn husband had so recently disappeared.

'Ah, well, you never can tell,' agreed Polly, and made departing gestures with her coat.

'Well, anything you want, just drop in,' said Maisie. 'I'm open all hours, look.'

'She works all the hours God sends!' hissed Fred suddenly, shooting a look of adoration at his postmistress. She was raising the cup to her lips, and smiling sensuously into the rising mists of the tea.

'See you, then,' called Polly, at the door. ''Bye!'

As Polly left the shop, a BMW drew up and a middle-aged woman in a Burberry stepped briskly out.

'Excuse me!' she called, and Polly stopped, surprised to be addressed. The woman walked boldly up to her and extended her hand. 'I'm Joyce Lillicrap,' she said. 'Gloria has told me so much about you.' *I hope not*, thought Polly, and murmured something polite.

Joyce Lillicrap's eyebrows had been judiciously pruned. Her hair had been coaxed towards blonde, her nails painted tactful pink, and her earlobes celebrated with flashing studs of gold.

'I live at The Hall,' she said. 'Perhaps Gloria has mentioned me.'

'Oh certainly,' Polly deceitfully assured her. 'Mrs Swain was telling me about your extension.'

'Really?' Mrs Lillicrap looked pleased. 'You must come and have a look. We think it's quite successful. It's nice to be able to have tea in the garden at this time of year. It's double glazed of course. I was saying to Ronnie only this morning, it's not many people who can admire their Chinodoxias over their cornflakes!'

'Well, quite.'

'Look here, dear,' Mrs Lillicrap moved closer and cocked her head at a protective angle, as if about to confide things which yokels had no right to overhear. 'If you're not completely comfortable at the Swains', I do hope you'll let me know. I've got a spare room and I'm quite at a loose end since Angelica went off to college—she's at London University, you know.'

Polly made an admiring sound.

'Only the Swains are sweet, but you know . . . if it all

gets a bit too . . .' Mrs Lillicrap's mouth assumed an expression suggestive of sour milk, '. . . or if you just want a change . . . don't hesitate. It would be a pleasure.'

'Well, that's really very kind of you, but I'm quite comfortable at the moment, thanks.'

'At least come to tea! Tomorrow. No—the day after. I've got to go to Exeter tomorrow to get my hair cut. Would Wednesday suit you? There are one or two friends of mine you really must meet. They'd adore you.'

Polly accepted the invitation, not without a quiver of apprehension. Mrs Lillicrap was delighted.

'Well,' she said, 'I must see if Maisie has got any Perrier left. I don't expect so for a moment. What do you think of our village shop, dear? Hopeless, isn't it?'

'I think it's charming,' said Polly. 'And Maisie is quite a character.'

'Ah yes.' Mrs Lillicrap leaned forward, her bird's beak of a nose almost touching Polly's. 'It really is . . . outrageous, what she gets away with. I don't quite understand how Bert copes with it all. But you never know—perhaps he thinks it takes the pressure off him? Who knows? Still. Mum's the word! More power to her elbow!'

And with a strange, malicious wink, she was gone.

Chapter  Ten

Polly had a hunch that if she climbed the first stile on the road out of Long Dangley and struck off across the field, three fields later she would be approaching the farm, saving herself several hundred yards of tedious lane-trotting. She would also avoid the occasional mad van driven by some rural lout whose only stimulant was the surging speedometer. And besides, she had to get to grips with the country. Here it was, behind this hedge.

She climbed the stile, trying to look as though she did this kind of thing every day, and then realised that nobody was watching. The lane behind her was empty. The field ahead of her was empty. There were a few modest rustlings in the hedge, but she doubted whether the small creatures involved would be grinning sardonically at her lack of elegance. How odd the country was! There was no *audience*.

So. Here she was in a field. It seemed to be only grass, so Polly set off diagonally across it. She knew the importance of not walking across crops. But grass wasn't a crop—was it? Oh God. She had so much to learn. A quick backward glance confirmed that she had left no impression on the grass. There were not even footprints. But the grass had left an impression on her. Her sweet little Italian ankle boots were deeply stained. It had rained heavily for hours earlier in the day and Antonio della Casa just wasn't up to it.

Polly groaned. Another Florentine delicacy gone west.

Once leather had got wet like that, it was ruined. The dear little boots, which Daniel had occasionally caressed, would henceforth be besmirched with a horrid white tide-mark. Polly sighed, but strode on. Her stockings and feet were soaked. What a prat she was. Why hadn't she stuck to the lane? It was too late now, however. She was almost at the next stile.

She clambered over it and continued on her way, though this field seemed even soggier. Great lakes of mud forced her to make detours; huge, appallingly fresh cowpats were scattered everywhere. Polly picked her way hesitantly along, never raising her eyes from the ground before her. Wet and mud were unavoidable, but Antonio della Casa would feel a trans-European telepathic frisson of horror if his dear little boots sank into a mire of excrement.

So keenly were Polly's eyes fixed on the ground before her that she was practically on top of the cows before she saw them. She sensed something large moving, looked up and found herself addressing a herd of cattle.

'Oh my God,' she said aloud. 'Shoo! Bugger off!'

The cows stood their ground and stared at her. Polly's heartbeat quickened. If she had seen the cows in the field, she would never have climbed the second stile at all. She would have squelched her way right back to the lane. But now the lane was far away. She had to face these animals, and not run. A postman had told her once that one should always keep eye-contact with a dangerous dog and walk slowly away from it, backwards. But Polly had to get past them before she could back away in the desired direction: uphill, towards the distant farmhouse.

Gingerly she skirted the main group. A few moved back timidly; other, more distant ones came forward. Polly glanced nervously at them as she walked. Were they cows? Some of them seemed to have udders, but others—well, she simply couldn't tell without getting down on her hands and knees like a garage mechanic. She had heard that bullocks could be maddened. And heifers, she was sure, were unreliable.

'Hello. There, there!' she murmured soothingly as she went. She smiled at them, but they did not reciprocate. 'Good girls. Or boys. Or whatever. It's all right. It's all right.'

But just how bloody all right was it? There was a sudden bellow, of a deep and threatening type, and Polly stopped in her tracks. Twenty yards away, with his head stuck in a thornbush and yet somehow watching her, sideways, out of a rather nasty yellow little eye, was a bull. It was obvious even to Polly that he was a bull. Apart from the haggis-like thing hanging by his tail, he was twice the size of any of the other beasts. His head was massive, his snout square, and Polly felt sure he would be capable of reducing even quite a large Volvo to a heap of twisted metal.

Polly looked at him. He looked at her. Who was that woman in Greek mythology who was carried off by Jove in the form of a bull? *Europa*, said Polly's brain promptly. Paralysed by its education, it could offer the names of any number of Greek deities, but not the hint of how to make an elegant withdrawal from an unexpected interview with a bull. Polly remembered the postman, and backed off, keeping eye contact. The bull raised his head and gave a series of bellows which started deep in the earth—well, in Australia, probably—and ended in a ringing tenor shout that echoed in the sky. He fixed her with his eye, but remained sideways on.

That was the way Polly wanted him to stay, whilst she retreated—backwards. Splashes and pongs underfoot informed her that she was staggering backwards through liquid cow manure: an ordeal spared those happy mortals who even now were walking home along the sweet, dry, fragrant pavements of Knightsbridge. But she did not care. Let ordure cloak her from head to foot! Let it spatter the light olive-green Jasper Cachet mac she was wearing. Just so long as Jove there didn't charge.

He was still watching her. Not surprising, really, thought Polly. I must be a ludicrous sight. There was something unnerving about the way the cattle didn't laugh at her. She had an audience now, all right, but applause seemed unlikely. A quick glance informed her that there was a stile about eighty yards away which led into the next field. And she could see the welcome roofs of Harrow Hill Farm rising above trees beyond.

Then, all of a sudden, the bull whirled round, bellowed . . . and dived headfirst into some more thornbushes. The need to scratch his head was evidently more pressing than the need to trample a townie. Sensing her chance, Polly ran like hell. Safe on the far side of the stile, she paused, panting, for a backward glance at the bull. He reminded her of a floor manager she had once known called Gerry. Poor Gerry. All glowering musculature and no action. Ah well. She breathed the sweet air of relief and set off across the last field. Now everything would be all right.

Five seconds later, though, something hard hit her on the brow. For a split second she thought it was a stone. Then she realised that this was country rain and that she was out in it. City rain was never a problem. There were umbrellas, taxis, bars, the porches of churches, bus shelters, shop doorways and awnings. Here there was nothing between her tender skull and the malicious marble-pelter in the heavens.

Polly gasped aloud as the skies opened above her. It seemed personal, somehow. The noise of it hammering on her head was deafening. In a few seconds her hair was soaked, plastered, and rivulets were streaming down her face and—even more uncomfortable—down the back of her neck. She staggered on, of course, but the sheer malice of the elements was hard to believe. The Jasper Cachet mac gave up the unequal struggle and became a sopping dishcloth that bunched itself up between her thighs as she ran. The dear little Italian boots disappeared at every step into a sucking morass of mud.

'Oh Christ, Christ, Christ!' Polly sobbed in fury and helplessness. The complete exposure of her position was somehow shocking. There was nowhere to shelter: not a bush, not a tree.

It's a bit like that scene in King Lear, isn't it, really? remarked her educated brain. *You know, when he's lurching about on the heath:* Blow winds and crack your cheeks, rage—*or is it* roar?—ye hurricanoes.

'Shut up you stupid bastard,' seethed Polly to her brain. 'From now on you can forget all this Shakespeare crap and stick to nice helpful simple things like: *wouldn't it be sensible to take the car?'*

Eventually, whimpering with exhaustion, she fell against the farmhouse door. It opened, and Mrs Swain received her with open arms.

'You poor thing, oh dear me, let's get this off!' Polly was aware of Joe watching satirically from the kitchen. She knew she did not present a delectable spectacle. And though the last thing she wanted was for him to get a crush on her, it was irritating to appear before anybody looking like a drowned rat.

'You must get those wet things off, dear,' said Mrs Swain. 'Dear oh dear, this little mac of yours wasn't really up to the job, was it?'

'Don't you get rain in London, then?' said Joe with a grin. Polly was irritated. This was not the best moment for him to come out of his shell. She was not in a position to draw on her usual reserves of dry wit.

'Leave the poor girl alone, Joe,' snapped Mrs Swain. 'You go up and jump straight in the bath, dear,' she went on, 'I'll deal with this mac and your boots for you, and when you're dry, you come down and have some goulash.'

'Oh, lovely,' said Polly weakly. 'Thank you so much.'

She was reluctant to go upstairs without answering Joe's jibe, however. She paused on the second stair. He was still watching her, with an infuriating grin.

'We do have rain in London,' she said, 'but it knows its place. Your weather here isn't all that well trained, I'm afraid.'

Not very distinguished by the usual standards of Polly's repartee. But she felt defeated by her situation. And even as she spoke, an outrageously impertinent raindrop rolled down across her collar bone and insinuated itself into her bra. It's a bit much, thought Polly, climbing the stairs. In town one did have to put up with sexual harassment, but meteorological harassment was in some ways worse. One couldn't slap its face. One had to, as it were, take it lying down. But never mind. Here was the blessed comfort of her warm bathroom. For the first time in her life, however, Polly avoided the mirror.

Chapter  Eleven

'Here you are, dear—I found this old jacket of Joe's.' After breakfast next day, Mrs Swain handed Polly an olive-green waxed-cotton coat of great antiquity. 'It's a bit the worse for wear, but it'll keep the wet out, look.'

'Oh, thank you very much!' cried Polly, fortified by a hot bath, a good dinner and a long sleep. Life seemed slightly more bearable today. 'That's lovely—it'll just tide me over till I get something suitable.'

Mrs Swain was a dear. Polly had often bridled, in the past, at being suffocated by motherliness (not, thank goodness, something her own mother specialised in), but being safely tucked up under Mrs Swain's wing was rather comforting, somehow.

After a morning working on the middle section of *Cold Comfort Farm*, she would drive into Sedgeworth and get herself some decent weatherproofs. Then, fortified against the elements, she could start to explore the surroundings without fear of drowning; although the wind had changed, and today was cold and bright.

At one thirty, Polly set off. It was nice to be in her car again, with its leathery smell, its obedient nose, and above all, its roof and watertight windows. The drive to Sedgeworth was pleasant enough, and Polly listened to Vivaldi's *The Seasons*—although since her experience of yesterday, she began to feel that Vivaldi had rather underestimated Winter.

Parking was no problem—the car park at Sedgeworth was almost empty. This is where the country scores, of course, thought Polly. Parking in London could drive a sane person to screaming pitch in minutes. And there was no charge for the car park here. Extraordinary. The streets were fairly empty, too, and Polly admired the handsome eighteenth-century houses and the market cross before strolling into The Eagle and enjoying a leisurely pub lunch. There was an open fire, desultory country conversations and, best of all, no muzak.

As she leaned back to relax for a moment or two after her sandwiches, however, she was disturbed by the faintly rustic stink in which she sat. It was rising out of Joe's old coat. She wondered if anyone else could smell it. What she needed was a streetwise T-shirt which read: IT'S NOT ME THAT STINKS, IT'S THIS BORROWED COAT.

She got up, eventually, and went out. Her spirits revived, as usual, at the prospect of shopping, albeit menial. A brisk wind was funnelling down the High Street. Polly zipped Joe's jacket up to her chin and thrust her hands deep in the pockets . . . odd! Something unusual met her fingertips. She fished it out. It was a small red rubber ring, about the size of a Polo mint but very stiff and springy. Impossible to thrust a finger through its fierce grip. Polly wondered what it was for. Wedding rings should hurt, she thought with a secret smile. That would be a useful deterrent.

Now: where was the shop that would sell waxed jackets and other country gear? Polly looked around her, and instantly saw it across the street. A dark little shop called Hunter's. She crossed the street without any effort—there was only a transit van and a Morris Minor within view—and admired, in the window of Hunter's, the very waxed jacket she required. But wait! The shop was dark. Nobody was inside. On the door hung a notice of opening times. Oh no! It was early closing day.

'God in heaven!' exclaimed Polly in a fury. She looked up

and down the street. Most of the shops had the same sad, shuttered look. A newsagent's was open, and a small chain supermarket. But everything else was firmly locked. Early Closing. She'd forgotten such a phenomenon even existed. It didn't exist, in London. There, shops were open all day and sometimes half the night as well. Thursdays always felt particularly delightful because most of the big stores in the West End stayed open till eight p.m. And here in blasted Sedgeworth they couldn't even stay open beyond noon. Damn it!

Polly felt cheated. This expedition was to have been her little treat. Buying clothes was always enjoyable, even practical clothes like these. And it meant another day in Joe's stinking old jacket. She sighed, and trailed off towards the car park. Oh well. At least she'd been out to lunch, even if she hadn't said a word to a soul.

Next to the car park was a phone box. Feeling suddenly lonely, she nipped inside and dialled Daniel's number. But yet again she was addressed only by his answering machine. He was probably out to lunch, himself. No doubt with someone beautiful or marvellous. Polly banished from her mind the brief hallucination of a cosy London restaurant, with the beep and swish of taxis outside and street upon street of shops, all *open*, for God's sake, their lights gleaming like jewels in the dusk. She was tempted to phone her mother, but decided against it. She had to feel on top of the world to deal with her mother. She would just have to drive home and admire the blasted landscape.

That evening she was invited into the kitchen to eat with the Swains, instead of the solitary splendour of the guests' dining-room. She was glad of a little company. It had been a frustrating day.

'Enjoy your little trip, did you, dear?' enquired Mrs Swain.

'Oh yes, thank you. I just drove around a bit,' answered Polly. She would not admit to her fruitless trip to Sedgeworth. She did not want to offer Joe any more opportunities for scorn. He seemed to progress straight from shy silence to relentless teasing with no civilised middle ground in between.

'How did you get on with our Joe's old coat? Keep you warm did it?'

'Oh yes, thank you,' smiled Polly, tucking in to an unidentifiable but delicious meat dish. 'It's a bit too big, of course, but that's nice at this time of year. You need a couple of sweaters really to keep the wind out, don't you?'

'Old Sheila had her last litter on that coat,' said Joe with a sly smile.

'Joe! She did not! Don't tease Miss Partridge, now!'

Polly serenely ignored him. After the horrors of trench warfare yesterday, a whiff of canine confinement was nothing. Polly tried not to remember the smell of Joe's coat. She had a delicate appetite and it was easily discouraged.

'I found something rather odd in the pocket, though,' she recalled. For a split second Joe looked embarrassed. He even blushed. Polly enjoyed the moment.

'What's that, then?' he asked defiantly.

It seemed to Polly that for a moment everybody around the table was trying not to think of condoms.

'A sort of tiny rubber ring thing,' she explained. 'About so big, and red.'

'Ah,' Joe smiled. 'Castration ring, that'd be.' Polly went a little pale.

'C-castration?' she enquired nervously.

'For the sheep, look,' said Joe. 'Sometimes we use rings; sometimes we cut them.'

Polly held on to the edge of the table. This was not the kind of talk which sharpened one's appetite. *With this ring I thee castrate.*

'I see,' she said. 'I thought it seemed rather tight. I couldn't think – '

'More sweetbreads, dear?' asked Mrs Swain.

'Er—no thank you. It seems awful really, that they should have to be castrated. But I suppose that's farming, isn't it?'

''Course it is.' Mr Swain emerged from his scrutiny of *Farmer's Weekly* and pushed back his chair. 'Couldn't have the buggers all entire. And there's a few members of the human race I'd like to have a go at, too.' He smiled grimly. 'That auctioneer bloke. Frank What's his name. Smug bastard.'

'Oh well,' sighed Polly. 'Poor sheep. But I suppose they don't know what they're missing.'

She had to be careful. The conversation was veering dangerously away from the nauseating to the titillating.

'Makes a nice dish, too,' added Mrs Swain, heading for the uncontroversial waters of the culinary.

'Really?'

'Don't you realise what you've just been eating?' asked Joe, a glint in his eye. Polly hesitated.

'Well, sweetbreads . . .' she pondered. 'I didn't really . . . What are sweetbreads, exactly?'

'Sheep's testicles,' pronounced Joe with sadistic relish. 'This lot was, anyway.'

'What . . .?' Polly gazed in dawning horror at her empty plate.

'Aye. Tasty, I reckon.' Joe winked at her. 'Want some more?'

'No. I – ' Polly rose hastily from the table. 'Do excuse me—I think I – '

There was no time to make an elegant and convincing exit. Polly raced upstairs and was sick.

When she had recovered, she threw herself on her bed, raging. She had made an absolute fool of herself—*again*. In front of that sneering young man. Above all, Polly dreaded losing her dignity. Her fortune, her virtue, her good name—anything rather than her dignity. She would not go downstairs again, and she would avoid him determinedly for the rest of her stay.

Half an hour later there was a soft knock at her door. Polly opened it feeling very sheepish.

'Are you all right, dear?' enquired Mrs Swain. 'Only I brought you a cup of tea, look.'

'Oh Mrs Swain!' exclaimed Polly. 'You are an absolute angel.' Mrs Swain set down the tray on the table. She had brought biscuits, too—how tactful and thoughtful. Polly was hungry again, and craved something bland. Something worlds away from sheep's testicles. Luckily they were custard creams, not ginger nuts.

'Don't take no notice of our Joe, now, will you?' warned Mrs Swain on her way out. 'He will have his little joke. But he don't mean nothing by it.'

'Oh, don't worry, it's quite all right,' Polly reassured her. 'He's a real laugh.'

As the door closed, however, Polly began to wonder if it might not be enjoyable after all if Joe did get a crush on her, so she could subject him to a series of delectable cruelties.

Chapter  Twelve

'Keep still, you bugger! Keep still!'

Polly was instantly awake; summoned by bawls. She had abandoned her quaint urban notions about the deep peace of the country. It was three a.m. Down in the barn, something was stirring.

Continuing sounds suggestive of struggle, and a hunch that it was the younger Mr Swain who played a starring role, led her to tip-toe to the window. The barn was lit within by a lantern, but the substance of the drama was hidden deep inside: she could see only a knot of writhing shadows. Was Joe consorting with some local wench of curiously stubborn chastity? Looking down, Polly felt drawn by the open door of the barn, with its mounds of straw gleaming in the lamplight as on a Christmas card.

She pulled on five layers of clothing, and tip-toed out onto the landing. A deep bass snore came from the bedroom door of Mr and Mrs Swain, answered by a faint nasal crooning. They were singing their nocturnal song in unison. Polly was glad. She felt like a child in a storybook setting forth on some terrific adventure for which the parental generation need to be dead, or failing that, unconscious.

Polly crept downstairs and pulled her new wellies on. (Sedgeworth on a Saturday had proved a lot more accommodating.) As she walked across to the barn, she heard extraordinary sounds: a kind of coarse agonised cry. She quickened her pace. Was Joe strangling an innocent rambler who had left a gate open? She ventured into the lamplight. Several fat sheep nestling in the straw got up, startled, and bleated at her. In the corner, Joe appeared to be wrestling with a particularly large one.

'I – ' But Polly was spared conversation.

'Come over here,' interrupted Joe, 'and sit on 'er head.' Polly obeyed.

'What – ?'

'It's back to front. Got to try and turn it.'

Back to front? What the hell did he mean? What was this, anyway? Some rural sport? A preamble to a dreadful sacrifice? Then she realised that Joe's arm was buried elbow-deep in the creature's birth canal and the problem of back to frontness was an internal, rather than an external one.

'Oh, I see!' she exclaimed, with all the force of revelation. 'The lambing's started.'

'No,' said Joe with the deepest scorn, 'I'm just lookin' for my wallet.'

Polly laughed aloud, and the ewe struggled harder.

'Oh dear, I'm very sorry, I frightened her.' She stroked the creature's head, half expecting it to respond like a cat: be comforted, rub its ears against her. 'There, there,' she soothed it. 'There, there, it's all right.'

The sheep shied away. It felt hard. Its head was bony and its wool dry and scratchy. Polly had imagined it would be soft, yielding. It was also full of panic and pain: it was strong, it was desperate, and its hooves were frantic and sharp.

Polly remembered a book she'd picked up once in the Belsize Park bookshop: Jane Fonda's Birth Guide . . . she couldn't remember the title exactly, but she'd dipped into the section about how to help and coach your partner through the pangs of parturition.

'Breathe deeply, darling!' she urged the sheep. 'You can do it. You're doing brilliantly.'

The sheep gave a sharp convulsive twitch and uttered another wild cry.

'Oh dear, she does seem upset.'

'You'd be upset if I had my arm up your fanny,' commented Joe, struggling. The sheep, stung by some deep pang, gave a huge kick.

'Christ, I said sit on 'er head, can't you? D'you want me to get kicked in the nuts?' Polly pressed all her strength against the sheep's shoulder and tried not to think about fannies and nuts.

'Trouble is, she's a theave,' he commented dourly, with a curl of the lip very like his father's.

'A—what?'

'A theave. This is her first lamb, see? She doesn't know what it's all about.'

Polly felt sorry for the helpless creature, lying on its side in this freezing barn suffering such indignities. It seemed unfair that epidurals were available only to human beings. Polly felt an overwhelming urge to make the sheep a cup of tea, but conquered it.

'Hand me that thing there.' Joe indicated a strange instrument lying on the straw: a kind of small lasso-like contraption of cord and plastic. Polly dumbly passed it to him. The word *garotte* sprang foolishly into her mind.

Joe applied the instrument to the sheep's back end, however, and pulled. Polly exerted every sinew to keep the creature on its side. It was the hardest work she'd done since the sofa had got stuck on the stairs when she'd moved into the Hampstead flat. Between Joe's hands, encircled by the helpful cord, two infant hooves appeared, covered with slime and looking curiously black and hard. One more heave, a deep bellow from the sheep, and she was delivered.

The lamb lay twitching in the straw, covered with patches of blood and what looked like egg-yolk. It trembled and shivered; faint spirals of steam rose from its flanks. Joe briefly inspected it, picked it up unceremoniously by its feet, and laid it at its mother's nose. She sniffed, and licked. The lamb lolled about, dazed by the light and the sudden cold. Its first glimpse of a freezing and dazzling world. It must be rather like arriving in heaven, thought Polly.

'She'll be all right,' observed Joe, and then returned to his inspection of the sheep's ducts. 'Thought so,' he commented after a moment. 'She's got another one in there.'

'Oh, twins!' gushed Polly foolishly. 'How wonderful!' Luckily Joe wasn't listening.

A second lamb was delivered, and lay blinking in the straw; its mother received and licked it, and its elder sister gave a faint bleat of greeting, or protest. Joe surveyed the scene.

'She's motherin' them well,' he commented. 'It's marvellous, to see the instinct comin' out.'

Polly suddenly found her nose full of tears. For a moment she could not speak. She felt opened up, somehow: vulnerable, tender. Hastily she scrambled to her feet.

'Shall I make you a cup of tea?' she asked, falteringly. 'You must be exhausted.' Joe smiled, and she felt warm.

'That's the first sensible thing you've said all night.' Polly ran back to the house.

As she tip-toed down the hall, the phone rang, sudden and shrill. On impulse she grabbed it, and heard the familiar swirls and currents of a transatlantic line.

'Hello?'

'That you, Polly?'

'Daniel! Have you any idea what time it is here?'

'Well, what's the problem? You answered right away.'

'Yes but—it's three a.m.!'

'Sorry, sweetheart. I got confused. I'm in San Francisco now and I was thinking New York. How are things?'

'Oh, fine. I'm helping with the lambing.'

'Yeah. Very picturesque. How's the script coming along?'

'Well, I haven't actually got as far as that yet. How are things with you?'

'Dismal. This guy MacAlistair is a complete fucking crook. He's trying to do all kinds of clever stuff with the rights. But I think I've nailed him.'

Polly did not even bother to try and remember who MacAlistair was. And despite the fact that she'd been longing for Daniel to phone, she felt a curious urge to get back to the important business of Joe's cup of tea.

Chapter  Thirteen

Polly was half-asleep the following afternoon as she walked to Mrs Lillicrap's. Mind you, it wasn't hard to deduce which was The Hall: a beautiful little Queen Anne house next to the church. Its pale gold Bath stone gleamed in the late winter sunlight as Polly passed between the wrought-iron gates and walked up the drive, and her eye was pleased by its symmetry and elegance. How sad that such jewels should pass into the hands of such as Mrs Lillicrap! But there you are,. money talks, meditated Polly regretfully, casting an admiring eye on a drift of dainty streaked crocuses.

Suddenly a large black dog bounded out of the shrubbery and barked in her face. Polly recoiled, emitting a frigid little squeak of terror before holding her hands out to the dog in the recommended manner—though it went very much against her instincts to offer it anything more friendly than a stout stick.

'Orpheus! Down!'

A figure rose from the shrubbery, where she had clearly been involved in gardening of the most fundamental kind. She was an untidy, greying woman in her late fifties, with a distracted air and faraway eyes. Mrs Lillicrap's gardener, Polly assumed.

'You're doing a splendid job,' breezed Polly. 'Wonderful crocuses!'

The woman gave a thin, hesitant smile.

'Yes, aren't they good?' She appeared to be waiting for Polly to say more.

'I've come to tea,' beamed Polly. She was good at putting half-witted middle-aged women at their ease. Speaking of which, she must write to her mum.

'To tea . . .?'

The gardener looked around with the perplexed, lost air of Lewis Carroll's White Queen. Polly was sorely tempted to ask her if there was jam today. Instead she became businesslike.

'Is Mrs Lillicrap in?'

Understanding spread over the White Queen's features.

'Ah,' she said gently. 'You must be looking for The Hall.'

'But—isn't this The Hall?' faltered Polly.

'This is The Manor,' said the White Queen, with the quiet air of one producing the Trump of Trumps. 'My daughter Charlotte will show you The Hall.'

Brisk footsteps were approaching from the house. Polly turned to see a brace of black labradors—Orpheus and, well, Eurydice, possibly, straining at their leashes. A woman of uncertain age, but possibly rather younger than Polly, had the dogs well in hand. She was small and squat, with the awkward air of one who has never quite worked out what sort of clothes suited her. Horn-rimmed glasses completed an ensemble of ill-tempered tweeds and gaberdines so inexpertly thrown on that Polly longed to take her to Knightsbridge and spend a couple of days transforming her from waddling frump to . . . well, waddling vision of delight, possibly.

'The Hall?' barked the waddling frump. 'C'mon. 'Snot far.'

'I'm so sorry!' Polly turned a deferential face to the White Queen, with a conviction that she had somehow committed a monstrous *faux pas*.

'Not at all!' was the reply, in a kind of half-mad whisper,

and the Lady of the Manor sank with evident relief back onto her laurels.

Polly ran after Charlotte, who was striding off down the drive and exchanging barks with the dogs.

'Oh dear, I am sorry! I simply thought this must be The Hall.' Charlotte did not bother to look at her.

'Happens all the time. It wasn't The Hall originally, you see. She changed the name when she moved in.'

She, Polly assumed, was Mrs Lillicrap, and she thought she detected a hint of scorn in Charlotte's voice. Well, to be honest, not so much a hint as half a ton of scorn. It seemed as if it might be Charlotte's favourite tone.

'We find it rather over-restored,' she went on. 'But then we're hopelessly old-fashioned in our views. I like things plain and unimproved.' She shot Polly a defiant glance as if to say *including myself*. Polly felt the prospects for a make-over in Knightsbridge were slim.

'Oh well, absolutely,' Polly agreed. 'That's one of the things I like so much about this village.'

'It used to be all right,' conceded Charlotte gruffly, with the air of one who clutched to herself certain grim secrets. They walked on for a moment or two in silence, until it became clear that Charlotte was not going to reveal exactly what had gone wrong in Long Dangley.

'Well, I find it quite pretty,' said Polly eventually. 'I'm just staying here for a few weeks.'

'Holiday?' barked Charlotte, in tones of semi-contempt.

'Working holiday,' corrected Polly mildly.

'What sort of work?'

'Oh—er, research.' Polly thought it might not be tactful to mention television. Charlotte was unlikely to feel that television had done much to keep the world plain and unimproved. 'I'm a writer.'

'What sort of writer?' demanded Charlotte.

'Oh, all sorts of things. Historical fiction, mostly.' Polly felt uneasy about the lie, but squeamish about the truth.

'Mother adores Mary Stewart,' commented Charlotte, pulling Orpheus away from a leg-up situation by someone's gate. 'I prefer Len Deighton. Not that I get much time to read at all.'

'What . . . what do you do?' ventured Polly rather timidly, wondering if Charlotte was perhaps a member of the SAS, a Customs Officer or nightclub bouncer.

'I run the estate,' she snapped. 'Mother's impossible and Father's gaga so there you are.'

Polly made what she hoped was a sympathetic murmuring sound, and decided not to ask how extensive the estate was. That would surely sound rather common. *How big is it* is never an elegant question and Polly had learned long ago that size was not important. What they did with the estate was likely to be much more interesting.

'You don't get much time for Len Deighton,' grumbled Charlotte, 'when you have to keep farm managers and foresters in order.'

'I suppose not,' said Polly, feeling a pang of sympathy for the foresters and farm managers.

'There's The Hall, down there,' Charlotte pointed to white gates between clipped privet. The contrast with her own wrought iron and yews could not have been more obvious.

'Thank you so much,' said Polly. 'I hope we'll meet again.'

'I wouldn't bank on it,' said Charlotte. 'I never meet anybody.' And she showed her teeth in what Polly later realised must have been a smile.

The Hall was a long, low house, perhaps originally a pair of Elizabethan cottages, now one dwelling, and disfigured with aluminium window-frames, double glazing and a burglar alarm. Never mind, thought Polly, the double glazing will come in handy. A chill wind had sprung up, and as she rang the doorbell Polly observed an early daffodil, of rather an over-ornamented double type, being thrashed by the wind against a stone.

'My dear! Come in!' Mrs Lillicrap wafted her into the heavily patterned fug, and as Polly took off her coat she was dismayed to detect sounds suggestive of Gloria's children in the sitting-room beyond.

'Hi, Polly!'

Gloria had invaded the sofa, and Aqua was sitting huddled up next to her, sucking her thumb wanly and looking martyred. Terry was on the floor arranging a series of transport disasters between a train, a lorry and a car. Sky, thank God, was not apparent.

'This is Mildred,' said Mrs Lillicrap, briefly gesturing towards a thin woman perched on a chair by the fire. She had the air of a stork or crane, her long nose and glasses gleaming in the light from Mrs Lillicrap's teak candelabra. Polly assumed that Mrs Lillicrap had withheld Mildred's name to demonstrate her inferior social status.

'This is Polly Partridge, Mildred.' At least Polly had managed to hold onto her surname. 'Gloria's friend. The Writer. You must be so very clever.' Polly received this gush with reluctance.

'I'm not all that clever,' she shrugged. 'I couldn't even manage to find the right house. I went to The Manor by mistake.'

'Went to the bloody Manor by mistake!' shrieked Gloria. 'Oh Polly you are a berk!'

'Indeed, so much of a berk was I,' admitted Polly, 'that I mistook the lady of the house for your gardener.'

Mrs Lillicrap, Gloria and Mildred all roared with laughter. Terry laughed too, to feel grown up. Only the awful Aqua demurred.

'Mummeeee!' she whinged. 'What are you laughing at?'

'Well!' exclaimed Mrs Lillicrap, smoothing down her red polyester jacket with evident satisfaction. 'So you thought Lady Fairfax was my gardener, eh? What a hoot! My dear, you deserve the biggest cream cake of the lot for that!'

Polly didn't argue.

Chapter  Fourteen

'Gloria won't tell me what you're up to,' beamed Mrs Lillicrap, handing Polly a cup of tea, 'but I know you're up to something! And I'm famous for my intuition. I say no more, but . . .'

She tapped the side of her nose and winked—a ghastly sight. Polly smiled in what she hoped was an inscrutable and mysterious manner.

'I'm not really up to anything,' she said. 'Just taking a few weeks off.'

'Ah, but, my dear, you're a *writer*!' Mrs Lillicrap's eyes narrowed in excitement. 'Writers are always up to something. My mother knew Ronald Hislop-Learing, you know.'

Polly raised her eyebrows in polite admiration.

'Have you ever read any of his stuff? *Heartbeats in Havana*, that was a terribly exciting one. But my favourite was always *A Hot Gun in Guadalajara*.'

Polly regretted that she had not had the good fortune to encounter Ronald's work, so far.

'Well, he was always a terribly dark horse. He used to come and stay with us in our house down at Pratt's Bottom. And Mother always used to say, "Don't look at me like that, Ronald—I know you're doing research!" He had a terribly researching kind of look, you know. Mother was always convinced that the Mexican Chief of Police in *Guadalajara* was based on Father.'

'What was your father?'

'An accountant, dear. But Mother said she knew it was him by the way he cleared his throat.'

'How extraordinary.'

'Terry, don't touch that!' Gloria had been trying to urge the whinging Aqua towards a crumpet and had, for a fatal moment, failed to notice Terry's terrifying lurch towards a little coffee-table adorned with figurines. Polly privately thought that the best thing that could happen to the figurines would be a visit from Terry with his sustainably managed hardwood hammer, but instead she removed him, with a graceful swoop, and placed him reluctantly on her knee.

'Isn't he a little darling?' drooled Mrs Lillicrap.

'Isn't he?' agreed Polly, pinioning the child in a penal embrace. However, though in works of fiction childless women often descend on lawless broods and civilise them with effortless authority, to the envy of their pathetic incompetent mothers, Polly felt that such a triumph was beyond her. With a few furtive kicks Terry regained his freedom, and rolled away towards the electric sockets.

'I'm afraid my house isn't designed for toddlers,' smiled Mrs Lillicrap with evident satisfaction, taking in with a single self-congratulatory glance the glass giraffes, the plates adorned with the features of the Prince and Princess of Wales, and the strange lamps made of shells which glowed invitingly upon small tables conveniently draped with pull 'n' smash lace cloths.

Gloria abandoned Aqua and the crumpet and rescued Terry within seconds of electrocution—rather unsportingly, Polly thought.

'Bloody kids!' puffed Gloria. 'Still, it's the natural instinct, isn't it, to explore and all that. But all the same—when it says in the Bible, *she wrapped him in swaddling clothes*, well, you've got to admit, the girl had her head screwed on.'

'Oh Gloria, you are a one!' Mrs Lillicrap evidently enjoyed the frisson of Gloria's blasphemies. Mildred, hith-

81

erto silent, opened her handbag a seductive crack and beckoned Terry like an old witch in a fairy tale.

'Terry?' she coaxed. 'Do you want to come and see what's in my handbag?'

Terry obliged. *I just hope she hasn't got the remains of her breakfast in there*, thought Polly. Aqua cranked up her discontent a gear, from whinge to snivel. She, too, wanted to examine the handbag. Mrs Lillicrap handed her a strange knitted doll with a huge crinoline skirt, whose normal function, Polly suspected, was to disguise rolls of lavatory paper in Mrs Lillicrap's dainty little toilet. Aqua examined the doll listlessly.

'It hasn't got any legs,' she complained.

'I've heard you're a writer of historical romances, Polly,' said Mrs Lillicrap with a sudden purposeful pounce, 'but I've been to the library and asked them to look you up on the computer thing and there's no mention of you at all. I was so disappointed. I so much wanted to read one of your books before you came to tea!'

Polly blushed. She wished she'd never concocted this historical romance story. Gloria gave her a startled glance. They really had to get their act together and agree a decent alibi for her.

'Ah, well, Polly writes under a pseudonym!' brayed Gloria in a rescuing manner. 'You wouldn't expect her to write under her own name, would you? I mean, some of her stuff . . . it's really *sizzling*!' Mrs Lillicrap's eyes flashed in excitement.

'Really? did you hear that, Mildred?'

'Oh yes,' Gloria went on, with a naughtily conspiratorial glance at Polly. 'Polly's at the leading raunchy edge of historical romance. She's famous for her ripped bodices.'

'How splendid!' gurgled Mrs Lillicrap. 'Let me guess. Are you Virginia Buchanan? Holly Daventry? Pearl Savage?'

'Not telling!' grinned Polly. 'State secret!'

'I did hear . . .' Mrs Lillicrap's eyes played speculatively over Polly's noncommittal features, 'that somebody's bought the film rights to Pearl Savage's *Wet Swords at Dawn*.'

'Really?' smiled Polly. 'Nice for Pearl.' Mrs Lillicrap gave her a culminating leer.

'We'll say no more about it now, dear,' she winked. 'But let's say I think I know what you're up to.'

Polly shrugged, as charmingly as possible.

'But what I was really hoping,' she went on, 'I asked Gloria and she thought you might—I was hoping you might be prepared to talk to the WI.'

Polly's heart sank. 'Of course! I'd be delighted. What about?'

'Oh, anything. Being a Writer. The City and the Country. The Person in History I Most Admire.'

'Who do you admire most in history, Pol?' asked Gloria through a mouthful of the half-masticated crumpet Aqua had rejected.

'Catherine the Great,' said Polly immediately.

'Oh really? Why?'

'Well, she did just as she liked. She got through masses of lovers—wore whole generations of young men out.'

'Ah! I see a new book taking shape!' pounced Mrs Lillicrap. 'With Meryl Streep in the title role!'

'Hardly,' objected Polly. 'Catherine was quite stout, I believe.'

'Good for her!' Mrs Lillicrap offered her rather baroque cream cakes around yet again. There were no takers, except Terry, and his acceptance was vetoed by Gloria—the first sensible parental act Polly had detected in her friend.

'Well, I'll certainly talk to the Women's Institute, with pleasure,' said Polly between clenched teeth. 'About Catherine the Great, if you like.' She was uneasily aware, however, that she might be mixing Catherine the Great up with another, lewder, queen. Queen Somebody or other of Sweden, perhaps. She would have to do her homework.

'Oh thank you so much! Everyone will be thrilled!'

'It's no trouble,' lied Polly. 'I might as well make a modest contribution to village life whilst I'm here.'

'Ah, but we've got another much more exciting little project lined up for you, Pol,' said Gloria with a dangerous grin.

'What?'

'Seduce Joe!'

Mrs Lillicrap hissed in suppressed pleasure, and the hitherto silent Mildred burst out in an astonishingly filthy cackle. Polly felt faint.

'Seduce . . . Joe?'

'Well, he's twenty-eight, you see, Polly, and as far as we can tell, he's sound in wind and limb. But no sign of a girl.'

'Gloria thinks he's gay!' whispered Mrs Lillicrap, with an electric sense of pure thrill. 'But Mildred says not. Don't you, Mildred?'

Mildred shook her long nose solemnly to and fro, and settling Terry down to play with the hologram on her bank card, she hunched her shoulders up in the time-honoured stance of one about to share a saucy secret, and let fly.

'It was about six year ago, I'm sure of it, there was this little girl come to do for Lady Fairfax, Danish or Dutch she was, I can never remember the difference, anyway her name was Martje or Marthe or something, I saw them in Blackstone's Wood when I was taking Queenie for a walk, they saw me, too, mind, and they got up double quick and dashed off, but I'm sure it was Joe, I recognised his bottom. Not a bare bottom, you understand – ' Mildred blushed hastily, 'proper corduroy trousers and that, to be honest it was the corduroy I recognised – '

'Mildred is a great connoisseur of men's bums,' teased Gloria.

'Lay off, Gloria, you are a one! But anyway I've heard the odd thing since, that there's a woman over in Nether Swell he's been seeing. And that Martje she didn't half disappear quick. She was packed off back to Denmark or whatever.'

'Lady Fairfax wasn't pleased, then?' asked Polly. 'That was a bit old-fashioned of her.'

'Not her,' confided Mildred with deepening significance. 'That *Charlotte*, she's a terror.'

'Jealous,' sighed Mrs Lillicrap disapprovingly. 'She was always jealous of my Angelica, too. That's Angelica.' She handed Polly a framed photograph of a vacuous blonde girl wearing a Swiss embroidered blouse of a particularly naff kind.

'Good heavens, she is pretty,' said Polly obligingly, avoiding Gloria's eye. 'But tell me more about Joe, Mildred.'

'She's interested!' cried Mrs Lillicrap. 'She's taken a fancy to him already! I can tell!'

'Not at all,' Polly corrected her calmly. 'I'm just naturally intrigued to know more about my hosts. And since Mr and Mrs Swain are the picture of respectability, I assume the only possible source of entertainment is the unfortunate Joe.'

'Picture of respectability, eh?' Mildred directed a deft snigger at Mrs Lillicrap, who smiled in a pursed, omniscient way. 'You'd be amazed at what that Arthur Swain has got up to in his time. I had it from my cousin Ellen at Langton Coombe.'

'What was it, then?' asked Polly.

'She says—and mind you, I'd trust her word any day— she used to be in the Police, you know – '

'Who?' Polly was confused.

'My cousin Ellen—her friend Annie Taylor, you know, *lived in the same village*—anyway apparently, twenty years ago this was, mind, Arthur Swain had got twins pregnant!'

'Got . . . twins pregnant? You mean, got somebody pregnant with twins?'

'No, no, dear—there were these twin girls, Eva and Alice, worked at the Co-op they did, and he got them both pregnant!'

'What—simultaneously?'

'Some people say, *on the same night!*'

'Good Lord!'

'And that's not the end of it.' Mildred's eyes widened behind their spectacles in glorious anticipation of some final coup. Polly held her breath. 'He got them pregnant—with twins! They had a set of twins each! Alice had boys and Eva had girls!'

Polly was stunned. Compared to the epic, almost Greek, ingenuity of Mr Swain's peccadilloes, what passed for perversity in Hampstead was but a lame, tame thing.

'What, Mr Swain? . . . I can hardly believe it.'

'Still waters run deep,' pronounced Mrs Lillicrap heavily.

'Yes, but honestly . . . was he already married to Mrs Swain at the time?'

'Oh yes. What that poor woman puts up with!' Mildred shook her head sadly at the price some innocent human soul had to pay for such a prize slice of misdemeanour.

'Well, it's obvious why Joe's a slow starter, then,' mused Polly. 'He feels nothing but contempt for his father's wild oats, and he's determined to shame him by his own legendary celibacy.'

'Ah, but it's such a waste, Pol!' groaned Gloria. 'All that lovely muscle—and those curls. What he needs is a woman of sophistication and experience. To draw him out. Bind up the old wounds. Teach him a thing or two. And then set him on his way.'

'Oh yes, Polly dear!' urged Mrs Lillicrap. 'Do! Please do! He's begging for it. And I'm sure it would be a labour of love.'

'The one thing I can absolutely assure you,' said Polly putting down her cup with a regal finality, 'is that I am never, under any circumstances, going to teach Joe Swain a thing or two, as you so crudely put it, Gloria. Apart from my aesthetic objections to the whole thing, I do not fancy him in the least.'

Luckily, at this point, Aqua wet herself—a useful diversion. All the same, thought Polly, *vis-à-vis* wetting one's knickers, there but for the grace of God go I.

Chapter  Fifteen

Next day, Polly set about her task. Not seducing Joe—researching for the TV series of *Cold Comfort Farm*. She was uneasily aware that she had done little enough towards it in the few days she had already spent in Long Dangley, and had instead lounged and mooched about rather aimlessly, and enjoyed long hot baths in her own little bathroom followed by long hot books in her bed. She had, she told herself, been resting and absorbing things unconsciously—the best way, because the least effort. But now she would consciously reconnoitre.

Polly surveyed the interior of Harrow Hill Farm with increasing perplexity. It was old, with beams and stuff, but it had felt the hand of the late twentieth century and could not be transformed to *Cold Comfort Farm* without a comprehensive ripping-down of Mrs Swain's twee Laura Ashley wallpaper, a ripping-up of acres of cosy twinkling polypropethylene carpet and a ripping-off of the sensible corrugated asbestos roof of the barn.

Where so much that was convenient had been ripped, it would then be necessary to install much bare, dank, stinking stone, with bloodstains and dungstains and God knows what. Polly was depressed. Her first conclusion was that it would be far easier to build the whole interior in the studios at Granada. She could just imagine the ingenious techs getting cracking with their aerosol cans of COBWEB and SLIME. But such a thought was disappointing. Polly resisted it.

Where Cold Comfort Farm was large, bare, stony and decrepit, Harrow Hill Farm was trim, cosy and welcoming. But might not some of the more ancient and ramshackle outbuildings be pressed into service? Polly had noticed several tumbledown barns apart from the handsome new one: there was a choice of rural hovels scattered here and there. She would put her coat on and go and look.

It was a cold, sunshiny day: with the fur hat Daniel had, brought her back from Moscow, and her gloves, and the copy of *Cold Comfort Farm* vibrating hotly in her coat pocket, she was looking forward to some exercise in the bracing air. As she was putting on her wellies in the porch Mr Swain thundered up the path in his huge boots. He gave her a sour nod.

Then Joe came out of the barn and hailed his father. Polly did not catch the exact form of address but she feared it fell short of perfect filial duty.

'The Jersey's calved,' Joe announced. 'Twins. A bullcalf and a heifer.'

'Oh, how lovely!' Polly burst out, unable to contain her delight. 'At least—I suppose twins are a good thing?' Then suddenly she recalled Mr Swain's history of misbehaviour with twins, and blushed.

But Mr Swain took no notice of her. He gave an enigmatic grunt and went into the house. Perhaps he always reacted thus to any mention of twins. Polly did not detect in his demeanour much in the way of remorse, guilt or repentance, however. He just looked peeved, as usual.

'Twins a good thing?' said Joe, wiping his hands on what had once been a cloth. The spring sunshine danced on his curls, reminding Polly of Caravaggio's glorious boys who glowed in many an art gallery around the world. 'What do you think? Would it be a good thing if you had twins?' And he grinned at her, rather saucily for one entirely dedicated to celibacy.

'Oh yes,' said Polly. 'An excellent thing. Get it all over with at once. Do cows often have twins?'

'Aye,' said Joe. 'We had a cow once, had twins by different bulls.'

'Really?' asked Polly, intrigued despite herself. 'How did that happen?'

'Well, we had this Friesian cow, and at the time we didn't have a bull, so my father took her down to be served by old Grainger's bull. Down in the next valley. An Angus, he was. Well, he did his work all right, and my father was just leading her back, when he passed this field with a Hereford bull in it. Blimey, you should have heard him bellow! Like Placido Domingo, he was. And blow me if our little Friesian cow didn't jump through the hedge to him and he served her an' all. And she had twins: an Angus and a Hereford.'

'How extraordinary!' said Polly. 'If that sort of thing happened in human society, there'd be a bit of a scandal.'

'It happens all the time,' said Joe with a wink, and then he suddenly strode off.

'How is the lambing going?' called Polly after him, annoyed with herself for not asking earlier. He turned round and paused briefly.

'Hectic,' he called, with something of his father's martyred air.

'Well, look, if there's anything I can do – '

'Just bring me a cup o' tea at three o' clock in the morning, again,' he grinned, challengingly.

Polly's heart gave a curious little skip. *Stop that at once, you idiot*, she commanded it. Sometimes it just went off into adrenalin overdrive all by itself. Polly thought that perhaps it was due to her having taken too many sleeping pills in her time. She hadn't needed her pills here in the country, at all, though. The country air simply felled her at nine thirty p.m.

She would get up at three o'clock and make him a cup of tea, however. There was something about the way he insulted her that was curiously bracing. Polly was developing an ambition to wrest a compliment from his lips—not to her personal appearance, fie upon that, but to her competence. She would make the best cup of tea he'd ever tasted, the bastard.

And now to inspect the ruins. Polly ventured out of the main yard and through a gate that led behind the house to a clump of Scots pines. There was a long low building on the left which looked quite promising. Cautiously Polly opened the peeling door and went inside. Ah! This was more like it. Various bits of furniture and relics of industrial machinery lay about, covered with a pale film of filth. In the centre of the room was a huge box, like two tea-chests put together, and over this box hung a sun lamp.

Perhaps this was where Joe came and stripped off and did a bit of sybaritic lounging, thought Polly with a smirk. He did have an unusually healthy glow. It would be satisfying, somehow, to know that it was caused by a solarium rather than the winds of heaven.

Whatever its present function, this room would make a perfect kitchen for Cold Comfort Farm. Or even the hovel of Meriam Beetle, the hired girl who was regularly served by Seth Starkadder every year when the sukebind hung heavy, as a result of which Meriam herself hung heavy and in the fullness of time was delivered. Yes, this would make a perfect hovel. Polly took out her copy of the book to check a few details.

Ten minutes later she was sitting on an upended box, roaring with laughter, when the door burst open and Joe came in, carrying a small, very feeble-looking lamb. Hastily Polly stood up and hid her book.

'What you doing lurking in here?' he asked, putting the lamb in the box and switching on the lamp.

'Oh, it just seemed a nice peaceful place for a read,' said Polly, trying to sound innocent.

'Oh yeah?' Joe straightened up. '*Cold Comfort Farm*, eh?'

My God. Not only could he read, but he had eyes like lasers. Polly felt foolish.

'Yes.'

'It's a great book, that'n,' affirmed Joe, leaning down to give the lamb a little shake.

'Is this the intensive care unit?' enquired Polly, trying to direct the conversation away from dangerous areas such as literature. She did not wish, yet, to mention her project. She did not want to scare the Swains off at the thought of TV cameras before she had even got to know them properly.

The lamb's wan eyes blinked at them. Polly's heart felt squeezed by pity. She wanted to pick the lamb up and cuddle it. Joe gave the tiny creature a long, thoughtful look.

'Aye. Intensive care.'

'What's wrong with this one?'

'It's poor,' he said. 'Cold. Needs warming up a bit.'

'Will it live?' asked Polly, trying not to sound desperate.

'Might. Might not.'

They both looked into the box. Warmth flooded over the lamb. Its tiny life flickered in the straw.

'Give it a couple of hours,' said Joe. Then he turned to face Polly with a strange, taunting light in his eyes. '*Cold Comfort Farm*, eh? Fancy me as Seth, do you?'

'I don't fancy you at all, to be honest,' said Polly, suddenly descending, in panic, to gross flirtation. 'I prefer chain-smoking wimps, if you really must know.'

A naughty look crept into his eye. 'Oh, so do I. Especially those Filipinos.' He turned to go, then paused at the door.

'You ever been to Glyndebourne?' he asked, suddenly.

'Well, actually—yes.'

'You must tell me about it some time,' he said, with a curiosity which sounded genuine.

'I'll tell you at three o'clock tomorrow morning,' said

Polly, feeling she had recaptured some essential dignity, but only just. 'When I bring your tea.'

'Thanks,' said Joe. 'I'll see if I can lay on any chain-smoking wimps for you.'

Chapter  Sixteen

'Hi, babe! I'm back. So warm the bed up. I'll be right over.'
Daniel's voice crackled ominously across the wire.

'What! When?' Polly felt seized by a mysterious panic.
Dan couldn't come over—not now.

'How 'bout tomorrow? I've slept off my jet-lag and I've
got a nice little duty-free treat for you. I'm corn fed and
raring to go, sweetheart. What time shall I arrive?'

'No—wait! I can't talk now.' Polly was aware of Mrs
Swain dusting quietly in the next room. 'I'm a bit busy. I'll
ring you back in half an hour. OK?'

'No need, Pol. No need. Name your hour and I'll be
there.'

'It's—a bit difficult,' faltered Polly. 'Let me ring you back
in half an hour. Really.' And she put the phone down,
palpitating.

Blindly she ran to her room, grabbed her bag and coat,
and drove to the phone box in the village. She did not dare
to investigate the cause of her panic. Polly was not the sort
of person who lifts stones up to see what's underneath. She
well knew it would be slimy, or have too many legs. But
the important thing was, Daniel mustn't come.

This was curious, given her desperation to see him only
a few days ago. But it was irrevocable. The farm, Long
Dangley, all this—it must be out of bounds to him. She
seized the phone.

'Listen, babe—what's going on?'

94

'I'm sorry, Daniel. I couldn't ring from the house. It's a bit awkward, you see—the the farm's got—got an exclusion order slapped on it.'

'A *what*?'

Thank God Daniel was so ignorant of agricultural legislation. Thank God she was, too. She could improvise happily without being distracted by real knowledge.

'One of the cows died a couple of days ago. You know—mysteriously.'

'What? Murdered for its money, you mean? Well, call Miss Marple.'

'No. Listen, Daniel. This is serious. They don't know what it died of. It could be FHB.'

'What?'

'It's a notifiable disease. The police came and everything and put us in quarantine. No one can come here. We all have to dip our wellies in Dettol every time we cross the yard.' Polly rattled on eagerly, warming to her theme.

'Well, how long's all this going to go on?' demanded Daniel grumpily.

'Not long. Just—till they've got the results of the tests and things. Listen. I'll come to London instead. Next weekend. It's my mother's concert anyway. With her choir, you know.'

'But I thought you were in quarantine?'

'Er no – ' Polly skated on thin ice. 'It's all right for us to go out as long as we're properly—er—disinfected. But no one's allowed to come to the farm.'

'Well look—I'll stay in the village. At the pub or whatever. And you can visit me there. I can pretend you're the chambermaid and fall on you. Like Byron.'

'Shut up! No. Listen. I'll come to London. I'm dying for a breath of stale air. It's ghastly here. You know how you hate the country. You'd die of boredom. It's awful. I'll come to you. I'll ring on Friday.' Polly slammed the receiver down and waited for a cock to crow. There was a merciful silence.

She stepped out of the phone box and filled her lungs with the fresh, dewy nectar that passed for air, down here. It was like inhaling Baume de Venise.

Polly walked along blindly for a moment or two, recovering from the ordeal of lying to Daniel. It was odd, but a tribute to their relationship, that she had done very little of it, so far. Mind you, she wasn't so confident about him. She suspected he might have done more than his fair share of lying to her. So it wasn't really a tribute to their relationship—it was a tribute to her. This thought was strangely comforting. Polly looked up from her reverie, and found herself at the church.

She went in through the gate. Polly liked churchyards. As a spinner of fictions she fed off the wonderful names on the tombstones, the tantalising glimpses of the history of dynasties. Poignant childhood deaths, lifelong marriages, and always the distant devouring combine harvester of war.

A figure was kneeling at one of the more recent graves, arranging flowers in a vase. By the breadth of the back and the fortissimo of the blonde hair, Polly deduced it to be Maisie the postmistress. She was talking as she worked. Polly ducked behind a tombstone (*In Memory of Henry Puddle, a loving husband and father*—and a confirmed wet, thought Polly).

'It's not been a bad week,' Maisie addressed the air, and presumably, the Departed. 'But we had to send back a whole crate of custard creams. Weevils! Honestly. Still, what can you expect. They came from Europe. They weren't even proper custard creams. Sort of wafery things. Still, Fred said, what can you expect, from Belgium.'

She paused and sighed.

'You did love yer ginger nuts, didn't you, you poor old sod.'

She lumbered to her feet.

'Oh yes. Bert told me to tell you that England avoided the follow-on by thirty-four runs but Peter Power's got a groin strain.'

Maisie gave a soft little giggle.

'Remember that groin strain you got in Gateshead? Still, it was well worth it, like you said. No need to worry about groins now, eh? Poor old sod. Tara then. See you later.'

Polly had no time to ponder the sinister undertones of this farewell, for Maisie was upon her.

'Hello, dear,' she beamed. 'My first husband. Len.' She indicated the grave.

'I'm so sorry,' murmured Polly.

'Wore hisself out. He had a rapture and it perforated his spleen. Or sommink. Search me. I hear you're going to talk to the WI.'

'Er—oh dear. Yes.'

'What's it all about, then?'

'Catherine the Great.' Or was it, Polly wondered, Queen Christina of Sweden? She must find out—urgently.

'Who's she?'

'Oh well, a Queen of Russia two hundred years ago. Bit of a man-eater, actually.'

'Great!' grinned Maisie. 'Maybe us can pick up a few tips, eh?' Polly doubted it. They bade a cordial farewell.

Polly noticed a door in the churchyard wall. It led directly into the garden of The Manor. Polly was devoured with a great desire to inspect the house from this angle, and perhaps receive another glimpse of Lady Fairfax's splendid garden. Though Polly hated gardening herself, she admired the results. There was a tiny knothole in the door, conveniently situated at eye level. Polly glanced furtively around. No one in sight.

She tiptoed to the door and applied her eye to the hole. A ravishing fragment of an antique portico gleamed between dark shrubs. There were columns, on a modest scale. It was a kind of verandah—south facing, Polly noticed. It must be warm even at this time of year. A couple of wicker chairs were set out, and a rather large old man was slumped in one of them, covered with rugs. He was fast asleep with his mouth wide open. Sir Whossname Fairfax presumably. Charlotte's father. Whom she had described as gaga.

Suddenly Polly received a strange and most unwelcome shove up the backside—which hoisted her briefly into the air. For a split second she thought it must be Daniel, spirited here by magic carpet, but the panting and wetness which accompanied the assault suggested a canine assailant.

'Orpheus! Down!—Miss Partridge?'

Polly recognised the bark as Charlotte Fairfax's and turned, in deepest misery, from her peep hole. Caught spying on The Manor by its heir! How very cringe-making.

'I'm so sorry,' she said, hastily producing her most gracious smile and winning manner, 'I simply had to admire your house.'

'Well, perhaps you'd like to admire it in more detail tomorrow?' said Charlotte. 'Down Orpheus!' For Orpheus was again thrusting his nose into Polly's Underworld. 'Mother would like you to come to tea.'

'How very kind!' exclaimed Polly eagerly.

'How are you getting on at the Swains'?' demanded Charlotte. Polly flinched. Everyone seemed to know everything about her. And since she'd started to scatter the odd self-protecting lie about, this was dangerous.

'Oh fine. Very comfortable, thanks.'

Charlotte snorted. 'I don't know how you can bear it. Especially that awful yob Joe.'

Polly thought she detected here a malaise that Vita Sackville-West might have diagnosed as suppressed randiness.

'Oh, he's all right. Rough diamond.'

'Managed to do much work?'

98

Polly could not remember exactly what work she had told Charlotte she was doing.

'Oh. Not much.'

'You must tell us all about it!' insisted Charlotte, with the air of a gauleiter interrogating a Resistance spy.

'I'm looking forward to hearing all about *your* work, too.' Polly determinedly turned the tables.

'My work. Hah! Well. Yes. Speaking of which – ' Charlotte turned on her heel, with the brisk authority of a drill sergeant. 'I must go and stick a boot up a backside. See you tomorrow. About four.'

And two nights in the cooler if you're late on parade, thought Polly.

Chapter  Seventeen

'Father, this is Polly Partridge.'

Sir Antony Fairfax looked up from his book, flung back his rug and held out his hand.

'My dear! Good morning! How do you do?'

Polly was a little disconcerted by this greeting, as it was mid-afternoon.

'Sit down, my dear. Sit down! G'morning!' He patted the sofa beside him. Polly obeyed, whilst Charlotte hovered nearby, a look of pained patience further disfiguring her features. It appeared that *Good morning* was an expression of senile high spirits. Sir Antony peppered his conversation randomly with it, as his seventeenth-century predecessors might have made free with the Egads.

'Forgive me for not rising, my dear. You see me tragically struck down.' He thumped his left leg, which was bandaged and propped up on a stool.

'I'm so sorry,' said Polly, wondering if it was gout. 'Is it painful?'

'A kind heart, you see,' he observed to Charlotte. 'A kind heart— a wonderful *ornament*, you know, to the female soul.'

Charlotte glared in a particularly unornamental way.

'Fell out of a tree,' he confided. 'One minute, teetering on the brink, my pruning knife poised, my dear, for the kill—the next—Good morning!—the brute tosses me off and I'm up to my arse in *terra firma*.'

'The branch broke,' observed Charlotte vindictively. 'I told you not to climb up. It's ridiculous at your age.'

'My dear,' Sir Antony leaned towards Polly like a tottering old tower in need of a buttress, 'at my age, everything is ridiculous. And that's the wonder of it. Good morning!'

'Well, I hope you soon recover from your accident,' said Polly. 'I've been admiring your garden. It really is quite splendid.'

'Elizabeth, Elizabeth . . . my wife, you know,' murmured the old knight. 'A bad breeder, but a gardener of genius, my dear. Good morning!'

'But you're a gardener too?' asked Polly. 'Hence the accident . . .?'

'I have a project,' he proclaimed majestically. 'I am creating a nymphaeum. At the bottom of the garden.'

'A nymphaeum?' Polly hesitated over the few broken shards of her Latin.

'Next to the river, you know. A place where water nymphs come and torment old men with the memories of past loves.'

'We're giving Miss Partridge tea in the drawing-room, Father,' said Charlotte, indicating to Polly that she should detach herself from Sir Antony's recollections before they became too indecent. 'Birgit will bring you yours in here.'

'I eat alone,' confided Sir Antony, 'on account of my teeth. Too distressing to behold, apparently. Good morning! If a man can't take his own teeth out under his own roof, what's England coming to, by God?'

'What indeed,' agreed Polly, rising serenely. 'When I get removable teeth I shall whip them out whenever I like, to annoy people.'

'My dear, you are a champion of your sex!' cried Sir Antony. 'I wish to see more of you.'

'This way.' Charlotte led Polly briskly into the drawing-room.

'God bless you, my dear!' cried Sir Antony, giving a military salute as they withdrew. 'Good morning!'

The drawing-room was dim grey and green. Cool, and old, and beautiful. A few Regency chairs, a silvery looking-glass spotted with age in the Venetian manner, huge fire irons before the massive hearth in which a meagre fire sputtered, and a smell of damp books and faded rose petals.

Lady Fairfax rose from the sofa, extended a limp hand and gazed abstractedly over Polly's left shoulder.

'Miss Partridge,' she murmured. 'How delightful. Do sit down.'

'I'll tell Birgit to bring the tea,' said Charlotte, and disappeared.

Lady Fairfax and Polly sat in silence for a moment. A clock ticked in an antique stately way. The fire crackled. The dogs Orpheus and Eurydice were sprawled on a faded Persian hearthrug where they gleamed in black unison, cocking the occasional ear or eye.

'How beautiful and peaceful it is here,' smiled Polly. 'It was so kind of you to ask me.'

'We'd heard about you,' said Lady Fairfax, staring vaguely at Polly's neck. 'And when we met the other day, I didn't realise . . . there wasn't time. You're staying in the village?'

'At Harrow Hill Farm. With the Swains.'

'Ah. The lovely valley!'

Lady Fairfax's gaze wandered to the fire, and Polly relaxed, although she felt a little cold. She wished Sir Antony had been allowed to join them. Lady Fairfax's conversation was not half so compelling. It was like being draped in damp cobwebs.

Charlotte returned and at length Birgit appeared, bringing tea. She appeared to be a Swede of the morose and brooding sort, handsome but remote. She looked as if her father shot elk.

'Thank you, Birgit,' murmured Lady Fairfax. Polly smiled encouragingly but there was no response. Birgit's every move was slow: she withdrew, eventually, rather like the Ice Age.

'A good-looking girl,' commented Polly.

'She's a halfwit,' said Charlotte.

'Oh, I don't think so, dear,' Lady Fairfax demurred. 'We've had worse.'

Polly was tempted to mention the girl who had tangled with Joe all those years ago, but refrained. Lady Fairfax would probably be pained by the memory. Polly herself was beginning to feel uneasy at the thought of Joe's past amours: and even more uneasy at the thought of her uneasiness. It was like the first intimations of seasickness. Polly put it aside.

'My daughter tells me you're doing research?' said Lady Fairfax with a faraway smile. All the same, her grey eyes were fixed quite purposefully on Polly.

'Well, in a way—yes.'

'Is this for another of your historical novels?'

'Er—yes.'

'I gather you won't reveal your *nom de plume*?'

Not in a million years, thought Polly, shaking her head in a playful way.

'Otherwise, what's the point of having one?' she shrugged—gracefully, she hoped.

'Of course . . .' Lady Fairfax's gaze wandered approvingly over Polly's grey Ralph Lauren gaberdine suit—packed for this very occasion. *You never know*, Polly had mused, back in Hampstead, *I might get asked to tea at The Manor*. And here she was, sipping Lapsang Souchong and nibbling cucumber sandwiches.

'So what's this new book going to be about, then?' demanded Charlotte.

'Ah!' Polly's mind went blank. 'Yes. The book. Well, I'm working on the doomed love idea, actually. You know.

There's the Lord of the Manor, a wealthy man, ambitious, and so on, and his daughter falls hopelessly in love with a serf, or a shepherd, or something.' Charlotte blushed violently, and Polly realised with a sickening lurch that Charlotte had taken it personally. The cucumber sandwich turned to kapok in her mouth. Nevertheless she swallowed it.

'Dreadful, in those days, life must have been,' Polly gabbled, frantically trying to paper over the cracks. 'I mean, when girls had nothing better to do than fall in love all the time. Dreadfully boring. We're so lucky,' she exposed herself bravely to Charlotte's glare, 'to have work—important work—well, yours is at any rate . . . here, the estate'— she faltered, thinking perhaps she should include Lady Fairfax in this hymn of praise to female labour—'land, and gardens and so forth, well, what could be more important? Custodians of the very fabric of the land.' She wasn't sure about *Custodians*. It sounded a bit temporary. *Landowners* might have been better. She sipped her Lapsang, trying not to choke.

'Oh, work is a bore,' sighed Lady Fairfax. 'I love a good romance. Mary Stewart and Pearl Savage. You're not Pearl Savage, I suppose? But then, you wouldn't tell us if you were.'

'Oh no,' said Polly with a laugh. 'That's right.'

'But how exactly can you do research for a novel like that?' demanded Charlotte. 'I expect I'm being awfully thick, but I just don't see what it would involve.'

'Oh, it's just the place,' said Polly, desperate to deflect attention away from the protagonists. Especially the daughter of the Lord of the Manor. 'Just the setting, you know.' With a throwaway smile.

But at her words the demeanour of Lady Fairfax and her daughter underwent a subtle change. They seemed to stiffen slightly in their chairs, and Polly began to suspect that she had committed a catastrophic blunder. She recalled, with a sickening qualm, the moment when Charlotte had caught her spying on The Manor through her peephole.

'What do you mean, the place?' Charlotte went on.

'Oh, you know—one has to have in one's mind a particular setting. Just the shape of the village, you know.'

'Minus the bungalows, of course,' said Lady Fairfax with a dying fall.

'Oh yes. It just helps, you know, consistency and that sort of thing.'

'So you're setting your next book in Long Dangley?' concluded Charlotte with a grim air of triumph. 'Recognisably as such.'

'Oh not recognisably, no, not at all,' said Polly desperately. 'I'll probably move it to Yorkshire or something. Or even Provence. You know.'

'All the same,' persisted Charlotte. 'That's what you're up to.' She seized the poker with such homicidal energy that for a moment Polly feared she was about to have her brains bashed out, but Charlotte only attacked the fire. Maybe she should fall onto her knees between Orpheus and Eurydice and cry *Forgive me it was a pointless lie I am not contemplating such a novel at all I am merely a harmless drudge inspecting a few derelict farm buildings and reporting on their scenic potential for Granada Television.*

But perhaps that would be even worse. In any case, it was too late. The temperature in the room had plunged into fathoms of icy disapproval. Lady Fairfax was staring, with a pained expression, at the portrait of an ancestor over the fireplace, as if contemplating the catastrophic fall of the House of Fairfax: from Lords of the Manor to Victims of the Bodice Ripper. Charlotte was still cradling the poker and frowning ferociously into the flames.

'Well,' said Polly, rousing herself towards a dignified retreat, 'isn't it extraordinary how cold it is for the time of year?'

Chapter  Eighteen

Polly sat at her window looking down the valley. There was the faintest hint of spring creeping green among the roots of trees, and in the hedgerows. She tried to imagine the view as it would be in high summer, with the woods in full bosky leaf: the cloudy domes of beech and ash catching the summer light. She would be back in Hampstead by then. At the thought, a slight pang passed demurely through her ribs like a stiletto.

The thought of these meadows drenched in sunlight, these trees casting heavy shade, fascinated her. And those lambs she had seen being born—she would like to see them grow fat, browsing on lush grass. She would have to come back: for a weekend, maybe. For several weekends. Perhaps she could buy a little –

A BMW suddenly appeared in the farmyard, and Mrs Lillicrap got briskly out. She cast a brief, perturbed look around her at the oceans of mud, held her camel coat tightly around her, and tip-toed towards the front door. On her way, she cocked her bright buzzard's eye upwards to Polly's window, saw her and flashed a conspiratorial smile. She also beckoned in a way which reminded Polly of an illustration of a witch in one of her childhood fairy tales.

Oh God, thought Polly, *what now*. She got up and went downstairs. Mrs Swain was just showing the visitor into the parlour.

'It's Mrs Lillicrap come to see you, dear,' she crooned. 'Shall I make a cup of tea?'

'Oh – ' Polly hesitated. Should she accept? Mrs Lillicrap rescued her with a masterful swoop.

'No thank you, not for me, Mrs Swain,' she beamed. 'I'm fine. I was just wondering, Polly, could I come up and see your room? I hate to intrude, but there must be a quite wonderful view from up there.'

'Why yes, of course, come on up,' said Polly, glad that her visitor could be thus tidied away. She was somehow too polished, too elegant, too flashy for this farmhouse. Polly herself resorted less often to Jacques Lefroq, these days. Today, for example, she was in jeans and a rather dull mud-coloured sweater which Joe had given her after she complained, in the barn at three a.m., of not feeling warm enough in her mohair-and-appliqué purple and silver number from Covent Garden.

She showed Mrs Lillicrap into her tidy, and rather beautiful, little bedroom. Mrs Lillicrap made straight for the window and peered out. Looking down on things seemed to suit her.

'Dear me, dear me, how magnificent,' she murmured. 'It must be the best view in England. Wasted on them, of course!' she whispered, and whirling round suddenly, closed the door with a theatrical flourish. Polly hoped she was not going to have to listen to an anti-Swain tirade. The faint smell of Joe crept off his jumper and stole up her nostrils in a particularly pleasant way. Polly was beginning to feel a curious loyalty to her hosts.

'My dear, do forgive all this cloak and dagger stuff!' she hissed, sitting down on Polly's bed with an expression of intense drama illuminating her face, like lightning playing over the Peak District. 'But the fact is, I've just heard the most frightful rumour!'

Polly's heart stopped. The memory of all her peccadilloes rose like a horrible apparition. For an instant Mrs Lillicrap became Polly's headmistress. The similarity was striking. Which of Polly's naughty escapades had come to light? She sat down, trying not to look guilty, and snuggled deep into Joe's jumper, for comfort.

'Mildred has a friend who works in a solicitor's office in Sedgeworth,' whispered Mrs Lillicrap. 'And she'd heard that someone has made an offer for the farm!'

Horror seized Polly. Pure, instinctive horror overwhelmed her, though God knows why. She, who was normally so careful, prudent, worldly; so well defended against her own misfortunes, let alone other people's. She let out a strange natural cry, like a cry of pain.

'No! Surely not! But why . . .?'

'It's all conjecture at this stage, Polly,' Mrs Lillicrap rattled on, 'but of course one realised that the Swains were likely to be in dire financial straits, like all farmers, poor things. I mean, the market's flat as a pancake, prices have gone through the floor, and this is quite a small farm really—and depending heavily on beef and lamb, well, one suspected—especially since Mr Swain – ' she dropped her voice to the merest hiss, 'took on rather a lot when he bought old Mathers out.'

'When?'

'Oh, ten years ago, I think, that's what Mildred said, well, it had to be done, old Mathers was hopeless, well past it, DTs and senile dementia, and in those days of course the wretched banks were practically twisting one's arm to borrow, but now, well . . . with these interest rates . . .'

'So you think they're selling up?'

Polly could scarcely believe it. There had been no sign, no clue. Indeed, part of the charm of the place was the sense that the Swains had been here for generations (even though she knew very well they hadn't—they had come across, Joe had said, from the the Vale of Ashridge, when his father was thirty-five).

Polly somehow liked to think that Joe was going to grow

old here, carrying on these timeless tasks, with a babble of little Swains, eventually, at the cottage door, and a wife . . . the figure of the wife retreated modestly indoors before Polly could identify her.

'Well, Mildred's friend says contracts are being drawn up and everything. My dear, it's a tragedy. Don't you think so?'

Polly was forced to agree wholeheartedly with Mrs Lillicrap, which went against the grain.

'But who's buying?' asked Polly.

'Ah, well, now we come to the mystery!' Mrs Lillicrap's eyes widened, and a small bead of hectic saliva flew from her lips and landed on the carpet. 'Mildred's friend says it's some company or other based in Hertfordshire, and she's sure it's developers!'

She spat out the last word as if it were a curse: which indeed, it often is, these days. Polly felt a cold hand seize her heart: something she had never before experienced outside the covers of pulp fiction. But there it was, all frigid and squeezing. She gasped, and stared out of the window, down across all the lovely tumbling tussocks of land, its joyous green emptiness.

'Think of that,' hissed Mrs Lillicrap, 'think of that, all covered with wretched bungalows! It's an outrage! It's got to be stopped!'

'But how?' faltered Polly. 'Planning permission . . .?' Planning permission was one of those subjects, like most things to do with local government, of which Polly had been hoping to remain totally ignorant to the end of her days.

'What you must do, my dear, is sound them out,' said Mrs Lillicrap. 'You're perfectly placed, here. Keep your eyes and ears open. Probe Joe gently—I'm sure that'll be a pleasure for you both – ' She paused long enough for a brief flash of vicarious lust. 'Find out what's going on. Get the inside story.'

Polly nodded. Though she did not like being made Mrs Lillicrap's lieutenant like this, the cause was just. She escorted her downstairs.

'The view from your first floor is really quite stunning, Mrs Swain!' Mrs Lillicrap called. Mrs Swain stuck her head round the kitchen door, wiping her hands on a tea towel, and nodded.

'We were just organising Polly's talk for the WI,' Mrs Lillicrap lied urbanely. 'A week next Thursday, we agreed, didn't we, Polly?' Polly nodded obediently. 'You are coming, now, aren't you, Mrs Swain? Or you'll never be able to look Polly in the eye over her breakfast bacon again.'

'What's it about?' asked Mrs Swain.

'Catherine the Great,' said Mrs Lillicrap. Polly went cold at the thought of her ignorance of Catherine the Great. She must get hold of a biography of her, and fast. 'She was an absolutely fascinating woman, Mrs Swain—and quite naughty in her way! You must come.'

Mrs Swain readily agreed to attend, in the hopes of picking up some tips from Catherine the Great, and Mrs Lillicrap went out to her car. Joe was on his way across the yard.

'Joe!' she called, in an ecstasy of matronly lasciviousness, 'you're looking unbearably gorgeous with all that dung on your shoulders!' Joe gave her a playful grin.

'How's the BMW going, Joyce?' he called back. 'Had any more trouble with the motorway police?'

'We won't talk about that, you cheeky boy!' She leapt in, slammed the door and reversed out of the yard with a crashing of gears.

'Good job she's not dealing with livestock,' observed Joe, arriving at the house door, 'she'd give 'em all mastitis.'

'She gives me mastitis,' agreed Polly.

'Ah. I know a good cure for that.' Joe looked boldly at Polly's rather modest bosom, almost invisible in the folds of his own brown jumper. 'Get your coat on,' he commanded. 'I've got something to show you.' Polly obeyed. She quite liked obeying Joe. Just for a laugh. She hadn't obeyed anyone for over twenty years: since the fifth form. It felt quite playful at times: as long as she always privately reserved the right to disobey him, at some time in the future, whenever she felt like it.

I also obey him because this is his kingdom, she thought, pulling on her waxed jacket, which had become adorned, in the past days, with any amount of cowdung and sheep's afterbirth and now therefore had become the real thing. It was his kingdom, and she was but an ambassador from another planet. Where was he taking her now? She stumbled along after him, anticipating a treat.

He led her through a gate behind the house, and up into a small wood. After a couple of minutes the trees thinned, and beside a hedgerow at the wood's edge, Joe fell to his knees and groped about amongst the leaves.

'Look,' he said. 'Here. The first violet. It's early. Very early this year.'

Polly bent down and there, between his big fingers, the modest little flower lifted up its dark face to them.

'How—how beautiful!' Polly found a strange ball of tears gathering behind her nose. 'Don't pick it.'

'I wouldn't,' he said. 'Even for you. It lives here.'

Polly, feeling a strange impulse, leaned forward and kissed it, and then sat back rather hastily and looked at her knees. Her instinct was to say something sardonic to protect herself, but she bit it back. She did not dare to look at Joe, somehow, but she could feel him smiling.

'Lucky old violet,' he said softly. Polly scrambled to her feet; Joe got up too. She stumbled on a tree root; he caught her hands and steadied her. For an instant he looked directly into her eyes, and Polly felt her whole body leap inwardly like a dog tied up.

'Thanks,' she muttered, and moved away. Then she paused. 'Thank you for showing me,' she said, a strange shyness paralysing her habitual ease with words. 'No one's ever shown me the first violet before.'

'Ah well.' Joe's brown eyes shone. 'You've been sadly neglected, sweetheart.'

Sweetheart, thought Polly, stumbling back through the wood, *Lucky old violet*. Her heart was hectic. She stopped by the gate and looked down at the farm in its strange haunted valley.

'There's something so lovely about this place,' she said. 'I think it's because you can't see another building. Not a single one. It's lonely. But I like it.'

'Oh, there are thousands of places lonelier,' said Joe, pausing at her side. 'In Africa. Lonelier and wilder.'

'But it's so rare in England,' Polly went on. 'Especially the south of England. It's so special. It must never be allowed to change.'

'Everything changes.' Joe pushed open the gate. 'You know that. Don't be daft.'

'It mustn't be spoiled, then,' Polly persisted. 'Surely you'd want to protect it? You wouldn't want, say – ' she became reckless, 'bungalows where your violet grew?'

Joe shrugged. 'What they do who come after us,' he said, 'we can't do bugger all about.'

A sheep bellowed from the barn, and Joe registered it.

'One of my old girls needs me,' he said.

'Would you like some help?' asked Polly.

'Yeah. Go and get a bucket of water and some soap,' said Joe, going off. 'An' I'll cure your mastitis afterwards if we get the time.' He gave her a very lewd wink. Polly jumped in wicked delight, and ran to the house.

'Oh, hello, dear,' said Mrs Swain. 'I didn't know where you'd gone off to. Only there was a phone call for you. Somebody called Daniel. He said to tell you he's stayin' at The Fleece and would you ring him right away soon as possible.'

Chapter  Nineteen

'Got to go, I'm afraid. Friend of mine has turned up at The Fleece. Nuisance.'

Polly grimaced apologetically and handed the bucket of water to Joe, who gave her a strange penetrating look. It wasn't often Polly dropped her articles, and Joe was perceptive where livestock behaved in an unusual way.

'Pub lunch, eh?' he grinned. 'All right for some.'

Polly shrugged, sighed, and departed.

On the way to the village she felt her spirits sinking. Two weeks ago the thought of a visit from Dan would have had her panting and wagging her tail: now she felt uneasy. Her stomach fluttered and her toes curled. Some great transformation was taking place within her, and she didn't dare to look what it was. It wasn't just Joe –

'Don't think about it,' she instructed herself out loud, parking rather carelessly in the pub yard. 'Automatic pilot. That's the answer.'

On automatic pilot, therefore, she pushed her way into the lounge bar, and before she had time to register Dan she was greeted effusively by Maisie, Bert and Fred from the Post Office.

'Hello dear!' cried Maisie. 'How are you? Have one on me—well, have one on Fred. I can recommend him. He's got a bottomless purse—ent you, love?'

The ferrety Fred stood up and produced a large wallet.

'That's ever so kind of you, but I'm meeting a friend . . .'

Polly faltered, catching sight of Dan's moody features, romantically lit by the firelight, watching her from the snug. Polly smiled at him, but her heart sank another few centimetres, somehow. It was deep in her pelvis by now. Maisie turned to inspect Polly's friend.

'My word,' she breathed, 'he ent half good lookin'. Look, Fred! He's like Dirk Bogarde, ent he?'

'Not unlike,' conceded Fred, evidently jealous. Bert inclined his huge red face towards Dan for an instant.

'More like Imran Khan,' he commented and buried his face in his beer.

'Get him over, love,' whispered Maisie. 'Tell him to join us, like. Go on!'

Polly backoned Dan: she was only too glad to postpone privacy with him. He heaved himself reluctantly out of the most comfortable chair in the pub, and slouched over with a slightly unforgiving air. Polly introduced everybody.

'So that's why the Post Office is closed,' commented Dan.

'Open again at two,' simpered Maisie. 'Or a minute or two earlier, for you.'

'Have you got a fax?'

Maisie fidgeted. She did not like to disappoint a customer.

'Well, no, not reelly, but we have got a Xerox.'

Any machine with an 'x' in it was something to boast about, in Long Dangley.

'Fred is going to get me a fax next Christmas, ent you, Fred?'

'When my ship comes in,' said Fred rather sulkily.

'You'll hev to go to Sedgeworth,' Bert pronounced. 'They'm got one there. At Andrews'. In the High Street. Faxes and Xeroxes and all that mallarkey.'

'Oh damn,' Dan scowled. 'And I drove through blasted Sedgeworth only an hour ago.'

'Come on,' Maisie coaxed him. 'Don't let it spoil yer dinner, eh? Have one of Elsie's pies.'

A savoury smell was spreading through the pub.

'Her's got Egon Ronay stars for them pies,' affirmed Fred. 'One o'they inspectors came round, you know—incognito. Like a spy, sorta.'

'What a good idea. Come on, Daniel! Let's share a pie,' Polly urged.

'Let the lad hev one o'his own,' commented Bert. 'He needs feedin' up a bit. From London are yer?'

Dan nodded.

'Ever bin to Lord's?'

'I'm afraid not,' said Dan with a graceful smile. 'The arcane mysteries of cricket are completely wasted on me.'

Bert retired, hurt, to the deepest folds of his face and took no further part in the conversation.

'Dan prefers American Football,' said Polly, organising a pie for her long-lost lover.

'Oooh I loves American Football,' agreed Maisie, setting a fervent hand on Dan's knee. 'Those tight trousers they wear, eh? Me and Mildred was watching it one night, and she says, "Maisie, I never thought it would be legal to sit here admirin' men's bums on the TV." She's a card.'

'Well, there you are then,' said Dan, lazily offering her a flash of his whitest teeth, 'it just goes to show that there is real progress in modern life.'

Polly could not, in the end, avoid a visit to Dan's room. It was pleasant, looking out onto a grassy bank at the back, and amusingly furnished with a four-poster bed, chintzy curtains and an en suite bathroom of the ripest pink. Dan kicked off his shoes and threw himself dramatically onto the rose-strewn bed cover.

'Come here,' he drawled in mock-Missouri. 'Too long time my woman been gone.'

'Just a minute,' said Polly. 'I must go to the loo.' She ran the water loudly and washed. The face staring back looked almost as pink as the decor. Polly had caught the sun, or the wind, or something. Quite an achievement in early March. But there was more to it than that. It was a flush of embarrassment, of curious unexpected guilt.

'Come on!' called Dan. 'Don't wash, for God's sake. You remember the letter Napoleon wrote to Josephine: *Battle won. Back on Thursday. Don't have a bath.*

'How disgusting.' Polly emerged, nevertheless feeling that she could do with a little Napoleonic courage right now.

'Still so fastidious after a fortnight in the country?' Dan grinned. 'Up to your eyebrows in muck? Well, well, you don't change. How's it been? Come here and bore me with it for a few seconds.'

Polly clambered onto the bed, and winced.

'This bed's horribly soft.'

'Never mind. Won't do us any harm for a couple of nights. Bad for sleeping but great for sex.' He inserted his tongue between her lips, but Polly struggled free.

'I—I can't stay here with you, I'm afraid.'

'Why the hell not?'

'I've got to help Joe with the lambing.'

'Bullshit! Someone else can do it.'

'There isn't anybody else. His father's too busy to stay up all night. And too old.'

'So you stay up all night with Joe, do you? And how old's he?'

'Oh, just a kid.' Polly felt herself blushing. 'Only twenty or something.'

'I know these bloody yokels,' grumbled Dan. 'He'll have his hand up your skirt in no time, my dear.'

'I don't wear skirts. I wear trousers.'

'Yes. So I see. Most unfortunate. The country's having a bad effect on you. But listen—you're sleeping here tonight and that's an end of it. I won't have all this lambing crap.'

'Don't you start ordering me about!' Polly's eyes flashed.

'Well, for God's sake! He'd have had to manage on his

116

own if you hadn't turned up, wouldn't he? Can't he hire a hand for a few days to take the pressure off? What sort of an outfit is it, anyway?'

'The trouble is, it's only a small farm.' Polly sat bolt upright, seized by her message. 'Just a family farm, you know, father and son. And the awful thing is, Dan, that things are going so badly they're having to sell up! And we think it's going to get bought by developers!'

'Well, never mind,' sighed Dan. '*C'est la vie*, darling. I mean, this is happening all over the country. It's just one of those things. As long as you can shoot your series there, it doesn't matter, does it? I mean, sales always take forever. Surely you can get *Cold Comfort Farm* in the can before the bulldozers move in?'

'I don't give a damn about *Cold Comfort Farm*!' cried Polly, not without a momentary quiver of guilt towards dear Stella Gibbons. 'Can't you understand what I'm saying? It's such a special place, it's so beautiful, there are these lovely woods all around, and there's violets in bloom there. Already. And it's so wild and remote. It's just—well, it's got to be saved.'

'Well, if it's so bloody marvellous,' pondered Dan, 'why don't we go and stay there? Make whoopee in your little room. Shake the old farmhouse to its foundations. Keep young Joe awake all night. Torment him with the sound of bouncing bedsprings.'

A wave of horror swept over Polly. For a second she could not speak.

'I would've suggested staying with you in the first place,' Dan went on, 'if it wasn't for this cattle bug you told me about.'

'Oh that,' said Polly hastily. 'That's all over now. It was just a scare. I think I got hold of the wrong end of the stick, to tell you the truth.' She did not like to think of Dan offering Mr Swain his condolences on the outbreak of FHB.

Or was it PMT or GBH? Never mind which. She had to keep Dan away from the farm.

'No, you can't stay at my place, Dan. I'm really sorry, but I just couldn't. It's too—public, you know. I don't think the Swains would approve of my importing a man.'

'To hell with the Swains! You're paying them their whack, what you do in the privacy of your own room is none of their bloody business.' Sentiments which, in a former life, Polly might well have uttered herself.

'No really, Daniel: listen! Please! Don't be difficult about it. It's all rather delicate. I don't want to offend them. You must sleep here and I'll sleep there. But I can always come over here and take part in outbreaks of rampant lust.' She nerved herself up to nuzzle against him. She was going to have to succumb to violent coupling in self-defence. It was all very ironical, really.

'Well, for God's sake let's get on with it, then,' groaned Dan, 'I've got a fortnight's pent-up lust to unload.'

And he fell on her.

Polly closed her eyes, and co-operated with what was going on. How very extraordinary it is, she thought, that feelings can change so utterly in a couple of weeks. It's just as one of those sixteenth-century poets had said—Michael Drayton, possibly: *Love is a still growing, or a constant, light, And his first minute, after noon, is night.* What was she going to do about all this? Not in the long term: that would be easy enough, though painful. She and Dan had never lived together. In fact, Polly had never lived with anyone, preferring the luxury of her own territory, decorated in her own austere taste, with her own front door and sturdy lock. It made partings so much easier.

In the long term, there would be no problem. Dan was dazzlingly attractive and would fix himself up with someone new, pronto. She wouldn't be surprised if he had a little something going on the side already. In San Francisco, maybe. It made Polly uneasy, especially these days, when a little bit on the side could turn out to be the Angel of Death.

Here I am, she wondered, lying here and feeling totally indifferent to a man who was my lover a couple of weeks ago. And why? It wasn't just Joe—but it was Joe, of course. Polly had to accept that she had started to feel things for Joe that were desperately inconvenient and tending towards the downright foolish. Nothing had happened yet, at least nothing venal, though the airwaves had been getting pretty vibrant recently. But even if it came to nothing, picking up with Dan where she had left off was out of the question.

Because it wasn't just Joe. That was an unfortunate lapse, a schoolgirl crush, whatever. There was the whole business of Harrow Hill Farm. This place. Those tumbling woods. Those rushing streams where Polly had explored, on her own, welly-deep in mud and ooze. The broken walls zig-zagging up the hill; the shelter of the hanging beechwoods; the delicious smell of the hay; the kiss of the first violet.

Polly realised, with a wry smile, that she was closing her eyes and thinking of England.

Chapter  Twenty

'What a way to earn a living, eh!' Joe sat back on his heels and looked at the lamb. It sprawled feebly in the straw, only a twitch of the ear and a heave of its ribs indicating the possibility of life.

'Will it make it?' asked Polly.

'Who knows. What he needs is a spell in the solarium.' Joe picked up the lamb and went out of the barn. Polly followed.

'Yes. What a way to earn a living. But still . . . you enjoy it, don't you? And it's, well, a reasonable living, isn't it?'

They entered the outhouse where two weak lambs were already lying in the big box under the lamp.

'Shove up, lads, make room for another!' Joe arranged the lamb gently in the warm nest, briefly inspected the original two and straightened up.

'Well, they're not dead yet,' he said. 'But even if they live, they're not worth half what they were last year. And they're not worth a third what they were three years ago. I don't call that a reasonable living. As for enjoying it . . .' He paused, took Polly's wrist and looked at her watch, then let her hand fall again. There was nothing seductive about the gesture. Joe was dead tired.

'Four thirty in the morning for the tenth night in a row. No, I don't enjoy lambing. It's a pain in the arse.'

Polly followed him back to the barn. 'But there's a lot of satisfaction in it, surely? When you save a lamb's life? Or get a ewe that's lost her lamb to accept an orphan, or one whose mother's not got any milk?' Polly had learned some basic principles of shepherding and found fostering a fascinating subject. Joe arranged surrogate mothers for his needy lambs with a mixture of authority and guile. If he had a lamb he wanted to foster, he might rub it against the newly born lamb of another mother, covering it with her blood, her slime, her smell. Then he would present the mother with both lambs, watch her sniff and lick them.

'She thinks she's had twins. Look at that, eh,' he would grin. 'She says, "Well, Joe, that wasn't no trouble at all. Twins? I never even felt the second 'un. I reckon I could do triplets next year."'

Sometimes a ewe that had lost her lamb would not accept an orphan immediately. In this case she was put in a pen, and secured in a kind of pillory, her head held fast for a couple of days whilst the lamb lay beside her and suckled her. Eventually, when she was released, she would accept the lamb and mother it.

'It's a wonderful thing, the mothering instinct,' Joe mused, watching one such ewe now, licking her lamb as it lay by her nose. 'Yes. I suppose I do get a lot out of it.'

'And you've got such a talent for it,' added Polly. 'It's rather marvellous to think of you carrying on doing this work, very similar to the work of the shepherds long ago— before Christ, even. And I can imagine you still doing it into old age.'

'Give me a break, girl,' smiled Joe. 'I'm going to put me feet up soon as I get to retirement age. You won't find me grovelling about knee deep in sheepshit when I'm sixty, mate. If I ever get to sixty.'

'Of course you'll get to sixty! You're the picture of health.'

Joe looked sombre for a moment. 'None of us knows that.'

'Well, by the time you're that age your son will be out here.'

'Maybe. Bein' distracted from his work by some artsy-fartsy artiste from Hampstead.'

Polly laughed. 'Sorry. Do carry on.'

Joe swept an expert eye around the barn, marked a certain ewe and heaved a sigh.

'I'll have a go at her in a minute or two,' he said. 'Let's just have a cup o' that tea, first.'

Polly eagerly opened the flask. It was one of the things she could do: be nimble and quick in small ways. As she unscrewed the lid, she noticed how different her hands looked. The long, polished nails had given way to ragged stubby ones, and grime threw into relief all the intricate whorls of her skin.

'I may never have children, anyway,' Joe went on, sitting on a bale of straw for a moment to rest. He looked weary, and his hands, worn like the hands of a much older man, hung from his knees in complete relaxation. 'You may never have any either. None of us knows. Not sure I want any.'

'Oh but surely – ' Polly hesitated. 'I mean, here you are, working with life and death, it would seem so natural for you to become a father. Watch your own little lamb grow. Take pride in it, like the rams do.'

'The rams don't give bugger all about their lambs. As long as they get their ends away, that's all they care about.'

'Yes, but for us, wouldn't it be natural – '

'Natural? What's natural?'

'Life. Seed-time. Birth. All this.' Polly swept her arm around the barn.

'And that. That's natural, too.' Joe nodded to where the corpse of a lamb lay, amongst some sacks at the side of the barn.

'Well, I suppose so. Still, I like to think of you as an old man, here. Maybe leaning on that barn door, in fifty years' time, making sarcastic remarks about the mess the young lads are making of it.'

'Fifty years?' Joe drank his tea. 'I won't be here in fifty years, girl. Doubt if I'll be here in five.'

Polly leapt at the lead.

'Why ever not?'

'There's more to life than this place. I want to see a bit of the world.'

'You mean, you're thinking of leaving your parents . . .? Could they retire here? It seems a pity if they have to leave such a beautiful place.'

'My folks want to retire to Bournemouth. For me mum's rheumatism. Cruel, it is, here, when the wind's in the east. You're lucky, you've come to us in a mild spring. But it can be cruel.'

'Would they sell up, then? At a certain stage? When they're ready to retire? And you wouldn't mind? Would – '

Joe turned round at a step in the yard. There, leaning over the barn gate and looking sardonic, was Daniel Birnbaum.

'Who the hell are you?' asked Joe.

'Only a friend of Polly's,' said Dan, with a simper. 'I'm staying in the village. Couldn't sleep—bloody awful bed. Thought I'd come over here and take a look at this mysterious lambing business she's been telling me all about.'

'I wouldn't come in here if I were you,' said Joe, with a slow appraising look taking in Dan's elegant suit, which he had bought in Milan last spring. 'You might get those smart trowsis all covered in shit.'

'I'll watch from here,' said Dan. 'It's all right.'

'Well.' Joe got up. 'I must see to this old girl.' He followed a certain sheep round the barn, caught her by the leg, pulled her down, and delicately but firmly pushed his arm deep into her birth canal. Polly joined Dan by the barn door.

'What a way to earn a living,' said Dan, with quiet condescension. Polly wanted to hit him.

The sheep struggled and Joe swore. Dan watched with a wry amusement which was unbearable.

'How about a romantic little stroll in the freezing muck?' murmured Dan. 'Unless you're brave enough to take me up to your rural boudoir and give me a few agricultural embraces.'

'Come over here, Pol!' shouted Joe. It was the first time he had ever called her Pol, and it felt like a claim. Polly was torn between pleasure and guilt. 'Come over and sit on 'er head. I've got a breech here.'

Polly went, like a bullet. When the lamb was delivered, the ewe had stopped groaning and struggling, and the lamb lay at her head, being licked, Polly thought she would ask Dan to tip-toe through the straw and come and feel the lamb: its warmth, the strange rough feel of its wool, the adult hardness of its big black hooves. She turned to ask him, but he had gone. Joe saw her turn.

'That your boyfriend, was it?' he asked, with a curious expression on his face. 'Good-looking bloke.'

'Not really,' said Polly with a sigh. 'He used to be, but— I feel worlds away from him, now.'

'He must still be keen on you, though,' said Joe. 'Coming all this way in the middle of the night. Reckon he's jealous? Jealous of me?' he grinned. 'Did you tell him you were up all night with dirty old Joe?'

'Oh, Dan's not the jealous type,' said Polly, getting up, and wishing she could change the subject. 'He's the sort that says, "I don't own you. We're free individuals. You can do what you like when you're not with me."'

'Big of him to bloody say so,' snorted Joe with contempt. 'I think it's crap. All that kind of thing. *Do what you like*. Crap. That's not what it's all about, to my mind.'

'What is it all about, then?' Polly's tone was almost meek. She was desperate not to offend or intrude. It was an extraordinary feeling: painful, embarrassing, vulnerable. Everything she hated. Yet she could not help it.

'Not now, girl,' he sighed, looking back round his flock. 'Not now. Christ, can't you see I'm up to my bloody eyeballs?'

'Sorry,' said Polly. 'Maybe I'd better go. See if he's hanging around somewhere.'

'You go and get a bit of kip,' said Joe. 'You look bloody awful, to tell you the truth. Go get a bit of bloom back into your pretty cheeks.'

And he turned back to his work.

Chapter  Twenty-one

'I must say, I'm surprised.' Dan lit a Marlboro and tossed the match away with a disdainful hand, then sprawled across the oak settle with his customary lean grace. Jeans, Breton fisherman's sweater, Quentin O'Hara's Bond Street version of the Donkey Jacket, '*Le Donqué*'; distressed-leather wilderness boots: he looked the complete . . . well, he looked a complete prat, actually, thought Polly.

Dan's entire ensemble was an artful urban parody of a working man's clothes. No doubt it had all cost him the best part of a grand. He was a grandee in prole's clothing.

'I didn't realise you were susceptible to beefcake, my dear.'

'What?'

'Well, he's prime one hundred per cent British Beef, isn't he? You want to watch your step. You could end up with mad cow disease.' Dan grinned through the smoke. It was the grin of an Oxford gargoyle: educated, superior, suave.

'Whom are you talking about?' Polly enquired, with a deliberate airy innocence.

'What's his name. Joe *Joe—Joe—just an ordinary schmo* . . .' Dan broke into sardonic song.

'Good heavens.' Polly smiled, as irritatingly as possible. 'You're jealous.'

'Jealous? *Moi*? Leave it out, dearest.' Dan blew smoke in her face—something he knew she detested. 'I've got a bit more self-respect than to be jealous of a two-bit ploughboy with overdeveloped pectorals and a brain the size of a pea.'

Polly felt her arteries harden with hatred.

Dan's pint of Guinness (he-man drink) stood untouched upon the table. Polly gave in to a terrifying impulse. She stood up, picked up the glass, and poured it over his head. It cascaded satisfyingly over the Breton sweater and Quentin O'Hara's *Le Donqué*, spattered the jeans and gave the wilderness boots further cause for distress. It also—very pleasingly—extinguished his cigarette. Most gratifying of all, however, was the expression of incredulity and outrage which seized and paralysed his expensive face. Polly enjoyed the spectacle for a moment before walking out. She was dimly aware of scattered applause behind her.

'I hear you tried to drown your boyfriend in the pub yesterday.' Joe peeped mischievously at her from his habitual station near a gravid sheep's arse.

'Ex-boyfriend.'

'I should think he's got the message by now,' mused Joe. 'If you ever do that to me I'll tan your bloody hide for you.'

'I don't suppose you'll ever give me cause.'

'What had he done, then, poor bugger?'

'He said you had overdeveloped pectorals and a brain the size of a pea.'

Joe burst into a glorious baritone laugh.

'If I thought I had a brain as big as that I'd be thrilled to bits.'

He returned, still grinning, to his accouchement.

'Twins,' he remarked a quarter of an hour later. 'We've had a lot recently. You've brought us luck this year, I reckon.'

'From what I hear you need all the luck you can get,' Polly blurted out, suddenly emboldened.

'Oh, yeah? What do you mean?'

'I've heard rumours that you're selling up.'

Joe did not look surprised. He washed his hands in the bucket and dried them on a rag.

'Selling up, are we? Any sordid details I should know about?'

Polly felt uncomfortable.

'Well, are you?' she asked. 'Because, listen, if you are, and you'd rather not be—I mean, I'm sure something could be done—look, I don't—I don't suppose I could do very much, but I'm sure you wouldn't want a housing estate on this land, would you? You'd like to go on working it, wouldn't you? For a while, at least?'

Joe sighed, then looked appraisingly at her.

'You're a soft-hearted little thing, ent you?' he commented. 'Under all that city-slicker tough-guy talk. But don't waste your sympathy on us. Or your time. It's dog eat dog in this game at the moment, sweetheart.'

'But I don't want you to be eaten by a dog!'

'You're the sort that comes to the rescue, aren't you?' He looked teasingly at her, his head cocked on one side. 'I bet you've sponsored an acre of rainforest and an elephant and a starving Indian kiddie an' all.'

'Well, what's wrong with that?' snapped Polly, annoyed at being categorised as one of a sort.

'Nothing the matter with it. I've sponsored an acre of rainforest, myself.'

Joe looked around the barn for his next victim, selected a sheep with a bottom like a ripe peach, brought her down and immobilised her, and commenced his obstetric routine.

'Gone back to London, then, has he?'

'I neither know nor care where he's gone.'

Polly was discontented. Joe had told her nothing about the sale of the farm, and she'd revealed that she was interested. Now he held all the cards, and she could see she'd never be granted a glimpse of them. It wasn't any of her business, of course, and that annoyed her most of all. He gave her a piercing glance.

'What's the matter with you, Missus?'

'Don't call me Missus!'

Joe watched her intently, feeling a sheep's insides the while.

'There's someone I want you to meet,' he proposed eventually. 'Charley Brewster the forester. Lives in the wood. He's your sort of bloke, I reckon.'

'Thanks very much,' said Polly icily, 'but I don't need any help from you to organise my social calendar.'

'Oooh, aren't we cobby tonight? Look, you're suffering from lack of sleep, girl.' Polly could not deny it. She was struck dumb by her own ineptitude and rudeness. And yet he seemed determined to provoke it. 'Off you go. Get a bit of shuteye. You're no good to me all stressed up like this. You'll set these old girls off.'

Polly stood up, reluctantly, and hovered for a moment. The lamplight fingered his dark curls, and Polly wished she could join it.

'I'm sorry,' she said. 'Yes. I am a bit low. I'd love to meet your friend.'

'I know,' said Joe softly. 'Run along now.'

But he did not look at her, which was disappointing. Polly trailed off to bed feeling defeated and foolish.

She who prided herself on her cool head and polite tongue; she who was so fastidious in her tastes and seldom fancied any man; she who had decided it might be amusing if Joe developed a passion for her, whilst she remained icily aloof . . . to be getting so desperate over this rustic hunk and to betray such incompetence, it galled her beyond endurance. She promised herself, in the moments before sleep, that she would root out this inconvenient weakness, tomorrow, chuck it away and be once more her whole self, serene.

Chapter  Twenty-two

Kathleen Partridge loved going to the theatre, but her husband was restless in confined spaces. He longed for his pipe, and had infuriated her all their married life by his fidgeting.

'You fidgeted all the way through Mozart's Requiem!' hissed his wife after one memorable concert. 'And I wouldn't put it past you to fidget all the way through through your own!'

How convenient, therefore, that Dan Birnbaum rang up, with a spare ticket for *As You Like It*. Would Kathleen like to accompany him? Since her daughter had so recklessly abandoned London and left him at a loose end.

'So how was it out in the country?' asked Kathleen as Dan's smooth car inched its way through the London traffic, a soupy bit of Brahms swooping about in the background. Brahms is fully upholstered music: Dan would never have dreamt of having any other sort.

'Oh, very scenic and all that,' said Dan. 'She seemed to have thrown herself into it with gusto.'

'What do you mean?' Kathleen's sensitive antennae detected a quiver of something unwelcome.

'Oh, the lambing, and so forth.'

'What, you mean she's actually working at it?'

'Up all night in the lambing shed, yes.'

'Never!'

'Oh yes. Holding 'em down while the shepherd delivered them. Being the midwife, I suppose.'

Kathleen Partridge wrinkled her nose.

'Who is this shepherd?'

'Oh, just some yokel. Not much more than a kid, really. With greasy hair and great big feet.'

'How ghastly! I can't imagine what Polly thinks she's doing. She's supposed to be doing research there, not messing about with that sort of thing.'

'Oh, I think it's just a little game, with her.' Dan smiled at his own reflection in the gleaming dashboard. 'You know. Getting the feel of it. It's her way of doing research, I expect.'

'Don't make excuses for her, Dan! You're too loyal, I think, sometimes. It sounds to me as if she's gone completely off the rails. We've hardly heard a peep out of her.'

'Polly's not the sort of girl who goes off the rails for long.'

'Polly's not the sort of girl who goes off the rails at all! That's why I'm so worried. She's always been so reasonable up till now. So sensible. Never jumping into things with her eyes closed. Always so cautious and sceptical.'

'Ah well. Perhaps she's got a bit tired of being sensible.'

'Oh don't say that! How dreadful! She can't go all adolescent on us now: not in her mid-thirties.'

'Crazier things have happened.'

Dan parked expertly, helped Mrs Partridge out of the car, and escorted her chivalrously to the theatre.

'I absolutely love *As You Like It*,' she whispered happily as the house lights dimmed and the stage, a huge tilted space, began to glow, Orlando and old Adam entered to set the ball rolling. The Duke's court was sumptuous, the wrestling scene was cleverly choreographed, and Rosalind, a new young actress with a lithe boyish figure, couldn't wait to get into her breeches. Dan thought privately that he wouldn't mind getting into her breeches either.

The Duke fumed, pronounced his excommunication, and Rosalind and Celia ran off to live in the forest.

'To Liberty, and not to Banishment!' was the ringing cry as the first interval arrived.

'How lovely!' purred Mrs Partridge. 'How absolutely lovely. It sort of takes you along with it, doesn't it?'

'An ice-cream or a drink?' asked the ever-attentive Dan.

'Oh, an ice-cream I think. I feel like a child on a treat. One of those Montezuma chocolate ones, please, Dan.'

Dan did not join her. He was always careful not to spill food on his sharp Milan suits.

'It's an adventure, really, isn't it?' said Kathleen, spooning the ice-cream in with gusto. 'I mean, the plot of the play. You can't wait to run off to the forest with Rosalind and Celia and see what they find there.'

'I suppose that's what Polly's done, really,' mused Dan, his dark eyes raking restlessly over the other members of the audience as they stretched their legs and relaxed, his alert scanners in search of the successful and the sexy.

'What do you mean?'

'Well, she's rushed off to live in the forest. It's the Maid Marian syndrome, really, isn't it?'

'Well, in her case, let's hope the novelty soon wears off.'

'Oh, I'm sure it will.'

Dan seemed reluctant to talk about it any more, and soon the play had taken off again and they were transported into a dappled woodland where various rustic couplings took place. In the end, Rosalind magically drew everyone together and paired off the true lovers, somewhat like a priestess, before bidding the audience farewell.

Dan wasn't entirely sure whether it would be farewell in his case, however. Her skinny legs and her huge bee-sting lips had interested him, along with her coltish grace and that ineffable sense of integrity that the best actresses have. He was sure she would never dare to empty a pint of Guinness over his head. She might be distinctly thrilled to receive a phone call from him suggesting lunch. He would soon be casting his latest series. They could do with someone like Stella Cavendish. He could make Stella a Star of Screen as well as Stage.

As he drove Kathleen Partridge home, however, his thoughts returned to Polly. There were many things about the mother that reminded him of the daughter. The way she held her head: rather proudly, looking down her nose. The sound of her laugh. The shape of her hands. Her expression when lost in thought: as Kathleen Partridge was now.

'Penny for them,' said Dan.

'You know, it's funny: I was thinking about my childhood.'

'Were you really? Did it stir a few memories?'

'Something must have.'

'And was it an idyllic childhood? Lincolnshire, wasn't it?'

'Not exactly idyllic,' said Kathleen Partridge grimly. 'I was the youngest child, and the only girl. Three older brothers! They were rather a brutal lot, to tell you the truth. And my father was a devil when the drink was on him.'

'Oh dear.'

'Yes. We got poorer and poorer, and he used to beat us with his belt. He knocked my mother about, too. I can still hear him now, roaring away downstairs. With little me up in my feather bed, crouching down under the covers, hoping he wouldn't come up.'

'How awful.'

'Yes. It was. My mother was a darling. Such a delicate, clever woman. But the life was so hard, it wore her out. She wasn't strong, you know. And he was such a brute to her. He'd come in, covered with dirt and dog-tired, on a freezing day, and he'd say, "Where's my dinner, woman!?" I used to hate the way he called her "woman". He was so coarse. Well, he was an absolute ruffian.'

'But you managed to escape.'

'Yes. I went off to college. He was outraged. He thought it wasn't worth educating women. "Throwing money away, that's what it is," he said. "Throwing money away." I went, though. I was determined. And my mum was on my side. But I don't think I'd ever have managed it if it wasn't for my Uncle Eric. He was a cut above my father, you see: an educated man. My father respected him, and Eric said I should go. And more importantly, he paid for it. And then of course I was free. I never went back.'

'What, never? Not even to visit?'

'Oh yes, of course, to visit. But my mother was trapped there. Doing all this hard manual work: scrubbing the kitchen floor at the age of sixty, with her delicate little hands covered with chilblains, and getting sworn at for her pains. And then of course she got cancer, poor thing. A quick sort. She was gone in a month. I blame him. People who are unhappy get cancer, don't they? And she was unhappy, if ever a woman was. Poor Mum!'

Kathleen got out her handkerchief and dabbed her eyes.

'I vowed that my daughter would never have to endure that kind of life. I brought her up to believe that a woman could do anything. The world's your oyster, Polly, I said to her. I can't bear the thought of a man treating her the way my father treated my mother.'

'I don't think Polly would ever put up with any kind of cruelty,' said Dan. 'I mean, look: here I am, Mr Nice Guy, weak as a kitten, never raised my voice in my life, even to a wasp, and she won't even live with me.'

'Oh dear,' said Kathleen Partridge, with a mounting sense of helplessness.

'Don't worry. I'm perfectly happy. We're perfectly happy, both of us, really. Honest. Chin up, Kathleen! You've done a good job on that girl and she's not going to come to any harm—believe me.'

'I hope so,' said Kathleen, blowing her nose. 'I hope so. Let's talk about something else. The play! Weren't those lighting effects marvellous, when they were in the forest?

Dappled light all over the stage. Just like being in a real wood. How do they do that?'

'Gobos,' said Dan.

'What?'

'Gobos. Little pieces of celluloid fitted across the lamps. With holes cut in. It's clever, isn't it?'

'I'll say,' agreed Kathleen. 'Just like the real thing—like being in a real wood, only without the flies. Perfection.'

Chapter  Twenty-three

On March 21st, traditionally the first day of Spring, Polly was down at the village phone box bright and early with a fistful of pound coins. She made a series of phone calls: to the estate agent who had sold her the Hampstead flat, enquiring about its current market value; to her building society, enquiring about the largest mortgage she was likely to be granted; and lastly to her mother, to wish her luck in the St Matthew Passion her choir was to perform next Saturday.

'Can't you come up for it, Polly, love?' Her mother's voice assumed its most wheedling tone.

'I don't think so, Mum. I'm up to my eyes at the moment.'

'Oh . . . never mind.'

A musical, and slightly ostentatious sigh wafted down the line. Polly felt a beast. In her mind's eye she could see her mother's disappointed face. And she *had* promised . . . not that her mother would remind her. She felt a huge, almost nauseated desire not to return to London.

'Daniel dropped by yesterday,' her mother went on. Polly's heart missed a beat. 'He said what a lovely place it is where you're staying. Dad and I were thinking of coming down for a weekend, maybe—if you can't get back up to town for a while.'

Clever old Mum! She was wasted, really, in the domestic arena. Only international brinkmanship would have given her talents full range.

'Well, maybe you should,' considered Polly, rapidly shifting into conciliation gear, 'although I think perhaps I will come to the concert after all. My work's been going quite well . . . I'm sure I could take the weekend off. And I do love Bach.'

She must also pay a visit to Dan and clear all this business up, properly. She was not the sort of woman to leave a man drenched in Guinness without tidying things up in a civilised way afterwards. They had to agree to part. And she didn't want him coming down here again. She wondered what he had said to her mother. Those two were as thick as thieves.

'Ooh, lovely darling, and maybe you and Dan can come to Sunday lunch.'

'Maybe,' hedged Polly. 'But he might be in Manchester. Or New York. Or God knows where.'

'Yes, isn't he wonderful?' exclaimed Mrs Partridge emphatically. Was some special pleading going on? Polly wasn't sure.

She agreed to go to London next weekend, however, and left the phone box with renewed weariness even though it was only ten a.m. A few minutes' walk in the March sunshine revived her, though: the daffodils and flowering quince were lighting up all the cottage gardens, and when she turned into the lane and began to climb up what she was starting to think of as her valley, she noticed that certain hedgerow plants were in tiny leaf.

Joe intercepted her that afternoon in the yard, threw open the passenger door of his Land-Rover and ordered her to get in. Polly obeyed, and they rattled off.

On the opposite hillside were thick woods, which Polly had often admired from her bedroom window. She had occasionally noticed a thin thread of smoke rising from a hidden chimney, and the source of this smoke was now revealed to her.

'The Bothy,' said Joe, pulling up beside the smallest

cottage Polly had ever seen. It was a single-storey building, whitewashed, with a central door and a window each side of it, like a child's painting. 'Charley's usually here for a cup of tea about now.' A van parked under a tree confirmed this suggestion.

'Oi! Charley!' Joe thumped on the front door and went in. Polly followed.

A slight young man with thick fair hair was sitting by the fire. He got up, produced a radiant smile and offered a pleasantly firm handshake.

'Charley, this is Polly,' said Joe. 'One of our guests. A longterm one. A lifer.'

'Well, hello!' said Charley melodiously. 'How lovely. Just having some tea—won't you join me?'

He had an educated voice, and a social ease which Polly had not been expecting.

They sat down on a sofa that had once been the back seat of an old car: leather upholstery, covered with a tartan rug. The smell of woodsmoke seemed to penetrate every inch of the place. It smelled very ancient, and very sweet.

'Enoying your stay?' enquired Charley, pouring the tea. 'Or is Joe working you too hard?'

'I'm afraid so,' said Polly. 'This lambing's a killer. Even more exhausting than cocktail parties in Hampstead.'

'Hampstead?' Charley pricked up his ears. 'I've got a friend who lives there. Right on the Heath. East Heath Road.'

'Oh yes,' said Polly. 'Everyone wants to live there.'

'Where are you?'

'Yorkshire Grey Place. It's tucked away, just opposite the tube,' Polly had the curious feeling that she was speaking somehow from the past. Memories of her flat were taking on a sepia tint.

'I tell you what,' mused Charley, 'I left a book there last time I stayed with them. I don't suppose you'll be nipping back one of these days? Maybe you wouldn't mind bringing it back for me.'

'Well as a matter of fact, I'm going back this weekend,' said Polly, with a hidden sigh. 'I could easily collect it for you. Of course.'

Joe gave her a quick look.

'Going to patch things up with lover-boy?'

'Certainly not! If it's any of your business. I'm going to hear my mother's choir perform the St Matthew Passion, that's all.'

'Ah! Bach!' sighed Charley. 'Then you're forgiven for deserting us. I wish I could come with you. I do miss concerts.'

'How's the coppicing coming along?' asked Joe, and Charley launched into an elaborate account of the weather, the pests, and the gods. He spoke with fascination and fluency. A university man, evidently. A drop-out, probably.

'It must be wonderful, planting your trees like this,' said Polly. 'Knowing your land will benefit from what you did in years to come.'

'My trees!' exclaimed Charley with a laugh. 'They're not mine exactly. It's not my land. It's the Fairfaxes.'

'Part of the Fairfax Estate,' explained Joe.

'What, managed by Charlotte? Of The Manor?'

'Ah, yes. Charlotte.' Charley exchanged a grin with Joe.

'Do they own a lot of land around here, then?'

'Masses. All that up there.' Charley cocked his head towards the wall, where a large map was pinned, with various woodland areas outlined and identified. Much of the land around Long Dangley appeared to belong to the Fairfaxes.

'How did old Sir Antony get his hands on all this, then?' asked Polly, her university Socialism stirring from its habitual slumber.

'Through his father's dick,' said Joe, and the men laughed. 'Inherited it, see.'

Polly ignored the coarseness and considered the map.

'Doesn't it make your blood boil,' she mused, 'to think of one family owning all this? I mean, it's like pre-Revolutionary Russia.'

'Little Hampstead bolshie, are you?' asked Joe. 'That's all a bit out of date these days, sweetheart.'

'Of course I'm not!' snapped Polly. 'But if I was a visitor from another planet, I'd think it was all a bit odd. And unfair.'

The men both looked at her: their smiles were uncomfortable to her.

'You are a visitor from another planet,' said Joe.

'Oh ho ho. Very funny. If you want to know, all this *we country people are superior to you stupid effete townies* stuff is wearing a bit thin.'

'Don't be cruel to the poor girl,' said Charley soothingly.

'I like a woman who speaks her mind,' commented Joe with infuriating condescension.

'Well,' persisted Polly, 'I just think it's a bit off, one family owning all this land. It's absurd. It should belong to everybody.'

'As a matter of fact,' Charley was pouring the last of the tea, 'it's in the best hands, sometimes, with these big landowners. Land that's kept for shooting and hunting is some of the least polluted and contaminated, you see.'

'So all your work is in aid of the gentry and their sport,' concluded Polly, trying to keep indignation out of her voice. 'So they can have fun killing things in an area of outstanding natural beauty?'

'Yes. Isn't it awful?' laughed Charley.

'And I suppose you'd say "The fox enjoys it"?'

'What the fox enjoys,' put in Joe, 'is tearing chickens' heads off for the hell of it. And lambs. And it shits in its own bed. Filthy animal.'

Polly was confounded, but not beaten.

140

'Filthy animal, eh?' she commented. 'No worse than some of the gentry themselves, I'll bet.'

The two men were silent, looking behind her at the open doorway. Joe's eyes were dancing with a sadistic delight which alarmed her. Polly sensed someone's presence, and turned round.

There on the threshold stood Charlotte Fairfax, a leather horsewhip in her hand. It took all Polly's dimly remembered Brownie training not to cringe.

Chapter  Twenty-four

'Your bullocks have got out,' Charlotte barked at Joe.

'Sorry, love.' He got up with a teasing expression. 'Only I washed 'em last night and I can't do a thing with them. Where are they?'

'Halfway down Water Lane. And you should mend that damned gate of yours. I told you about it last October.'

'Would you like some tea, Charlotte?' enquired Charley with a luscious smile.

'I haven't got time to sit around gassing all day,' snapped Charlotte, 'even if some people have.' She glared at Polly, who remained serenely seated.

'You can't deny the English working man his tea break, love,' said Joe tauntingly. She ignored him, and concentrated on Polly, whose presence seemed particularly irksome to her.

'How's your research coming along, Miss Partridge?' she enquired with ill-concealed scorn. Polly hesitated.

'Research? What research?' asked Joe.

'Oh nothing,' said Polly quickly. 'Just a bit of homework.'

'You ask her all about it some time,' said Charlotte in a menacing tone. 'You'll find it very fascinating. Well, Charley, I see you haven't got all that coppicing done yet. Too busy nattering with Miss Partridge, I expect.'

'All in good time, Charlotte,' Charley produced one of his most intense smiles, and soothing tones of voice, as if by sheer willpower he could instil into her some of his sweetness of temper.

'It wasn't Charley's fault,' said Polly. 'We just dropped in on him without notice—didn't we, Joe?' She felt briefly like a child making excuses to a particularly bristling primary-school headmistress.

'I'm off to sort my bullocks out,' said Joe. Polly got up. 'No, no—you stay here. I expect Charley will want to show you his plantations.'

'With pleasure,' said Charley, and then, turning with perfect manners to Charlotte, 'with your permission of course, Charlotte. Perhaps you'd like to come along too?'

'It's not a question of what I'd like,' said Charlotte sourly, whacking her boot with her crop. 'I've got the farm manager and the accountant to see this afternoon.'

'The accountant? Oh, bad luck,' smiled Polly. Charlotte glared, as at an intrusion. Well, thought Polly, though one does make allowances for sour temper caused by severe sexual frustration, I have come to the end of my patience with you, Miss Fairfax.

'Let's go, then,' said Charley, and soon Polly was rattling along in his van, along private drives through woodland areas.

'It must be quite difficult, working for Charlotte Fairfax,' she said.

'Oh, not really. Poor girl. It's just a question of having patience. Foresters have plenty of patience.' He smiled at his steering wheel.

'Have you always been a forester? I mean, how did you come to be one?'

'Well, originally I read geography at university. Then I did a bit of travelling, and then I went back to college and did forestry.'

'Did you grow up in the country? I mean, was it in your blood?'

143

'Good heavens, no! I'm from Pinner.' Charley parked the car, and showed her his young beech and chestnut trees.

'It is extraordinary,' said Polly, 'to think they'll still be young trees when we die.'

'Oh yes,' Charley fondled a twig. 'You're really working for the future in this job. I'll never see the results of my work. Well, I see the immediate results, of course.'

'I love trees.' Polly looked up, fearing she was going to say something daft but not really caring. 'I love their coolness and the way they toss about in the wind. And the smell of pines.'

'Yes! Although I prefer trees that do things, really. Shed their leaves and get new ones. I love the next couple of months. They'll just be coming into leaf. And all the different shades of green! Light delicate greens, lemony greens, buttery greens, silvery greens. You get quite drunk on it.'

Polly was surprised to hear him talk this way. It was like Joe with the violet.

'My mother's birthday's on May 28th,' Charley went on, 'and she always says that after her birthday the greens all tend to darken and merge. Up till then, it's sheer magic.'

'So it's all your mother's fault, then?'

Charley produced a huge grin.

'Absolutely.'

Charley resumed his coppicing, and Polly wandered about, feeling loose and cool, as if her soul softened and slid about in the quiet, faintly melancholy atmosphere. She watched Charley work: though slight, he was sinewy and strong. How old was he? In his thirties, perhaps. You could never tell, with these men who had untouched, boyish faces. He could even be forty. There was something other-worldly about him. He was a male wood-nymph, Polly decided, placed amongst his saplings and delectably bent about his work, to lead astray and ravish some hapless goddess.

She shook herself. This was getting silly. Twilight had crept up on them and the trees reached out towards each other through a blue mist.

'I love this time of day,' commented Charley, packing up his things. 'Some people say it's because I was born at dusk.'

'Were you really?' Polly was enchanted, though of course millions of people, statistically speaking, must have been born at dusk. 'I was born at noon.'

'How very central of you,' laughed Charley.

'When you do think Charlotte was born?'

'Oh, three o'clock in the morning, I should think. Which accounts for her always being so irritable.'

'If she *was* born,' Polly went on. 'I can't imagine her submitting to anything so undignified.'

'I expect she was grafted. It's quite hard to imagine the Fairfaxes coupling. Yes, I think a graft is about the most that Lady Fairfax would agree to.'

'A properly horticultural method,' agreed Polly.

'Poor girl! One does feel sorry for her,' sighed Charley. 'But the fact is, she can be a real pain. She gets these obsessions.'

'What obsessions?'

'Oh . . . about men. She had one about Joe, apparently. Before I came along. Never left him alone. Then she transferred her affections to me.'

'So she'll be furious that you showed me around this afternoon?'

'Oh yes. Desperately jealous. Never mind. One mustn't indulge that sort of thing. People mustn't be allowed to tyrannise.'

Charley suddenly stopped in his tracks and listened. Someone was crashing through the undergrowth. A strange growling or humming could be heard. Suddenly Sir Antony burst upon them, limping slightly, a gun under his arm.

'Good morning! In search of the squirrel. Not so much a lovable beast. More a damned rat with a fancy tail.'

'I'm glad to see you're up and about again, Sir Antony,' said Polly heartily.

'Thank you, my dear. An infusion of port, you know. And vine leaves. Port in the belly and vine leaves in the hair.'

'I'll remember that for when I fall out of trees.'

Sir Antony leaned heavily on Charley.

'You must never, on any account, permit this young woman to fall out of a tree, Brewster,' he rumbled. 'She is too exquisite for these rural exertions. Good morning! The girl's a blackstocking. Marry her, my lad, marry her: you won't regret it.'

And with a bow and a burp, Sir Antony was on his way.

Chapter  Twenty-five

'London? You are lucky, Pol!' Gloria's eyes glazed over for a moment, recalling no doubt moments of childless carefree spending in Covent Garden, like flashes of an impossibly remote previous life.

'Well, to hear my mum's choir, and to sort things out with Daniel.'

'Sort what out? Stop that, Sky!'

Sky had found a roll of unexposed film, pulled it out and was tying Terry up with it.

'He's an *Indian*!' she pouted sulkily.

'Well, even more reason to be nice to him,' insisted Gloria. 'The Indians are much better people than us. They're gentle, and polite, and they build wonderful buildings, and they—er—their music is lovely, and er . . .'

'They're *not* better than us!' shrieked Sky venomously, in a miniature re-enactment of colonial history. 'He scalped three of my best friends!'

'Ah, well, that's a different sort of Indian,' said Gloria. 'Red Indians. They – '

'Mummy! Why are they called Red Indians?'

'They—er, well, their skins are a bit darker than ours.'

'What red? Red like the postman's van?'

'No, not that red. Just a bit darker. But that's not interesting. The colour of people's skins doesn't matter a bit. It's – '

'Yes it does!' yelled Sky. 'We're better than the darkies!

147

And Darren's mum at school came up and told Miss Humphreys she wasn't to send any more reading books home about the bloody Indians.'

'Sky! We don't say that word.'

'Yes you do. You said it when you were trying to open that sardine tin yesterday.'

'The village school . . .' Gloria turned ruefully to Polly, 'leaves a little to be desired. Or at least, some of the clientèle . . . still, I suppose it's good for her to mix with all sorts. I mean, that's real social democracy, isn't it? Racists and all.'

Gloria bit her lip doubtfully. Polly privately thought that Sky could probably give the racists as good as she got. Although perhaps by now she had been unanimously adopted as their leader.

'What were we saying? Oh yes. London. It seems so far away . . .' Gloria sounded a little wan. Was it the bookshops she was missing? Or the day nurseries? 'Look, Pol— you couldn't nip down to Sutton's in Covent Garden and get me some seeds, could you? I'll give you a list. Only I had terrible trouble with my cauliflowers last year. They were all loose and straggly.'

'With pleasure,' said Polly, rising. 'Anything else? Is Chris in London at the moment?'

Gloria looked evasive. 'I'm not sure. I think he's at a book fair somewhere. Milan, would it be? Or is it Bologna? How's Daniel?' The best form of defence was, after all, attack.

'Daniel's for the chop,' said Polly firmly. 'I seem to have grown out of him.'

'Oh dear,' sighed Gloria. 'And he was so bloody good looking, too.'

'You said bloody, Mummy! You said it!' exulted Sky. And then the children launched into a sudden strange chant:

> Walla walla custard, green snot pie,
> Then you skewer out a dead dog's eye,

148

Put in in your mouth and swallow it quick,
Then wash it down with a cup of cold sick.

Gloria blushed, and pulled a disgusted face.

'I told you never to say that thing when we've got visitors! You've been very naughty! No flapjacks for tea!' Aqua burst into tears, but Sky was unrepentant.

'I don't care! I hate flapjacks anyway! And you taught us it! If you didn't like it why did you teach us it?'

'Had a bit too much Muscadet one day,' Gloria confided. 'And I suddenly remembered this ghastly rhyme from my childhood. My brother brought it home from school. Something nasty he picked up in the playground, like nits. And I thought, the oral tradition! So I told them it. But I thought the better of it in the morning.'

'How often one does,' agreed Polly, firmly removing the hem of her skirt from Terry's marmalade grip. Sky joined him on the floor and they both threw themselves vigorously into the project of catching a glimpse of Polly's knickers. Hidden by the table, Polly administered a sharp little kick to Sky's behind. The child erupted with an indignant roar, and flung herself on her mother, sobbing vigorously.

'She kicked me, Mummy! She kicked me! Horrible lady!' Gloria wrestled with the child as with an incubus, shooting Polly half-placating, half-accusing looks.

'I'm sorry, Sky,' said Polly calmly, 'but I always kick people who try to look up my skirt. They deserve it. And it was only a very gentle little kick on the bum.'

'I don't in general ever raise a hand to them,' said Gloria with veiled resentment, 'so they're not used to it, you see. No doubt there are those in the village who think a good hiding would solve a lot of my problems.' Polly privately considered there might even be someone in the same room who thought so. Gloria sighed again.

'Maybe they're right,' she said with an edge of desperation. 'But I can't really change my tack now, can I? I did so want to bring them up according to Rousseau.'

'Did Rousseau actually have any children?' asked Polly, edging towards the door.

'Christ! What a dreadful thought! Supposing he didn't! I just thought, here in the bosom of nature – '

At the word *bosom* all three children dived for Gloria's Greenpeace sweatshirt, and a violent tugging and tussling commenced, during which Gloria tried in vain to keep her dirty grey bra out of sight.

' – you know, here in the heart of the whossname, where they have all the room in the world, where they can be surrounded by Nature, there should be no problem – '

'Yes. I know what you mean. Look, I'm sorry, I must go. Joe is giving me a lift to the station.'

'Joe! How is he? Managed to get him going yet?'

'He's seduction-proof,' Polly shrugged. 'I can't be bothered with him.'

'What a shame,' sighed Gloria. 'What a waste. Perhaps he's one of these celibates. Like that comedian. What's his name. That one with the TV series. My God, Polly, I've completely lost my marbles since this lot came along. I can't remember anyone's name.'

'Never mind,' said Polly. 'I expect you'll get them back.' And she left, quickly. As she walked down the garden path, she could hear Gloria faintly wail, 'What about Sutton's?'

'I'll ring you later!' called Polly, 'from London. Don't worry.'

At the gate she met Mildred.

'Hello, Miss Partridge,' she winked. 'Just got somethink for those little dears.' She indicated a large carrier bag.

'Strait-jackets, I hope,' said Polly and marched away to her car.

'You are a one!' Mildred called after her. 'I'm reelly looking forward to your talk next Thursday. And so is

Joyce. And so's everybody.' Polly gave her a gracious smile, but felt a thunderous qualm. The WI talk about Catherine the Great! It had completely slipped her mind. Thank God Mildred had reminded her. She could nip down Charing Cross Road after her trip to Sutton's and get some biographies to mug up on the wretched woman.

Polly parked her car in the farmyard, hastily packed an overnight bag, and ran for Joe's Land-Rover which was humming by the barn. He had warned her not to leave her car in the car park at Sedgeworth station.

'Them Sedgeworth bastards'll have your cassette player out and everything. Like as not some kids'll take it joyriding and crash it into a wall.'

'Good Lord,' Polly had mused. 'And Sedgeworth looks such a sleepy little place.'

'When they get some Old Stonkey into 'em on a Saturday night,' said Joe, 'there's no stoppin' 'em.'

Polly had decided not to drive to London. For a start, she could not face the motorway. It seemed somehow monstrous and devouring after the lanes of Long Dangley. Also she had a curious feeling of wanting to leave a significant part of herself behind.

'I'll give you a lift,' Joe had said. 'I've got to go down to Sedgeworth in any case to look at some grass keep.'

So she found herself clutching her bag and jolting along the lane, with Joe looking searchingly into fields as they passed. Suddenly he turned towards her.

'What's all this research you're doing, then?' he asked sharply. 'What old Charlotte was going on about?'

Polly hesitated. For a moment she was tempted to let it all tumble out, and to suggest that if the farm were used as a location for a TV series, it might help towards their financial crisis, but she restrained herself. She hadn't done very well, in the past, when she'd let her feelings tumble out in Joe's presence. Some of her mother's political cunning asserted itself.

'I'll tell you all about my research when I get back,' she said. 'If you tell me the details about the farm being for sale.'

'All right,' said Joe. 'It's a deal.'

He drove in silence for the rest of the way, evidently lost in thought.

Chapter  Twenty-six

As she stepped out of the train at Paddington, Polly thought there must have been some kind of chemical disaster nearby, spreading fumes and stench over West London. But there were no ambulances, or fire engines, or police cars: everybody was just going about their business, getting off trains, queueing for taxis, gazing upwards at the departures board, or begging. Nobody apparently noticed the noxious fumes. Polly lifted the neck of Joe's brown sweater up and covered her nose and mouth with it, to keep out the smell of London with the faint scent of hay, muck and shepherd.

She took a taxi back to Hampstead. The driver was a squat fellow with a monkeyish face.

'Caw struth unbelievable ennit?' he said, as great miscellaneous dollops of traffic burst upon them at junctions, like rubbish cascading out of a split carrier bag. A fag hung from his lower lip, and wafts of smoke occasionally invaded Polly's sanctum. She slid the window to.

Now the smoke and the swearing, as it had become, were less intrusive. All she had to bear was the overpowering twee pong of air-freshener coming from two symmetrical green plastic holders fixed to the inside of each door. 'Woodland Glade' it said, but it smelt more like a bordello. Polly pulled the brown sweater up to her eyes and, as expensive cars whinnied and screeched past, she closed her eyes, too, and thought urgently of the first violet.

Down the spiral stairs to her front door . . . a pile of garbage had become trapped down there: a tabloid shrieking HAMMER MURDER MONSTER RAPED MY MUM SAYS TV STARLET; several polystyrene boxes which had contained fast food; a half-eaten hamburger; two cigarette packs; a broken bottle and a Coke can. And this was Hampstead. God knows what it must be like in Hackney. Hastily Polly let herself in and slammed the door.

How often she had heard that particular satisfying thud, and felt herself home and safe. The familiar smell of coffee had grown a little musty, though, and as she went down the dim brown corridor to the living-room and kitchen, the smell of stale cigars hung about the place. It was an expensive flat, it was a cosy flat, it had been Polly's home for years. She had been expecting to feel guilty towards it, returning: that it was reproachful for her abandoning it, but in the event she was irritated by the sordid smell of it, the absence of light.

In the living-room was a patio window which gave out onto a little yard. A determined gardener might have made ivy grow out there, or some such plant of shadowy places, but Polly had always ignored it. As she looked out now, a cat was defecating right by the window.

'Oh my God, this is ludicrous,' she said aloud, and hastily made herself a cup of coffee. She drew the curtains, so as not to observe the yard, and switched on the light. It was two p.m. on a bright Spring day, but the only place in the flat where a sliver of daylight penetrated was the kitchen. The window above the sink, heavily barred because it was just below street level, looked out onto a pavement. So as she stood washing up her coffee cup, Polly beheld the expensive ankles of Londoners walking up and down Church Row. Sunlight gilded the pavement and flashed upon the patent leather of the passers-by, but to Polly, for the first time, it seemed as if she was in a cage.

She pulled on her rubber gloves, opened the front door

and swept all the rubbish into a plastic sack. Then, because there was rather a nasty vomity smell hanging about, she swilled out the little area with disinfectant. But the smell of disinfectant was almost worse. It reminded her of times, long ago at primary school, when someone in the class had been sick. Usually Andrew Bowles.

Back indoors, Polly hovered by her phone. She had to get this business over with Dan. But if she didn't go down to Covent Garden now, she'd have to stay over till Monday and do the shopping then. Damn Gloria and her seeds. She rang Gloria instead, and jotted down what she needed, then grabbed her coat and crossed the road to the tube. Dan would have to wait.

She'd see to him on Sunday. 'And lo! For six days she laboured, and on the seventh day did she give unto her feckless boyfriend the old heave-ho.' What were Sunday afternoons for if not the severing of relationships? If not heads. Polly had a hunch that more domestic murders occurred then than at any other time. Not that she'd have to go that far with Dan. And she was pretty sure he wouldn't murder her, either. He was very careful with his carpets.

Sutton's proved quite charming—a tiny shop tucked away at the top of Drury Lane, the sort of place you might almost expect to find in a small market town like, say, Sedgeworth. Coming out and turning towards the piazza, Polly was hailed from the opposite pavement by a tall young man with a tawny beard and blazing green eyes. It was Matthew Tregaron—a fearless probing TV reporter who specialised in environmental issues. He'd met Polly at a party where Dan had taken her, dumped her and gone off to talk on a phone for hours in an antechamber. Matthew had quite pleasantly entertained Polly in the absence of her swain, and been rather dashed when he returned, full of important news from San Diego.

'Hello, Polly! You're looking fantastic! How are you?'

'Fine thanks, Matthew.' For a horrible moment she thought his name might be Michael or Maurice after all, but he did not flinch, so she pressed on. 'How are you?'

'Great. You're really looking stunning. You know, you've got a glow.'

'Ah. Well, I've been in the country.'

'Little holiday with Daniel? Lucky bloke.'

'No. On my own. Daniel's—well, that's all over.'

Matthew's eyes lit up horribly.

'Oh no! How awful for you. You poor love. Come on, let's go and have a cuppa in Tutton's and you can tell me all about it.'

Polly privately vowed she would tell him nothing at all about it, but the idea of an *orange pressé* was not entirely unwelcome. Besides, the hint of a cunning plan was appearing over the dim horizon of her mind. So once they'd found the nearest thing Tutton's could offer to a cosy corner, and she'd dispensed with the subject of herself and Dan with a couple of brisk sentences, she launched into the saga of Harrow Hill Farm.

Well, not the whole saga. She kept well clear of the handsome shepherd, concentrating instead on the wild beauty of the place, its remoteness, the first violet, the stillness, the silence, the way the smoke threaded its way straight up from the chimneys and a dog's bark could echo all the way up the valley . . . and then that all this might be threatened, the rumour about the sale, the possibility of developers, and the awful thought of 'Twelve executive-style detached residences' springing up overnight, with neat and inappropriate gardens fenced off with *Cupressus Leylandii* where toads once squatted and buzzards wheeled. If indeed they did wheel. She would have to ask Joe. Dan had never sent her that damned bird book. He was a dead loss.

Matthew was enthralled, not just by the sight of Polly free, animated and glowing, but by the project itself. If this was, as she promised, one of last beautiful wild valleys left in southern England, and there really was a threat from developers, it would fit very nicely as a ten-minute report into his regular fortnightly programme *Earth Talk*. He was hot for it. He couldn't wait to get out there to see it for himself—with Polly at his side, of course, and then, after a couple of hours of romantic scrambling in woods and stuff, they'd go back to the pub, get slaughtered on the local firewater, take a room upstairs and fuck all night like jackrabbits.

Matthew's imagination was unfortunately coloured by an overactive libido and by his dedication to the earth. His recurrent fantasies, which he exercised regularly in his studio flat in Bloomsbury, were of pinning elegant older women down in meadows, or under bushes, until their hair was full of goosegrass and his bare bum was bristly with furze. Even now he could see Polly unbuttoning her Jacques LeFroq suit with abandon under an oaktree, and exposing to the teasing wind the wild white opulence of her breasts (which were, alas, did he but know it, at least three sizes smaller in reality).

Polly's own imagination was racing with an altogether different scenario. In her version, her breasts did not figure except as the location of an excited pounding as Matthew's fearless probing lens captured for the nation the exquisite beauty of Harrow Hill, millions reeled in horror at the thought of the executive-style residences, and the Prince of Wales reached deep into his pocket to buy the whole valley and establish it protected for ever as an agricultural trust.

'So you're not sure about the identity of the purchasers, yet?' Matthew stirred his tea, stared into her eyes and, in his imagination, slipped off his corduroy trousers and stood magnificently erect above her, outlined against the sky, a bit like the Cerne Abbas giant made flesh. The rustic-style Tutton's café table creaked slightly under the strain. Polly stared innocently and beseechingly back.

'Do it to me, oh do it to me, Matthew, oh God you're so big!' she murmured.

No, wait a minute, she didn't. She was actually saying something about not being sure about the identity of the purchasers but she would find out.

'But look, hey, I'll come down there and we can suss it out together,' urged Matthew. He wondered how soon he could have her on her back under that oak. Given good weather, he reckoned he could manage it by Thursday.

'Oh no—that is, not yet,' said Polly quickly. 'It might arouse suspicion.' At the word *arouse*, Matthew's balls tightened like a couple of hedgehogs about to burst from prolonged hibernation and tear up and down the hedgerows devouring everything in sight.

Polly thought Matthew looked a bit odd for a moment. Disappointed, no doubt. Of course he had to come down to the farm. It was no use asking his help and then trying to keep him away. She was being silly.

'I'll ring you just as soon as I've found out a bit more,' she promised. 'Then you can come down sort of incognito and do a bit of nosing about'—at this thought, Matthew almost fainted—'and then, when we're sure of our facts, we can reveal all. And whilst you're shooting, I bet the whole village will come and watch us.'

Hastily Matthew added a hundred and fifty dazed countryfolk to the background of his seduction under the oak. As he brought Polly to a majestic orgasm, the entire parish burst into applause, old men clapped horny hands and young men threw their caps in the air. The young maidens, however, stepped forward and—but no. This was getting gross.

'Excuse me a moment,' he said. 'Must just go to the loo.'

'I'll order another *orange pressé*,' said Polly. 'And when you get back, you must give me your phone number.'

By the time Polly and Matthew had finished their plotting, it was dark.

'Good God!' cried Polly. 'Is that the time! I must dash. My mother's singing in the St Matthew Passion tonight. I don't suppose you'd like to come? Quite appropriate really. Your very own passion.'

Matthew, who had been on the point of suggesting dinner or a trip to the theatre, gracefully declined, helped her unnecessarily out of her chair and bent to kiss her cheek before she fled. It was soft, round, achingly dewy.

Matthew regretted he was going to be busy tonight. In fact, he'd be wracked, in his little studio flat in Bloomsbury, with a Matthew Passion a lot more venal, but perhaps, in its modest way, no less exhilarating. Maybe after a repetition of their drama under the oak tree, they would take their show on tour, culminating with a command performance at the Albert Hall.

Polly ran down Long Acre and jumped onto the Northern Line, with a dim sense that she had forgotten to do something vital. Never mind. She'd remember it eventually. Right now she was pleased with herself. This chance meeting with Matthew really might lead to something.

Chapter  Twenty-seven

The St Matthew Passion was performed with gusto, perhaps even brio; Mrs Partridge was pleased and proud to have her daughter in the audience, and they enjoyed a coffee in the bar afterwards with old friends Rose Gillespie and Anne Finch.

'Polly's taking time off from a special project in the country,' said Mrs Partridge importantly. 'I expect that's why she's wearing that awful brown sweater. What happened to that lovely appliqué one, Polly? The one you got in Covent Garden.'

'At the cleaner's.'

'Oh, yes. Well, your cleaning bills are bound to be astronomical if you insist on wallowing about in mud all day.'

'Are you really wallowing in mud, Polly?' asked Rose nervously. She was a thin spinster who lived in Marylebone Road and was rather frightened of anything more rural. To her, Willesden was a wilderness and Uxbridge the remote rim of the world.

'Not wallowing,' laughed Polly. 'But I have been helping out a bit in the lambing shed.'

'Have you really?' exclaimed Anne. 'How lovely!' Anne loved cuddly things. She made soft toys for charity shops and collected dolls and teddy bears which she kept in a large china cabinet in her front room. Her favourite creation was a scarecrow with a bird on his shoulder and a mouse

160

on his foot, and straw sticking out of his trouserlegs: all artfully contrived out of knitting wool in Anne's cosy flat in Swiss Cottage. A cottage industry, perhaps.

Polly's father sat nervously twitching his fingers and trying not to think about smoking his pipe.

'What's the weather been like here, Father?' asked Polly.

'Oh, nothing unusual. But did you hear about that typhoon in the Philippines?'

Polly wondered why terrible things always seemed to happen in the Philippines. Was it something to do with the presence of so many American sailors?

'If they could only harness all that energy . . .' mused Mr Partridge, struggling not with the US Navy but the elements, 'capture it somehow . . .'

'In a bottle?' asked Polly facetiously. Her father looked rather hurt. Hastily she put her arm across his tweedy shoulders and gave him an affectionate pat.

'I'm sure you're going to save the world eventually, you clever old thing,' she whispered.

'Oh, no,' he recoiled at the thought of such undeserved responsibility. 'Your mother would manage much better.'

Soon it was time to go. Polly made apologetic noises and rose from her seat.

'Are you going to Dan's?' enquired her mother, rather indecently, Polly thought.

'No. An early night at home, tonight, I think,' said Polly.

'Well you're both coming to lunch tomorrow, aren't you?' said Mrs Partridge. 'I've got a lovely piece of organic topside specially.'

'Well, I'm coming, certainly,' said Polly. 'Not sure about Daniel.'

'I've asked him!' said Mrs Partridge in a confident and controlling manner. 'He's coming. Definitely.'

Polly's heart sank. So she was going to have to endure a jolly family lunch before getting Dan to herself. The condemned man ate a hearty breakfast. Unless she seized the nettle in the morning. No. She couldn't do that: it would spoil her mother's lunch. The lunch was going to be spoiled either way: either by her nervous anticipations of the scene with Daniel, or the sulky repercussions of it. In the morning she would rest and summon her strength. She would walk on the Heath, and collect that book of Charley's from his friends in East Heath Road.

Apart from the rumbling of lorries, the yells of the intoxicated, the squalls of night laughter and the squeals of brakes, the relentless thump thump thump of music in the flat above, and the faint shaking of tube trains deep in the earth beneath her, Polly spent a quiet night.

Next morning she collected Charley's book from a bald but handsome man in East Heath Road. Then she walked up on the Heath. A few people were exercising their dogs here and there. The sun was shining. A month ago Polly would have felt restored and cheered by this contact with air and grass. But with the city shimmering and slumbering below in a kind of carbon monoxide soup, the air did not taste as clear as it was wont to do. And the grass, adorned with Coke cans and condoms, was not the same delectable green stuff that Joe's sheep loved to get down their necks. This place, once so dear to Polly, now seemed a parody of paradise.

'Excuse me.' A tall distinguished-looking man with silvery hair—a barrister, perhaps, or a minor diplomat—accosted her with the courteous accents of the British public school. Polly stopped and smiled politely. 'I've got cramp in my hand,' he said, holding out his right hand towards her. Polly was puzzled. What on earth was this all about? She raised an eyebrow, wondering what was coming next. 'When I get this at home,' the civilised voice continued, and the mild grey eyes fixed her with an expression of eloquent plea, 'my wife usually stamps on my hand. That always does the trick. I couldn't help noticing that you're wearing boots . . .'

162

Polly was off like a shot. Good Lord! Was nothing sacred? Could one not take a maidenly stroll on Hampstead Heath on Sunday morning, with churchbells rolling northwards on the spring air, without the Establishment pestering you with their perversities? She was seething. The man's class credentials had knocked her off guard. Had his manner or speech been more rough, she would never have paused, not for a moment. Stamp on his hand? She entertained a brief but fervent desire to stamp on his head.

Polly paused by a small tree, having reached what she regarded as a safe area. It felt safe partly because of the discreet presence nearby of several families, and partly because she had once met Michael Foot exercising his dog at this very spot. She needed to get her breath back. She would stand here for a moment and admire the view.

'What do you think of this, then?' came a sudden voice, and a man looking distressingly like Terry Wogan, only with a moustache, stepped out from behind the tree and exposed himself. Polly cast what she hoped was a withering glance at his ludicrous pink member.

'If it wasn't so small,' she said sharply, 'I'd think it was a cock.'

And she marched off, back towards the street. The families hadn't noticed anything, the kites were flying, the bells were ringing, and in Finchley her mother was probably by now basting a much more attractive piece of meat.

'More Yorkshire Pudding, Dan?' enquired Mrs Partridge sweetly.

'You spoil me, Kathleen,' smiled Daniel, with a curl of the lip Polly had always found faintly irritating, even when at her most besotted.

'Nonsense! You need feeding up. You've got that New York look again.'

'But I've been to visit Polly in the country since then! Up

all night at the lambing shed. I should look the picture of health.'

'I think I've heard all I want to about this wretched lambing shed,' said Mrs Partridge.

'Sheep, you know,' said Polly's father, secretly fingering his pipe in his jacket pocket, 'apparently emit quite a lot of the world's greenhouse gases.'

'Gordon, please! We are trying to have a civilised lunch.'

'No but really, dear—if only one could do something about it . . .'

'Fit 'em all with catalytic converters,' said Dan through a mouthful of beef. 'Or get 'em to fart into balloons. Then use the methane to generate electricity.'

'Daniel! Please! You are awful!' giggled Polly's mother. Polly knew by Dan's expression that he was joking, but her father seemed dangerously taken with the idea.

'The trouble is,' he said with solemn concern, 'I suppose you'd have to change the bags quite regularly, or the poor sheep might sail away into the next county.'

'We have had quite enough of this subject, thank you. Now, Dan, tell us: did you have a wonderful time with Polly at her country seat?'

'Not very,' he grinned. 'She tipped a pint of Guinness over my head.'

'What! You're joking.'

'No. Scout's honour. She can't deny it.' He smiled at Polly in his most charming manner.

'Well, you were being obnoxious.'

'Polly! I don't believe that Dan is capable of being even slightly obnoxious.'

'Oh yes I am, Kathleen. Thank goodness. It's sometimes jolly useful in a tight corner, believe me. I've been obnoxious in four continents, as a matter of fact. And nowadays all the schools who are on the ball are teaching their kids to be obnoxious in three European languages.'

'But really, Polly! A pint of Guinness! You didn't!'

'I did.'

'What, in public?'

'In the local pub.'

'Good heavens! You silly thing.'

'Never mind,' said Dan genially. 'I enjoyed it. It did wonders for my hair.'

He smoothed his black Byronic locks back off his brow and struck a pose suggestive of a shampoo advertisement. Polly had to laugh, against her will. For a moment she remembered what it was about him she had originally liked.

After lunch there was coffee, and talk of Bach, volcanoes and New York. Polly found herself steering the conversation away from Harrow Hill Farm, however. She could not trust herself to speak about it.

'You won't be stuck out there much longer, will you, Polly?' her mother asked irritably. 'This is getting ridiculous.'

'What do you mean, ridiculous?' Polly bridled hotly as if she was fourteen. 'Why shouldn't I spend a few weeks in the country, for goodness' sake—even if I hadn't got a work project keeping me there?'

'You have to tread softly around the sacred subject of the lambing shed, Kathleen,' warned Dan.

'Marie Antoinette went through all this,' sighed Mrs Partridge, as if she had been talking it over with Marie Antoinette's mother at the last coffee morning. 'Had these sheep parked outside *Le Petit Trianon*. Used to put on her best shepherdess frock and go out and pose with them once a week. Silly affectation. Those of us brought up in the country know what it's all about. And we know it's not picturesque at all, Daniel. Quite the contrary.'

Polly bit her tongue.

'Did you have a nice walk on Hampstead Heath, love?' Her mother turned sweetly to her, anxious to recommend the Heath as the most, in terms of fresh air and vegetation, a sensible girl should need.

'Yes, thank you, Mother,' Polly lied. 'Quite bracing.' She turned to Dan. 'There's that new Indian film on at the Screen on the Hill this afternoon. Do you fancy going?'

'Sure.' He looked encouraged. 'Then maybe we can have a curry—although after one of Kathleen's lunches even the best curry in town would be a terrible anti-climax.'

Polly liked the idea of a curry. She was deviously planning to end the relationship in a public place, and avoid going back to his Belsize Park flat at all, if possible. But Dan was knee-deep in devious plots of his own, and as an international entrepreneur, he had had a lot more practice.

Chapter  Twenty-eight

'Just want to pick up my inhaler,' said Dan, parking outside the moody Belsize Park mansion where he had the ground floor flat. 'Feel a bit wheezy. Come in for a minute. There's something I want you to see. Think you might rather like it.'

Despite hearing several similar invitations of this type from men in the last few hours, Polly did not detect any sinister undertones. It was a nuisance: she had hoped they would park the car and go straight off to the cinema, but now she realised this was rather an unlikely scenario. They went inside.

'It's in the kitchen,' said Dan excitedly. 'Come and see.' There, right across the far wall, where his collection of Provençal rustic copper pans used to hang, a huge oak dresser now stood. 'Looks as if it's been there for ever, doesn't it?' he mused, running an elegant finger appraisingly across its grain.

'Where on earth did you get that?' asked Polly.

'Oh, down Camden Passage. Amazing, isn't it? It's from Yorkshire, apparently.'

'Yorkshire,' Polly echoed. 'Yes. I can see it in a kitchen up on the moors. I can imagine Emily Brontë keeping her cartridges in a broken teapot on the top shelf.'

The dresser's dark and impassive face had been artfully dressed with Dan's collection of naïve art: plates decorated by peasants in Portugal; Moroccan and Indian silver; masks from Mauritius; parrots carved in the hill-villages of Ecuador and a large wooden fish from Mexico, with a heron painted on its belly. Polly had always been rather fond of this paradox, since herons ate fish. Was the heron in the belly of the fish or vice versa? But today she found the whole collection somehow irritating.

'It's getting a bit like a folk museum in here,' she observed.

'Ah, of course,' Dan was instantly defensive, sardonic. 'I was forgetting. You're an emeritus peasant yourself now, aren't you? So poor benighted inner-city bastards like me aren't allowed to own dressers, I suppose.'

'How much did you pay for it?' asked Polly.

'Mind your own bloody business,' smiled Dan pleasantly.

'Don't let's start snapping at each other again,' sighed Polly. 'In fact, let's talk. We need to. I haven't had a chance yet to apologise for throwing that beer over you.'

'That's all right.' Catching her softened tone, he instantly moved in close and placed his hands on her hips. She tried to back off, but her exit was barred by the dresser.

'Look,' she removed his hands, 'we need to talk. Please. Come on. Be fair.'

He tilted her chin upwards and flickered his tongue across her lips. In the past, this act had had an electrifying effect on her. Now it made her feel faintly nauseous. Polly wrenched herself away and sat down. He installed himself beside her, in his pride and joy: a seventeenth-century ladderback carver chair, upon which centuries of working bums had taken their aching ease before it passed out of their custody and fell victim to the slack buttocks of the intelligentsia.

'Come on, then. But be quick,' said Dan. 'I want to spend this afternoon either at the movies or making love. Not in a committee meeting.' Polly seized his hand. Not as an invitation, but as one might hold hands when battened down against a hurricane or typhoon: when the tender

168

human skull is threatened by the whirl and crash of flying garage roofs and fragments of corrugated iron.

'There's no future for us, Daniel.'

'Why not?'

'Because . . .' Polly hesitated. 'Because I've had time to think. On my own. And I've realised that we've grown apart.'

'No we haven't. Don't start trying to drag me into it. I haven't grown apart from you. Not at all. You're the one who's had enough. You should have the guts to say so.'

'All right then. I've grown . . . I've grown out of this relationship.'

'Oh, very organic. Like growing out of a pair of sandals? Look, why don't you stop being so bloody hypocritical? You know and I know what's the matter.'

'What do you mean?' But Polly felt herself blushing despite all her efforts to erect an invisible dyke in her neck, against the rising flood of embarrassment.

'Joe or whatever his name is. Your rustic toyboy. That's what's behind all this. I'm not stupid, Pol. I know you quite well. When I saw you in that shed with him, crawling about in that muck and gazing adoringly at his rippling pectorals, I knew what was going on. Christ, woman, I've been around. I'm not a dodo.'

'Rubbish!' cried Polly. 'Why is it that men can never accept that a woman might just have had enough of them, full stop? Why does there always have to be another man involved? There's absolutely nothing between myself and Joe.'

'I saw the way you looked at him.'

'I didn't look at him. Not in any particular way at all. He's not my type, not remotely. You're just being paranoid.'

'And you're lying in your teeth.'

'I am not!'

For a moment Polly was tempted to seize the Mexican fish and break it across his expertly gelled scalp.

'Look, Pol, if you'd come clean and say, "OK Dan, sorry about this, old sport, but your time's up, young Joe's giving me the old once-over now, time for a change, and I fancy a bit of rough, so on yer bike mate and good hunting," well, fair enough.'

'But that isn't the case!'

'Come on. Don't lie to me, darling. Deceit turns me on, you know.' Dan seized her wrist. Polly tried to struggle, but despite his sedentary job and effete tastes, he was surprisingly strong. He came from springy and resourceful immigrant stock and he played squash regularly with a member of the minor aristocracy. He could hold his own even against a woman brought to a rolling boil of fitness by extensive hill-walking and regular immobilising of sheep.

'Let go, Daniel. Don't give me all this chauvinist crap.'

'All right, then. One for the road. You've said your piece: that's it. I accept. Unreservedly. But let's just have a farewell bash, eh? Where would you like it? On the kitchen table? Is that what old Joe goes in for? Is that what turns you on nowadays, then? Well, this is an old farmhouse table, as it happens – ' Skilfully he immobilised her on it. 'And I can hand out a bit of rough if that's what you're after. Ooo ar, darlin', let's have yer drawers off!'

Polly struggled, but in vain. The dexterity with which Dan ripped away her defences and imposed himself on her made her wonder how many other women he had raped.

This is how the civilised New Man behaves, then, she thought, deciding that her best way of enduring the assault undamaged was to detach herself from her body, take up a position near the ceiling and watch like a disinterested anthropologist, *when his dignity is wounded. I bet if I struggled he could end up murdering me. It could happen by accident. He could bash me with one of these folk artefacts. I can see it all in the papers next Sunday. TV PERSONALITIES IN BELSIZE PARK SLAYING.*

When it was over, Polly just lay there, staring at the

ceiling. Dan withdrew himself and leaned, panting, against an old spice-chest. She could feel him glaring at her. He would be bewildered and guilty, already. She would just lie there, like a stone. For all the world as if he had killed her.

'There!' he said, finally, his voice trembling slightly. 'On the kitchen table. On the farmhouse table. Just to keep you going till you get back to Superman. Got a big cock, has he? I expect he shags twenty sheep before breakfast when you're not around.'

Polly reached for the Mexican fish and hurled it across the room. It struck Dan on the temple. His face suddenly seemed to close up, and he slumped forward, striking his head on the edge of the table as he fell. Polly leapt off the table.

For a horrible moment she stood in a prickling silence. His body lay utterly still where it had fallen. Without even pausing to retrieve the torn fragments of her knickers, Polly grabbed the fish and ran.

As it happened, a taxi was cruising up Belsize Park Gardens. Trying to hide her violent shaking, Polly got in. As they drove up the hill, she stared, mesmerised, at the side of the fish. If fish can devour herons, the prey can become the predator. But what sort of model was that for human behaviour? Her heart hammered in her ribcage. *Thank God I'm not a carnivore*, thought Polly. *Supposing I had to tear somebody's head off every time I got peckish?* And yet the lionesses never seemed to lose their nerve.

Polly wondered, as the taxi carried her back to her lair, whether she had become a murderer. Or that slightly more exciting and refined of species—a murderess. If this is what a weekend in the city can lead to, she thought, I don't think I'm ever going to risk it again.

Chapter  Twenty-nine

Polly leapt onto the train at Paddington with thirty seconds to spare. She felt like a criminal, and as far as she knew, she was. Repeated phone calls in the four hours since she had felled Dan, had connected her only with his answering machine.

'Hi, this is Dan Birnbaum,' it had chirped. 'Sorry I'm unable to talk to you personally right now.' *Only my ex-girlfriend just murdered me with a Mexican fish*, Polly had mentally added, with increasing panic.

She tried to sound calm, the one time she had actually left a message on the machine. (The police would listen to incoming messages. Of course. It would be act of an idiot to say, 'Dan, I'm really sorry I hit you so hard. Do ring and tell me you're all right. You didn't look too good when I left. Yours ever, Polly.') 'Er . . .' (Stay calm. Sound blasé. This is a casual call.) 'Um . . . Hi, Dan. How're you doing? Give me a ring when you can.' She did not identify herself. Dan, if alive, knew her voice all too well. The police, she hoped, did not.

'Good evening, ladies and gentlemen.' The voice of the British Rail guard broke in upon her anxieties. 'I'd like to welcome you aboard the seven fifteen . . .' Some of these guards were seriously stage-struck, thought Polly. Soon they'd be describing the scenery to us or reading little poems composed by their wives. London was slipping past outside, but it was already dark. Polly saw only the reflection of her own pale and hectic face against the black.

'Good evening, ladies and gentlemen, this is the senior steward speaking. I'd like to inform all passengers that the bar and buffet is now open offering a wide range of hot 'n' cold snacks, drinks and light refreshments including . . .' He launched into an ecstatic description of a chocolate chip cookie, and Polly discovered she was hungry. Murder certainly gave one an appetite.

Two Danish pastries later, with a gin and tonic cradled in her restless fingers, Polly closed her eyes. But every time she closed them she saw Dan lying on his kitchen floor. There had been no blood. But it was surely possible to kill people without spilling blood. Besides, Dan was too well bred to bleed in front of a lady, even when dead.

Polly snorted with laughter, surrendering for a moment to a desperate hysteria. The woman opposite glared at her over her copy of *The Sunday Times*. Polly looked out of the window, smiling to herself in as rational a way as possible. It was a highly suspect act, to laugh in public in England, when on your own. It was almost tantamount to a confession of murder, in fact. A couple more snorts and the guard would be alerted, they'd phone down the line, and have the police waiting for her at Chippenham. Polly raised Joe's sweater to her nose once more, to hide her guilty, hysterical face, feeling safe in its hayloft smell. She hoped she'd be allowed to wear it in prison.

She had rung Joe and asked if he could meet her. It seemed a cheek, but it would've been a long taxi ride and Polly wasn't even sure whether Sedgeworth rose to taxis at all on Sunday nights. Joe had seemed willing.

'Anything to get away from sheep for an hour or two,' he had said. 'Have a good time in London, did you?'

'No. It was absolutely ghastly. That's why I'm coming back early.'

'Ah.'

Joe could pack a lot into a syllable. Somehow his 'Ah' contained a certain grim satisfaction that city life had proved so unpalatable. It might have irritated Polly quite a lot if she hadn't been so preoccupied. There was something else nagging away at the back of her mind. What was it? Something she had forgotten to do . . . Gloria's seeds were safely packed in her overnight bag, together with the Mexican fish which in a frenzy of guilt, Polly had scrubbed with an abrasive cleaner to remove any forensic fragments of Dan's head that might have adhered to it.

Oh God! Catherine the Great! The awful imminence of her talk suddenly broke in upon her. She had been going to gen up on Catherine in the bookshops of Charing Cross Road, but that chance encounter with Matthew had put it out of her mind. There wouldn't be anything on Catherine in Sedgeworth, she was sure, let alone Long Dangley. And she had to give the talk on Thursday. Three days to go. Never mind. With any luck, she'd be arrested by then.

Being a murderer on the run certainly cleared from one's mind the mere debris of everyday anxieties. Even the predicament of Harrow Hill Farm had receded to a shadowy sideshow. So what if developers plastered the hillside with executive-style residences? Polly would willingly have sacrificed the whole valley to supermarkets and video shops if she could be sure that Dan was all right.

It wasn't that she loved him after all, or anything naff like that. It was just that Polly had always been reluctant to inflict pain. It was such a messy business. She would infinitely rather endure it herself than dish it out. She had spent hours chasing moths towards her windows, asking wasps to leave, scattering disinfectant along her skirting boards to deter mice: anything rather than cause suffering to a fellow-creature.

And yet the fellow-creatures would probably not have hesitated to cause suffering to each other. At Harrow Hill Farm she had woken several times in the night to hear small things shrieking in indignation at being decapitated by slightly bigger or fiercer creatures. Perhaps when she hurled that Mexican fish at Dan's head she was behaving like a natural creature for the first time in her life.

There was something very reassuring about the sight of Joe waiting in the station car park at Sedgeworth.

'I see you're still wearing that old thing,' he said, tweaking at the collar of his jumper.

'I find it strangely comforting.'

'Do you need a bit of comfort, then? Bad weekend, was it? Your mum sing out of tune? Did she shatter all the windows in the Wigmore Hall?'

God! Was it only last night she had been listening to the St Matthew Passion?

'No. The concert was fine. I like listening to music. You can sort your thoughts out. It's like a sort of meditation.'

'I know. I listen to classical music a lot. Viv, mostly.'

'Viv?'

'Vivaldi. The Seasons. I got it on cassette.' Joe flicked a switch on the dashboard, and a red-hot rush of harpsichord flooded incongruously through the vehicle.

'How extraordinary,' said Polly. 'I've been listening to The Seasons in my car, too . . . Ah! Lovely! It does make me feel better.'

'Terrible weekend, then, was it?'

'Not bad.'

'Did you see lover-boy?'

Polly hesitated. If she told Joe the whole story, including the rape, and the murder—and it turned out indeed to be a real murder, she was sunk. He would know: the police would have to know, that would be the end of it—and her. Better not to admit she had seen Dan at all.

'No.'

'Yes, you did.'

'Oh, did I indeed? And what makes you say that?'

'You had to think about it.'

'You're very observant, aren't you?'

'It's my job.'

'You always know when your beasts are lying, then?'

'They never do. That's why I like them.'

'Prefer them.'

'I didn't say that.'

'Well, do you? Prefer the company of animals to humans?'

'Depends on the individual animal. And the individual human an' all.'

A short silence developed, during which Polly wondered if she would be able to learn Chinese in prison. She had always wanted to learn Chinese.

'So how was he? Recovered from his wetting?'

Polly was silent for a moment.

'He raped me,' she said, finally, in a voice that shook. 'And I killed him.'

Joe said nothing for a while.

'Apart from that, Miss Partridge,' he drawled eventually, 'how did you enjoy the weekend?'

Polly laughed: a sudden, mad laugh. It seemed safe in this Land-Rover with Joe. She could sense that she was safe: Dan wasn't dead after all. That kind of horrible thing couldn't happen to her.

'You don't seem surprised,' she teased, 'that I've committed murder.'

'I'm not surprised. The bugger was asking for it. And besides . . .' he turned up the farm lane, 'it makes sense of this phone message we got for you.'

'Phone message? Is he all right, then?' Polly's voice jumped with eagerness, with fear.

'It said, "Please ring Metropolitan Police" and gave a number.' Joe's voice was measured and calm, but at his words Polly felt herself catapulted into a black abyss.

Chapter  Thirty

Joe parked in the yard, jumped out and slammed his door. Polly could not move. Her heart panicked, its great alarmed leaps paralysing her. She felt she had crossed a terrible frontier into a country where only anguish awaited her. The little inconveniences of her past life now seemed like heart-rending comforts. If only she could go back! Just twenty-four hours, just twelve. To a single moment when she might have acted differently. Polly had always been wary of passion. She had surrendered to it for a moment and ruined everything for ever.

Joe noticed she was still in the Land-Rover, came back and opened the door.

'Are you coming in?' he enquired. 'Or are you nesting? We had a hen once who made a nest in the passenger seat of the old van.'

Polly reached dumbly for his arm. She felt weak and stricken, like someone after a major operation. Joe helped her down.

'Gently does it!' he commented teasingly. 'Mustn't shake the old bones.'

Somehow Polly managed to walk across the yard to the front door: towards that phone message waiting for her. She still could not speak, however. Her whole body had become somehow tangled and mangled and unco-operative. Her thighs, in reality slim, seemed massive and heavy to move.

'My mum and dad are away,' said Joe, opening the door. 'They've gone down to Bournemouth for a day or two.'

Polly was relieved. Joe seemed to be taking the whole business in his stride. She sensed he would be a great source of strength in her present dilemma. He did not seem to be shocked by anything.

He handed her a small, folded piece of paper. Polly's heart thrashed even faster.

'That's the phone message,' said Joe.

She unfolded it. For a moment she could not comprehend what was written. A stupid blankness had seized her brain. *I'm still alive*, it said. *Better luck next time. Dan.*

A terrible shaking took hold of Polly. Joe was smiling at her but he seemed to be inhabiting a different, parallel world: the inches between them might as well have been thousands of miles.

'But . . . but you said . . . you told me . . .' At last she managed to get words out. 'You told me the Police had rung.'

'Sorry, sweetheart. Only kidding!'

Polly broke into racking sobs. Joe was aghast: immediately he put his arms round her.

'I . . . I . . . I . . .'

'There, there. Don't say anything. I'm sorry, love. I'm sorry. It was just a joke.'

'But how could you—how could you—didn't you realise—' The sobs tore at her throat, would not let her speak.

'Don't try to talk.'

Polly's legs gave way. Joe carried her upstairs and laid her on her bed. He covered her gently with the eiderdown.

'You lie there and I'll go and make you a cup of tea. I'm a bloody idiot sometimes. I'm very very sorry.'

As Polly lay on her bed, the sobs melted away. The room seemed to embrace her with its familiar faint smell of lavender. The window was slightly open and a timorous wind, coming in from the friendly dark, stirred the curtains. Her own reflected warmth started to return to her through the eiderdown and comfort her. Dan was all right. The nightmare was over.

Still she could not stop shaking. Shock, she supposed. There was no policeman waiting to talk to her. No death. No dishonour. Her life remained tremblingly intact, though the image of a horror had nudged its root. Passion did this. Passion had stupefied her, had caused her to throw that fish. But now that she knew Dan was alive and well enough to leave joking messages, a deep rage against him sprang up, just when she most wanted to be quiet. Another passion. Oh God. Polly turned and stared into the middle distance, trying to relax.

An unusual object on her bedside table caught her eye. She refocused and found it was a tiny jar full of violets. Their dark little faces seemed to stoop towards her with concern. It was if they knew how she felt, and sent their sweetness down to soothe her. Who had done this for her? Mrs Swain had never placed flowers in her room: it had only happened when Mrs Swain was away. She knew very well who had done it. Even now she could hear his steps coming up the stairs, and the faint china tremor of cup on saucer.

Eventually she would let herself be pleased about these violets, but now she could not face any strong feelings. Joe came into the room and put the tea down. He sat on the bed. Polly was still shaking from time to time, but she managed a weak smile.

'Thank you.'

Joe took her hand. 'I'm very sorry. I had no idea you'd take it like that. I'm stupid.'

'No. I'm the one who's been stupid,' Polly's voice sounded thin and wobbly. 'I hate being like this—collapsing like this. It's ridiculous.'

'Just lie still,' he squeezed her hand. 'Don't try to talk. Just rest. Then have your tea. A good night's sleep will make all the difference. We'll laugh about this in the morning. Just be quiet now.' Joe got up.

'No. Wait! I want to tell you—just tell you about it. Have you got a moment?'

''Course I have.'

He sat down again, and Polly told him the whole story. When she got to the bit about throwing the fish, however, a twinkle crept into his eye, and she seemed to catch it, and they both burst out laughing, and worse than laughing: they got trapped into a helpless hysterical attack that squeezed all the breath out of them, threw them about the bed, whinnying and screaming.

'I threw a fish at his head!' she gasped and choked. 'A fish!' The world seemed upside down, absurd, but at this moment, magically healed and joyous.

When the laughter had blown itself out, and the tale was told, Joe looked properly sombre.

'The only thing you can do about this, sweetheart,' he said, 'is put it behind you.'

'I know. The thing that upsets me most of all is I got so out of control. To collapse like that! I hate it. You having to carry me upstairs and everything. I can't stand being out of control.'

'Nothing wrong with feeling weak sometimes,' he said, getting up.

'You never seem to be weak,' she said reproachfully.

''Course I am. Weak as a kitten sometimes. I'll be crying on your shoulder one of these days.'

Polly smiled. 'Well, till then, is there anything I can do for you?'

'Yeah. Two things. First, you've got to pay me back with an even worse trick than the one I just played on you.'

'That'll be a pleasure. What's the other?'

'Bring me a cup of tea in the barn when you wake up.'

'Lambing all night again? How's it going?'

'Nearly finished now. Got the last few in there tonight.

180

Then I'll be able to take things a bit easier. Show you a few places. Find out all about this research of yours.' He paused by the door. He looked tired.

'Well . . . goodnight,' said Polly.

Joe hesitated. Then, awkward for a moment with a curious shyness, he stepped forward and placed a single chaste kiss on her brow.

'Goodnight,' he said.

Polly soon slipped into a blessed sleep.

She awoke at about five a.m., feeling restored. For a moment she thought about the events of the weekend, then remembered Joe's injunction to put it all behind her. Quickly she got dressed, diving into his old brown sweater with relief. One of these days she would have to wash it. But she was reluctant to. Washing it would spoil it.

It was odd, making tea in Mrs Swain's kitchen knowing she was not upstairs. There was a feeling of freedom, as if the grown ups were away and the children were free to misbehave, or to play at Mummies and Daddies. She put on her coat and carried the flask out to the barn.

A row of pens contrived from hurdles lay along one wall. In each of them there was a ewe with her lambs. Three ewes had twins. Polly inspected them with an eye that was becoming more discriminating. One ewe lay with her lamb behind her. Polly knew she was not such a good mother as the ones who kept their lambs literally under their noses and warmed them with their breath. But where was Joe?

Suddenly she saw him: sprawled on his back among some bales of straw. He had been surprised by sleep. He looked like a painting of a dead soldier, his clothes muddied and torn and bloodied by his long campaign. His face was relaxed, his mouth slightly open. She could see the breath moving across his lips, which gleamed slightly. A handful of damp curls lay on his brow in a dark tangle.

It seemed a shame to wake him, but it seemed a shame to go, somehow, so Polly sat and watched him sleep until dawn broke.

Chapter  Thirty-one

When Joe woke up he was rather crumpled and grouchy. Polly pretended she had just arrived. She poured the tea, and expressed sympathy with his fatigue and congratulations that the lambing seemed to be over. It felt good to be legal again after her brief few hours as a murderess. She felt restored, and anxious to be finding out more about the farm sale—if such a thing existed. On such a morning as this, with trees visible through the barn door decked out in pearly light, the question of what was to become of this place seemed more urgent than ever.

'What about our bargain, then?' she hesitated.

'What bargain?' Joe seemed exhausted and scratchy. Polly feared it was not a good time to ask.

'I tell you about my research and you tell me about plans for the farm's future.'

Joe gave a mighty yawn, and stretched till his sinews cracked. 'Later.' He clambered stiffly to his feet. 'Right now I'm so shattered I couldn't give a damn. You could be researching into voodoo for all I care.'

'Sorry,' said Polly, feeling foolish.

'It's OK. Just be patient. When I've had a good night's sleep, and some grub, and a bath, and a change of clothes, I might be able to manage a civilised conversation.'

'Are you going to bed now?' asked Polly.

'I must just water these ewes.'

'I can do that.'

'Thanks.' Possessed by another huge yawn, Joe glanced briefly at each of his nursing mothers, and then, evidently satisfied, he staggered off towards the house.

Polly gave each of the ewes a bucket of water, and reached in and caressed one or two of the lambs. The ewes, fiercely maternal, stood up and stamped their front feet at her indignantly. The lambs were curious and responsive. They were too new to be frightened of human beings.

'It's all right,' Polly soothed their anxious mothers. 'I'm only the barmaid.' She looked round the barn, wishing there was something else she could do—partly to be helpful, and partly because she felt like it. Her own work, the searching out of locations, the sketching of scenes, the drafting of framework scripts, hung about in the background of her mind like a heavy cloud, oppressing her spirits. Carrying buckets of water to the sheep, however, gave her a simple satisfaction she had not experienced before.

Since she was too ignorant to know what might be helpful, she went back to her room, tidied it, and was just inclining reluctantly to a folder with some notes in it, when the telephone rang. With the senior Swains away, and Joe—she hoped—asleep, she ran to answer it.

'Polly! This is Joyce Lillicrap. Can you talk?'

'Yes. Hello, Joyce.' Polly felt slightly uneasy. She had not done her homework. 'I'm afraid I haven't got very far, yet. I have tried, but – '

'Never mind, dear. I know those Swains! Secretive and sly! Mrs Swain wouldn't even let me have her recipe for marmalade cake! But don't worry—we've managed to unearth some news this end.'

'Oh really? What?'

'Well, Mildred has done some more sniffing around, and apparently the Swains are negotiating with some developers based in Croydon. I ask you, dear! Croydon! What can they possibly care about what happens to us here? I broke down in Croydon once, and the man who came from the garage was an absolute fool.'

Polly made a mild observation to the effect that she expected there were both pleasant and intelligent people living in Croydon.

'Perhaps there are, dear! Perhaps there are! Wonders will never cease! But we don't want them building all over your lovely valley, do we?'

'Well, no.' Polly was rather charmed, as she was no doubt meant to be, by the valley's being described as hers. 'Is that what they're going to do?'

'Apparently. Mildred's friend has found out a bit about the sort of things they've done in the past. They specialise in the top end of the market: big detached houses, you know, on greenfield sites usually. About twelve houses to each development, with names like Woodlands or Meadowsweet. Quite large gardens, each, no doubt, with its awful pampas grass.'

Polly shuddered. 'But are we sure that's what they're planning here?'

'Not altogether. That's where you come in, Polly. We desperately need to know what's going on from the horse's mouth. Contracts haven't been exchanged yet, apparently, so it's not too late. I'm sure the Swains will see reason. But once contracts have been exchanged we'll be slugging it out with the developers and my dear, you don't need me to tell you that will be an entirely different matter.'

Polly did need Joyce Lillicrap to tell her, actually. Her ignorance of planning permissions and associated matters was extensive. But she could see the thrust of Mrs Lillicrap's arguments.

'You must pump Joe, my dear. I'm sure you can get him going, with your charm and skill. Tell him if he wants to save the farm, the whole village will be behind him. We'll move heaven and earth.'

'Yes,' said Polly. 'And I've had a few ideas about how I might get certain TV people interested.'

'Have you? How marvellous!'

'Yes. I was in London this weekend, and I met an old friend of mine: Matthew Tregaron.'

'Ah! The boy with the beard who does that environmental stuff on Sunday mornings?'

'Yes.'

'I do wish he'd shave it off, you know. But never mind. And I do wish he wouldn't have his programme on Sunday mornings when I'm so busy cooking lunch.'

Polly explained that Matthew had no choice about when his programme was scheduled, and that in some quarters, programmes about the environment were still regarded as marginal.

'Rainforests and things are OK,' Polly went on, 'but local issues, things nearer home, like the stuff Matthew reports on, well, that's still Sunday morning material to some people. Unfortunately.'

'Still, you've got him interested? That's splendid!'

'Oh yes. I've definitely got him interested.'

'And he's coming down?'

'He's just waiting for me to give the word.'

'But that's terrific! I must get Angelica down if I possibly can. She's always fancied him. Well, I suppose I would too if it wasn't for that awful beard.'

Polly terminated the conversation with a promise to find out more, summon Matthew and place the mass media on red alert about the disappearance of a national treasure.

After putting down the phone, however, she felt disinclined to begin any of these tasks, but sat instead on the stairs for a few moments, picking her nose and thinking. Then she got up and went outside.

The air smelt different. You could smell the earth. Bleats echoed from the barn; everywhere, in the hedgerows and upon the banks, there was a dusting of green. This faint stirring scent of Spring mingled deliciously with the smell of diesel, straw and hay. Polly was looking forward to the summer when she would be able to smell the hot stones.

She walked down to the first field and sat there on the gate for a while, looking down the valley. If she sold her flat, and got the maximum mortgage . . . but something warned her that Joe would never accept financial help from her. The sun came out, and she turned her face towards it. It beat down with surprising strength. Summer was coming. But what was Polly's own harvest going to be?

Since she felt energetic, Polly walked across the valley to the Bothy, to deliver Charley's book. But though his van was parked outside, there was no sign of him anywhere.

Chapter  Thirty-two

'Good morning!' Sir Antony burst from a thicket, puffing and snorting like an old satyr who was finding his naughtiness more and more of an effort. 'Miss Pheasant, I believe.'

'Partridge.'

'I knew you were game, me dear. Ha ha! Good morning! Looking for Brewster?'

'Well, yes. I've just been to London and I brought a book back for him. I left it in the porch.'

'That'll do, ah yes! Are you . . . *inamorato*?'

'I beg your pardon?'

'Are you and Brewster . . .' he leaned towards her and winked, 'on canoodling terms, hey? Time he had a woman. Good morning!'

'Goodness, no,' smiled Polly. 'I've only ever met him once. And I don't really think he's my type.'

'Quite right, quite right. Fellow's too pale and peaky. Bit sickly if you ask me. Bad stock, bad stock. North London, you know. Too much lead in the air. What you need, my dear, is a man with blood in his veins. Tally ho!' Sir Antony suddenly loosed off a volley of shot up into the treetops. It provoked an outraged cawing, but no casualties.

'Were you after . . . a squirrel?' she asked.

'No, no, my dear,' he beamed at her. 'Just high spirits, you know. That one was in your honour.'

'Thank you.'

'Not at all.' Sir Antony eased himself onto his other

leg. He still seemed a little stiff after his plunge from the tree.

'How are you?' asked Polly.

'In disgrace,' he sighed. 'Shot me windows out this morning.'

'Shot your . . . windows?' faltered Polly.

'Only those high ones in the hall. Damned women gave me hell about it. If a man can't shoot his own blasted windows out, what's England coming to?'

'But why . . .?'

'Wanted a bit of air,' growled Sir Antony. 'And now I've got it, by Jove! Turned out of doors without a crust to roam the woods till lunchtime. Still, who wants to be cooped up there, all day? I walk my estates, my dear, and I survey my sheepies, and my Aberdeen Angusses, and my little deers. And'— he tipped his tweed hat to her —'my blackstockings. Good morning! I must leave you.' And he lurched off down a woodland path.

Polly returned to find a letter had arrived for her. It was postmarked Manchester. Polly recognised the typeface of Tony Lewis's secretary and experienced a minor panic. So far she had produced very little in terms of notes, sketches for locations, outlines of scenes. Tony would be expecting some progress to have been made by now. And she had not sent him anything since the initial postcard. She felt guilty, and tore the letter open.

Instead of the polite enquiry she was expecting, Polly was appalled to read that Tony had had one of his brainwaves. He was coming down to see her. He'd heard a bit about Long Dangley and Harrow Hill Farm from Dan, and it sounded really good, A1, and he was sure she'd been too busy to report back so far, and anyway he wanted to see it for himself so he'd come down for a day or so. He fancied a little break. She wasn't to worry about him: he'd find a place to stay, he'd be there on Tuesday.

Tuesday! That was tomorrow! Polly ran upstairs, grabbed

her notebooks, and went out into the sunshine. If she had to work, at least it would be outdoors. With a Mars bar in her pocket, she could keep going for hours. There was a nice cosy little sun-trap in the further barn: curling up among some bales of hay, Polly got out her project file and gave it some pencil.

Several hours passed: the sunlight moved quietly across the bales, and Poly wriggled after it. Towards three o'clock she began to feel a bit sleepy, but the Mars bar did the trick. By using very large handwriting (an old trick remembered from past exams) and only covering one side of the paper, Polly had managed to assemble a remarkably large dossier. Sketches and maps, however crude and useless, were another way of amassing a fair acreage of notes. She was beginning to feel rather pleased with herself.

'What a pretty sight!'

She jumped.

Joe was standing in the doorway. She had not heard him come. The sun was beating on his back: it lit up his dark curls. Polly's heart quickened.

'You look better,' she said.

'I feel better,' he smiled. 'I've had my bath, got me clean clothes on . . . feel civilised for a change.'

'Good. You must've been shattered.'

He paused and looked at her with his head cocked on one side. 'You look like a little hen,' he said. 'Dusting down in here. Found a nice cosy nest, have you?' Slowly he advanced towards her. 'What's all this stuff?' he looked at her papers. Polly whisked them out of sight. The evidence of her espionage. 'Ah,' Joe smiled. 'The research.'

'Yes,' said Polly, hiding them under her skirt. But Joe showed no further interest in them. Instead his eyes caught on hers, and for a long, long time, they lost themselves in each other's shining gaze. Then he leaned carefully down, she raised her head, and the kiss Polly had been longing for dropped into her mouth like the most luscious fruit, ripe at last. He was delicious.

They parted with a little groan, then sank into a deep embrace. His arms around her felt huge, and warm, and strong. Polly's notebook cut into her buttock.

'Let me . . . let me move my stuff – '

Joe carefully placed the papers behind a neighbouring bale. Then he took her in his arms again and his brown eyes melted over every detail of her face. With infinite tenderness he smoothed a lock of hair off her brow. He seemed to have all the time in the world. Polly's senses were swimming. She could not speak. She had feared this moment would never come, or if it came, he would be rough, or clumsy. But he held her as gently as the tiniest lamb.

'Aren't you a dear little thing?' he breathed. She felt his breath on her eyelashes. A remote, rather neglected compartment of Polly's brain reported that for a man to describe her as *little* was demeaning, and *thing*, well . . . downright insulting. Polly decided that that part of her brain was going to have its grant cut. Because, on hearing herself described as a dear little thing, her eyes filled mysteriously with tears.

'Oh dear,' she trembled, as a tear broke down her cheek, 'you are . . . you are awful. Making me cry like this.'

Then she noticed that his eyes were brimming too.

'I must kiss you again,' he whispered. 'I can't help it. You taste just like chocolate.'

Love was made on that warmed hay, more gently, and more tenderly, than Polly had ever known. They lay in each other's arms afterwards and listened to the birds' wings fluttering in and out above their heads.

'Nesting,' said Joe, and his voice vibrated against her cheek. She felt lapped from head to foot in sheer bliss, as if she was where she had always wanted to be. Outside, hens crooned and clucked. Far away in the valley, a dog barked. A little breeze ventured in and stirred her papers. One page of notes sailed down through a sunbeam onto the barn floor. Joe rescued it.

'It doesn't matter,' said Polly, sorry to lose his arms for a moment.

'Oh yes it does,' he said, replacing it carefully and handing it to her. 'Your work. Now tell me. What's it all about?'

So Polly told him. Joe did not mind at all. He seemed to think it would be rather a laugh, as long as it didn't interfere with the routines of the farm.

'I did wonder,' she said, 'I mean, if you're having to sell the farm, if we could help in anyway, I mean, there is a location fee . . . it might just . . .'

'Massive investment, this place needs,' said Joe with a sigh, looking out of the barn door. 'It's not viable, the way prices are at the moment. The bank manager's turned nasty. You should have heard the soft-soaping bastard a few years ago when the boom was on. But now he wants his pound of flesh.'

'So you're selling?'

'No choice, sweetheart.'

'To developers?'

'I dunno. They can cover it with concrete and build an artificial ski-slope here for all I care.'

'Don't! You do care!'

'I don't want to talk about it.'

'But what'll you do?'

'My mum and dad reckon they're off to Bournemouth. I fancy Australia.'

Polly's heart gave a gigantic bound.

'What?'

'Plenty of sheep out there. Sunshine, too.'

Polly felt a horrid pang of anxiety. He mustn't disappear.

'But not yet, surely? These things take ages to fix up.'

'Oh, I'll be here for a while yet.'

'Good. Because I want you to teach me everything you know.'

'I just showed you everything I know, sweetheart,' he twinkled at her. Polly laughed.

'Not that. I meant—to do with the farm. Well, the sheep, mainly. I don't know why I like them so much.'

'It's because they're poor helpless creatures, born to die,' he said thoughtfully.

'Is that why?' Polly sighed. The sun went in, and she felt cold. Joe smiled at her naked body.

'Come on,' he said. 'Cover up that enticing little bod, or I'll be after you again and my folks will come home and catch us at it.' He dressed quickly, his mind already on his next tasks. Polly lamented that the moment of sunlit splendour was past.

'I'm off, then,' he said quietly. 'Why don't you go in and make a cup of tea? Finish your work in the warm. It's turned cold now. I lit a fire before I came out.'

Polly stood up. She felt stiff and crumpled, but possessed of a raging inner joy.

'Are your parents coming home soon, then?'

'Search me. They might not come till tomorrow.'

Polly hoped they would not. She fancied an evening by the fire with Joe.

'I won't be around this evening,' he said suddenly, with telepathic directness. 'I've got to go and see someone in Exeter.'

'Never mind,' shrugged Polly, hiding a sudden bitter disappointment that flashed through her limbs like blue electricity. Damn it, she was in love again. All her dear freedom gone. It was two years, really, since she had stopped being in love with Daniel.

'Hey!' Joe stopped her on her way to the barn door, held her close, and placed a delicate kiss on her brow. 'If the folks are still away, I'll come to your room tonight. Maybe.

If I'm home early.' But he didn't. Polly lay awake and listened, her body twingeing with desire. But—and somehow this was a very painful thing—he never came in at all. He was out all night.

Chapter  Thirty-three

The farm kitchen seemed strangely deserted as Polly made her tea and toast. The ecstasy of her afternoon with Joe, and the misery of her night without him, coalesced uneasily in her stomach, forbidding eggs and bacon. Even the toast would have to be very dry and boring. She sighed. She didn't mind the way love destroyed your peace of mind: it was the peace of body she really missed. To cap it all, it was raining, out of a sulkily grey sky.

It's caring about it that I hate, thought Polly, stirring her tea listlessly, light-headed with lack of sleep. *Why shouldn't he stay out all night? There could be any number of innocent explanations—and even if the explanation isn't innocent, the fact that I lay in his arms for an hour yesterday afternoon doesn't give me the right to comment.* But her body had decided that it cared horribly, whether she had the right to or not. That was what happened when you fell in love. Your body slipped its leash and dashed off straight towards the thorn-bushes. And your imagination was off after it, like a shot.

Even as she washed her few dishes she was listening for the sound of an engine: every time she passed the window, she glanced out with a pathetic hopefulness which was extremely irritating. Her imagination lurched off from its usual orderly channels and ran amok in a personal video shop, trying out a series of sex-and-violence movies starring Joe's Land-Rover smashed to smithereens on the motorway; Joe's body monopolised by a voluptuous young tart in the

195

unexpectedly naughty city of Exeter. Eventually she had to marry him off to Jodie Foster, and shoot them both on their wedding night with her own fair hand. This made her feel a bit better for a while.

She put on her coat and wandered out to the barn which yesterday had been a golden boudoir shimmering with lovely scents and sounds. Now it seemed damp and forlorn. Polly closed her eyes and surrendered to the memory of that first kiss. She told herself sternly that it might all be over: nothing more than a quick thrash in the hay. Ships that pass in the night. But it hadn't felt like that . . . Polly's imagination seized a gross initiative, and she was too tired to argue.

To the swelling strains of Brahms's Wind Quintet (Polly's background music was always very high quality), Polly was dressing herself in ivory Edwardian lace and arriving at an exquisite little church tucked away down a legendary lane. It was not the church at Long Dangley—that was not quite picturesque enough. Inside the church Joe was waiting in his best suit, and the old organ was pumping out a wedding march.

Reeling from this kitsch onslaught, Polly attempted to call her imagination to heel, but it gambolled playfully just out of reach, and then streaked off towards a cradle: a Joeian baby with big brown eyes, another one . . . the whole family at the cottage door, which had become taste-fully festooned with honeysuckle and climbing roses. And Joe gazed rapturously into the faces of his son, his daughter and his wife, before walking off into the sunrise to milk his rams or shear his bulls or whatever.

Right, you bastard, Polly told her imagination, when it had returned, finally, to heel. *I'll teach you to do that all over the carpet*. And she marched indoors and went to the phone. She would hurl herself into the Save the Farm Campaign. That wouldn't give her wretched imagination time for even a peep into the chocolate-box world of cottage-door contentment. *I'm not going to end up on a bloody Victorian birthday card*, she promised herself.

'Matthew? This is Polly. It's all confirmed, they are selling the farm, and my spies tell me it's developers, though exactly what sort I haven't yet established.'

'Great! I'll be right down there,' Matthew's breath swished eagerly into Polly's ear. 'We'll soon suss it all out, don't worry. Er . . . just remind me—how do I get there? M40 is it? or M4?'

Polly was knee-deep in navigation when Joe burst in, his face grey and tired, and pushed past her. Matthew lost her for a moment.

'Polly? You still there?'

'Sorry, Matthew. Sorry. I just lost my train of thought for a moment. Then, make for Sedgeworth . . .' She completed her instructions and Matthew rang off. Joe came downstairs again.

Don't say anything silly and jealous, she urged herself, *don't, don't, don't!*

'Have a wild night out in Exeter, then?' It came flying out of her mouth before she could stop it, complete with bitter sneer.

'No,' said Joe brusquely, and went out.

It was as if the golden hour in the barn had never been. No—it was much, much worse. As if he regretted it. Well, he probably did. He was going to ignore her now. Perhaps it had been a challenge to him—a conquest. He'd wanted to score. To put her in her place. Polly's head ached with lack of sleep, and with the stupidity of it all. She went upstairs and had a nap. It felt like the first sensible thing she had done for weeks.

She was woken by a furious barking, and looked out of her window to see Tony Lewis marooned in his Mercedes, encircled by a rampant sheepdog. She opened her window and waved.

'He's only being friendly!' she called. Tony got cautiously

out of his car, and held out his hand to the sheepdog, who like all sheepdogs was eager for affection and shamelessly promiscuous. By the time Polly, rather crumpled, got downstairs, the dog practically had its paws round Tony's neck.

'C'mere, Scott!' barked Joe, who had just entered the yard. 'Goo back! Back in the van!'

'The dog's not supposed to get attached to anyone else,' Polly explained. 'It's supposed to just work with its master. No owner they're always desperate for a bit on the side. Sounds a bit like marriage.' Too late, she remembered that Tony's wife had left him for a bit on the side. Never mind. Distraction was at hand.

'This is Joe— Joe, this is my boss Tony Lewis. Down on a flying visit.'

'I won't shake hands,' Joe revealed dramatically muddy paws, 'but make yourself at home, mate.'

'Lovely place you've got here – ' Tony indicated the valley, the farm. 'Bit of a change after Manchester.'

Joe nodded, offered him a brief formal smile, ignored Polly, jumped in his Land-Rover, and roared off.

'Well,' said Tony. 'Bet he sets a few hearts fluttering, eh? Bit of a ladykiller, is he?'

'I really don't know very much about him,' admitted Polly, suddenly realising it was all too true. 'Why don't you go into the parlour and I'll bring my notes down? Then after we've had a chat maybe we can go to the pub for lunch.'

'I've already had lunch,' said Tony. 'It's two thirty. Great pies they have there.'

'Two thirty? Is it really?' Polly sighed. 'Had to have a little kip this morning. Bad night. Don't know whether I'm coming or going.'

After an hour's briefing, Tony began to get excited. He stood up, fiddled secretively with the seat of his trousers, and started to prowl up and down just as if he was in his office at Granada.

'We need to shoot it in the summer, really, you see,' he was saying. 'We can't possibly get it fixed up for this summer. I mean, you haven't even written any scripts yet—not that I'd expect you to, for a moment! But, well, and casting . . . what is it now, April . . . You need the long days really, you don't want to have to be on location in September, and the weather always breaks round about then in any case . . . It looks like next year really, doesn't it, Pol?'

'Well, next year . . .' Polly hesitated. 'The awful thing is, we don't really know whether there's even going to be a farm here at all, next year.'

'What?'

There was the squeal of brakes in the yard, and Polly looked out to see Matthew Tregaron getting out of an estate car. He bounded up to the front door and thundered on it. He looked ready for action, dressed in his country reporter's clothes of tweed and cord. Tony, uneasy in his shiny polyester suit and nylon shirt, greeted him cordially.

Matthew was dismayed to find Tony here, as he was used to being the only man from a TV company, but hid his disquiet effortlessly. He had been nurturing the most gross fantasies all the way down the M4, about Polly's legs, which had ended up wound round his neck like a college scarf. Still, at least they were not wound around Tony's. Polly did not betray any body language that suggested Tony was a lover. Not that any self-respecting woman would give him a second look, with his baggy trousers and paunch and faintly shining brow. Mind you, when it came to top executives, some women seemed able to put up with the most extraordinary physical disasters.

Matthew did not sit down. Instead he lounged gracefully against the door, to demonstrate his long litheness. Besides, he had been sitting down all the way down the motorway. What he wanted was action.

'Could we take a look round?' he asked.

'I was going to ask that,' put in Tony feebly. 'Why don't you show us round together. If it won't be too confusing. Minimise the, er, disruption.'

'It's not a bad moment, actually,' Polly agreed. 'The Swains are away.'

'Who was that I met, then?'

'Oh Joe. That's their son.'

Matthew pricked up his ears. He did not like the sound of Joe. Already he was planning to put him down with a few smart remarks, if he showed the slightest signs of rustic lust towards Polly.

'Could we look at the house, first?' asked Tony.

'Certainly.' Polly led them to the kitchen. 'Although I feel the house is really much too comfortable and twentieth century to be convincing as Cold Comfort Farm. Some of the outbuildings are better.' Tony looked around Mrs Swain's fitted cupboards and agreed.

'Is there an old dairy through there?' he asked. 'Sometimes there is, you know, in these old places.'

'It's the utility room now,' Matthew reported, lifting the latch and giving it a cursory glance. 'Mind you, if you got rid of the washing machine—and the tumbler drier – '

'The sink unit's all wrong,' objected Tony. 'Why do they get rid of those wonderful old stone sinks?'

'Probably because they're hell to work with,' said Polly sharply, suddenly finding herself defending the Swains' desire to modernise.

'Of course, of course,' said Tony. 'But still . . . might we go upstairs? There's Flora's bedroom, that's a problem. I think we might have to go to studio for quite a lot of the interiors, you know.'

They arrived on the landing.

'Fitted carpet, you see,' commented Matthew. 'I bet there

are beautiful old elm boards under here. If this was my place I'd strip all this horrible old synthetic rubbish off and sand the boards down. And seal 'em.'

'That would be better, yes,' agreed Tony. 'From my point of view, as well.'

Polly bit her lip, and felt a curious affection for Mrs Swain's violently patterned landing carpet, which up to this moment had struck her as bilious in the extreme.

'Might we have a peep in here?' asked Tony, indicating the bedroom of Mr and Mrs Swain.

'I . . . I expect so. It's their bedroom,' said Polly, realising with a qualm that the next bedroom along was Joe's and that any moment she might be required to peep in, and see—her imagination lunged at the morsel of opportunity, and served her up a whole tormenting wall covered with photographs of beautiful women—or worse, one particular beautiful woman. Very much more beautiful than herself. Which wouldn't be hard. Polly sighed, and pushed upon the door of Mr and Mrs Swain's bedroom.

It was a large room, above the parlour, and had two windows, one in each wall, which made it lighter than the other rooms. One window had a stunning view down the valley; the other, a stunning view up to the wood.

'Rip this carpet up,' said Matthew directorially, 'get rid of this bloody awful divan, and those curtains—it's a shame about the built-in wardrobe. And chuck out her nasty little vanity unit, and you'd have an absolutely brilliant room.'

Tony went to the window, opened it and looked out. 'Someone's just arrived,' he said. Matthew joined him. Polly recognised the slam of Mr Swain's van door, and glimpsed between the vile bodies of Matthew and Tony, the puzzled faces of Mr and Mrs Swain, returning, and staring up at their bedroom window in disbelief.

'It's all right!' called Matthew jocularly. 'We're not the bailiffs!'

Honestly, thought Polly. What a pair of prize arseholes. And I brought them here. For the first time for many a week, she wished she was back in Hampstead. Preferably with her head right under the sofa.

Chapter  Thirty-four

Mr and Mrs Swain seemed charmed, after all, to have their bedroom invaded by the men from the television. Polly noticed how media folk enjoyed an entirely undeserved prestige amongst the ordinary tillers of the soil.

'I've seen you on that programme of yours,' crooned Mrs Swain, putting on the kettle in a flustered and thrilled manner. 'Sunday mornings, isn't it? We saw that one—you remember, Arthur, when you had that boil—we saw that one about the watercress beds being poisoned. Where was it? Hertfordshire.'

'Aye, aye,' Mr Swain agreed.

Polly was surprised that, after all her weeks of subterfuge, the Swains seemed to take to the idea of becoming a film location, embracing it joyfully without a moment's hesitation.

'Could save our bacon,' said Arthur, a grudging note of hope softening his habitual sourness. 'Get this bastard of a bank manager off my back.'

'Well, yes, precisely,' said Matthew, who was trying, in the subtlest way he could, to draw the Swains into the idea of being interviewed on TV about the farm sale. 'It's a predicament so many farmers find themselves in at the moment. It's a scandal.'

'Too right,' Arthur took his cap off and smoothed his few remaining hairs down onto his pate. 'Ten years ago, see, they was forcin' their bloody loans down your neck.'

'And the Ministry and their mates in the agro-chemical industry weren't much help either,' added Matthew.

'I blame bloody Europe,' concluded Arthur, relaxing into a comfortable blast of xenophobia. 'I always said we should stay out. I voted to stay out. So did the wife. But no. We had to join the club. Bloody greed, that's what it is. Well, we're seeing the results of it now.'

Matthew, who was mentally framing Mr and Mrs Swain and trying to get a few old beams in the background of the shot, steered the conversation towards the sale.

'So it's on the market? And I suppose that means developers?'

'Well, we're tryin' to avoid it, of course,' said Mr Swain, with a secretive sideways look. 'It's all in the hands of the solicitors at the moment. Our boy Joe knows more about the details. It's more his business, you know, sortin' it all out. Us bein' so near retirement. We're off to Bournemouth.'

The Swains tried not to look too excited about Bournemouth, knowing that it would mar the tragic implications of their tale. Mrs Swain's hand hovered dangerously near the brochure about apartments on the seafront, but she recollected herself and opened a cake tin instead.

So, thought Polly, Joe is in charge of the farm's destiny after all.

'You're victims, really,' said Matthew, 'of a shortsighted government and an antediluvian farming policy.' Polly wondered if Mr and Mrs Swain knew what an antediluvian farming policy was. She certainly didn't.

'Aye,' affirmed Mr Swain. 'You said it.'

'I'm wondering,' Matthew went on, 'just thinking aloud here . . . your case might be a very good example of the way things are going . . . the small farmer being sacrificed whilst the big boys ride out the recession. I'm all right Jack.'

'Too bloody right.' Arthur drained his teacup.

'Would you . . . might you be prepared to talk about this on camera? I think it would make a really thought-provoking item.'

'What, him on TV?' Mrs Swain burst in anxiously. 'Ooooh, never, Arthur, for goodness' sake. You'll have to let him get a haircut first.'

'Wait a minute,' Mr Swain switched his suspicious glare to Tony. 'What's your part in all this, now?'

'That's different,' said his wife urgently, as though to a simpleton. 'That's the book, see? That Miss Partridge is going to make into a programme, isn't it, dear?'

'That's right,' said Polly, trying to sound reassuring, tactful and confident all at once—a severe strain even on her urbane range, 'that's the idea to use the farm as a location—that would be a much bigger—a longterm thing. But of course it wouldn't interfere with your work here, at all.'

'I won't have much more work here, if I get my way,' remarked Mr Swain caustically. He took off his cap and scratched his head. 'Orright, then,' he said, looking at Matthew. 'You're on.'

Mrs Lillicrap was on, too. The next morning, Matthew's cameraman joined them and they filmed her at the bottom of the valley, in her immaculate green wellies and new Barbour, looking sensitive and tormented in an area of outstanding natural beauty. Mildred had done some nosing about and the results were spectacular.

'As far as we've been able to find out,' hissed Mrs Lillicrap conspiratorially at the camera, 'there are plans to slap a factory right across the lovely meadow you're looking at. Light industrial units, they're called, and we know what that means. Lorries and noise and pollution. Ruining this lovely valley . . .' The camera zoomed in close on the burgeoning beech trees, which were freckled with the most delicious green. Mrs Lillicrap continued her lament, little suspecting that the famous Matthew Tregaron was planning to edit her down to a sentence and a half.

Polly watched, standing by the hedge, and wondering where Joe was. He had disappeared again to Exeter the previous evening, leaving her to the tender mercies of Tony and Matthew. They had sat in the pub till closing time, swapping bits of media gossip. Polly had tired of it rather soon—after about ten minutes. And it had been a full-time job keeping her eyes well away from Matthew. Irritated by the presence of Tony, Matthew had started transmitting the most obvious visual signals. His eyes had glistened sickeningly at her like boiled sweets. It had made Polly's teeth ache every time she slipped, unawares, into the sticky pool of his gaze.

Both men had stayed up later and later, like hopeful hangers-on at a party who each supposes the hostess will grace him with an invitation to her bed if he can outlast the other. In fact the hostess had been wondering most urgently if Joe had returned to the farm yet. When she finally got back, at eleven, his Land-Rover was still not there. She had gone to bed disappointed and had heard him come in just after midnight. What was going on?

All these late nights are playing havoc with my brain, she thought, stifling another yawn as Mrs Lillicrap completed her on-camera experience and instantly whipped out her powder compact to check that her image had been beyond improvement. Then she snapped it shut and fell on Polly.

'You must all come back to The Hall for lunch,' she swooped. 'I'm hoping my daughter Angelica has made it. She's such a fan of yours.' She turned to Matthew, who at the word *daughter* had pricked up his satyr's ears. He was beginning to feel a little discouraged about Polly. She had seemed preoccupied last night, and hadn't returned any of his hot looks. And today she was stupefied, yawning all the time.

'Well, to be honest, I really must have a working lunch

with poor Tony,' pleaded Polly. 'We've got to discuss his project before he goes. It's been a bit tricky, having you both here at once,' she smiled apologetically, but she trusted not erotically, at Matthew. 'Why don't you go and meet Angelica? She looked extraordinarily pretty in the photo I saw. I'll try and get along later. But I think I ought to try and find Tony. He's mooching about the woods somewhere.'

'Fine.' Matthew admitted defeat and turned gratefully to Mrs Lillicrap, as she was evidently willing to offer him a free lunch, and beyond that the possibility of something to fascinate. Angelica, eh? Sounded a bit heavenly. Maybe he could arrange a fall from grace.

Polly strode off across the fields. She had vaguely suggested to Tony that they should meet at Charley's bothy at around this time. The Bothy was perhaps the most picturesque building she had seen in the area, surrounded by trees, with its quaint old outlines unimproved by the twentieth century. Perhaps it would do for Meriam's hovel.

Yes. There he was, waddling anxiously to and fro. He had found it. Tony was not as daft as he looked. In fact, he had often in his younger days set off for a week's walking in the Peak District complete with Ordnance Survey map, cagoul and boots, before he reached upper management and the Mediterranean had become unavoidable.

He looked up and smiled rather nervously at Polly's arrival.

'Lovely place, isn't it?' he declared. 'I hope we're not trespassing, though.'

'Ah, Charley's here!' said Polly. 'There's his van. You really must meet him—and it's extraordinary inside. No mod cons. An open hearth. And he uses an old car seat as a sofa.'

'Bit of a recluse, eh?' wondered Tony, admiring the ivy growing in through the window.

They knocked on the door, and Polly put her head in and

called, but there was no reply. She did not feel like venturing further in. It was annoying. Still, they might meet him around somewhere, at work.

'Can I help you?' came a sudden bark.

Polly jumped. There, looking particularly forbidding, was Charlotte. Polly cringed—her usual response to the appearance of Miss Fairfax.

'I was just hoping to see Charley,' said Polly.

'He's off sick,' said Charlotte. 'Can I help?'

'Not really, thank you.' Polly hesitated. 'It was nothing special. This is . . .' Tony, and all that he implied, would be anathema to Charlotte Fairfax. Polly dreaded having to introduce him. This chance meeting could not have been more unfortunate. 'This is Tony Lewis. Tony, this is Charlotte Fairfax.' They shook hands.

'Another writer, are you?' asked Charlotte briskly.

'No. I'm with Granada Television,' said Tony, totally failing to detect the tidal wave of disapproval that was about to break over him. 'We're discussing the possibility of filming *Cold Comfort Farm* around here.'

Polly closed her eyes and wished she was anywhere else. Even the Costa Brava.

'What a jolly good idea!' exclaimed Charlotte. 'How interesting!'

Polly opened her eyes in amazement.

There was the rumble of an engine, and Joe's Land-Rover drew up.

'Afternoon.' He swept the company with a genial glance, then fixed his gaze on Polly.

'Can you come and give me a hand for a moment?' he asked. Polly leapt at the chance. Tony, forgotten for a moment, hesitated. Charlotte turned to him with a purposeful air.

'Come and have lunch,' she said briskly. 'And you can tell me all about this project of yours.' Tony obeyed. Then Charlotte turned suddenly to Joe.

208

'I can't make it till later, tonight,' she called. 'Say about nine?'

Polly's heart jumped in alarm as she strapped herself in. Never had minding her own business been such a strain.

'Fine,' answered Joe, and drove off in what Polly felt was a deliberately infuriating silence.

Chapter  Thirty-five

'Got a date with Charlotte tonight, then?' Polly burst out, despite her best efforts. She managed to keep the tone light and bantering, though. Well, nearly.

'That's right,' said Joe, keeping his eyes on the road. Polly told her internal organs to settle down and stop their unseemly riot, but they ignored her.

'Bet she's a hot little number,' Polly hazarded, between clenched teeth.

'Yeah,' murmured Joe. 'She goes like a train.'

Polly lapsed into silence and bit her knuckles in order to avoid screaming. *Look at me*, she begged silently, *just look at me, once. A kind word. A syllable. A shred of tenderness. A crumb. I need so very little. I just need to know that it did happen, and that you don't regret it.*

Joe seemed preoccupied and turned into a rough track, looking over hedges to his left.

'Some of my heifers have got out,' he said. 'You can give me a hand, rounding 'em up.'

'OK,' Polly agreed, wrestling desperately with her jealous desire to go on picking away at her own wound. A silence fell.

'You taking her out somewhere nice, then?' she heard herself sneer. Joe sighed.

'Give me a break, will you?'

Polly was deeply ashamed. 'Only teasing,' she explained swiftly.

'I should bloody well hope so,' said Joe.

The heifers were found, encroaching into a field that was not for them; gorging themselves on something or other that was not theirs to savour.

'They're naughty,' said Joe, as after much charging about and whooping they managed to get the heifers back into their field. 'There's one of them—I don't know which she is—but she's a showjumper. Jumps over the hedge. Then the rest follow. And when I find which one she is, she's had it, mate. Off to market. Right away.'

Polly felt rather sorry for the heifer who craved what was in the neighbouring field, leapt over the hedge, gorged in blissful delight for an hour or two, and was then driven back into her own bleak and boring pasture. But she bit her lip. These kind of metaphors were not helpful.

'Right,' said Joe, businesslike again but not, alas, tender. 'Where can I take you now? Got an assignation with the bearded wonder?'

'He's having lunch with Mrs Lillicrap,' said Polly. 'And Charlotte's having lunch with Tony. Everyone's having lunch with each other. Why don't we have lunch? Nothing much. Just a Mars bar in a barn somewhere.'

'You're a naughty thing,' smiled Joe, and it was like sudden sunshine flooding over her heart. 'You're trying to lead me astray. Now, you know I don't stop for lunch.'

'Not even for five minutes?' Polly engaged with his eyes, boldly trying to rekindle what had blazed there before. She felt ashamed of herself, lost in this naked need for tenderness. Joe turned his eyes away and went back to the Land-Rover.

'Hop in,' he said. 'I'll drive you home.'

When Polly got in, she was dismayed to find tears streaking down her face. Joe noticed it at once.

'What's up, girl?'

'Nothing. I'm sorry. It's just—nothing.'

'Look,' said Joe, taking her hand for an instant, 'I'm sorry. I've got things on my mind at the moment.'

'What things?'

'I'll tell you later.'

'Tell me now.'

'I haven't got time. It's not the right moment.'

'Is it something awful?'

Joe hesitated for a moment, staring through the windscreen at the hawthorn hedge.

'Yes.'

'Is it about the farm?'

'No. Now for God's sake—give me a break. I've got a lot on my plate right now.' He started up the engine.

'Can't I help?' cried Polly despairingly. She longed to tell him that whatever it was that caused him pain, she wanted to share it; she would move heaven and earth for him.

'No. I'm sorry. You can't. Not yet. Later, maybe.'

Polly dived for this crumb and clutched it pathetically to her breast. Joe drove her to the farm and dropped her off in the yard.

'What are you going to do now?' she asked, halfway out of the door.

'Going to move some sheep.'

'Can't I come and help?'

'Sorry, sweetheart. I need to be on my own today.'

Polly's face buckled for an instant, but she crammed it back into control.

'You take care of these TV guys of yours. Sort 'em out. Then when they've gone, you can take care of me and sort me out.' Hope flared in her breast. 'By the way,' he said. 'I hope you haven't led my folks astray about this TV business. They seem to think their ship's come home. You know the size of our overdraft, don't you?'

'Of course I don't.'

Joe revealed a sum of money which Polly, appalled, recognised as the equivalent of the budget of a whole TV series: studios, locations, writers' and actors' fees, technicians' salaries, the lot. What the Swains were likely to be offered as a location fee, Polly realised, wouldn't even reroof an old pigsty.

'Oh dear,' she said lamely. 'I hope they don't think—I mean, I didn't want to raise their hopes unfairly . . .' A hasty sum in her head convinced her that even if she sold her Hampstead flat at an exorbitant price, and was awarded a mountainous mortgage, she couldn't even come near to half the farm's debt.

'Don't you worry,' said Joe. 'This TV business is great. It gives 'em something to get excited about. Cheers 'em up.'

'And what about you? Do you mind?'

'Nah. It'll be a laugh.' He winked at her. 'We can take the piss of all your actory friends.'

Polly smiled gratefully. She was encouraged by the thought of her and Joe as some kind of team, in the future. Especially if it was a satirical one.

'Off you go, now.'

Sometimes he addressed her as if she was a child. And the trouble was, she couldn't quite manage to hate it enough.

That evening, Matthew had still not reappeared. Perhaps Angelica Lillicrap had provided a useful distraction. Polly surrendered to the more endurable company of Tony and the necessity of a final meeting with him, over supper at the pub. But she had never found it so hard to concentrate. Her watch informed her it was nine thirty, and by now Joe would be doing whatever it was he did with Charlotte.

'So really, from my point of view . . .' Tony burbled on, in rare good spirits evidently as another of the famous pies yielded itself up to him. Polly nodded, but her brain was miles away, in some corner of The Manor perhaps. The stables. Yes. That riding crop. In Polly's fevered imagination, Joe served Charlotte over a manger, as effortlessly as a graceful young carthorse saluting a bad-tempered mare.

Perhaps he liked the dominating woman. Perhaps she whipped him. In Polly's imagination, Charlotte placed an imperious boot on Joe's eager chest, and kicked him backwards into the straw.

'. . . everything sorted out by then. As long as you think . . .' Polly nodded. She could tell by his tone of voice Tony required little more than assent, leaving her free to torment herself with torrid images of Joe pleasuring the younger Lady of the Manor, indoors this time: on antique sofa, on floor, yea, on the very ceiling.

Perhaps Charlotte was sexy after all. The more she thought about it, the more Polly was convinced she was. Dan reckoned there was nothing quite so exciting as a thoroughly plain, frumpy woman. He had once got terribly excited in a train at the sight of a meek, bespectacled fifty-year-old spinster sitting opposite him, untouched in her tweeds. Charlotte offered that kind of attraction, certainly, but with the added ingredient of a fiery temper. And the paradox that beneath the uncompromising jodhpurs lurked a woman's vulnerability . . . no wonder Joe was hot for her. And of course the class war thing. Nothing would be quite so exhilarating to a local lad like him, as the thought that he was penetrating the upper class.

'Fancy another one?' asked Tony, taking Polly's glass.

'Yes, why not?' agreed Polly, in a mood of dangerous self-destruction. 'I feel like getting smashed tonight.'

'That's right,' said Tony, hoping she did not mean it. But no, she couldn't: Polly was never ever out of control. 'After all, we've got plenty to celebrate.'

'We certainly have,' agreed Polly with a strange, heavy emphasis. 'Make it a double.'

Chapter  Thirty-six

Next day Tony departed, and Matthew reappeared. Polly took him for a last walk across the fields. Matthew sighed.

'I hate having to go back to the smoke,' he waved an expansive arm at the landscape, 'having to leave all this.' The fields were wet, and twinkled demurely at him under a thin morning sun. Birds were nesting, with busy flutterings in hedges. A blackbird perched on a gate, its beak full of straw looking like a bizarre blond beard.

'Yes,' said Polly. 'In fact, I think I might stay on into the summer.'

'I don't blame you,' said Matthew, with a sidelong glance. 'It's a great place for healing, the countryside.'

'Healing?'

'You know—feelings, and so on. You must be feeling very upset about Dan.' Matthew lowered his voice solicitously. If she was broken-hearted, that might explain her indifference to him. And a tearful breakdown now might nicely loosen things up. But Polly's purposeful stride never faltered. Her wellies crushed the wakening grass with every appearance of cheerful purpose.

'Not really. It was one of those things, you know. Like a hollow tree. All dead on the inside but somehow still standing. Then one day an enormous owl lands on it and—it collapses.'

Matthew wondered what the enormous owl had been. 'So it's OK?'

'It's OK. Coming here made it all clear, somehow.'

'Yes. Nature has a way of sorting things out.' Matthew breathed deeply. 'Nature the healer.'

'And the destroyer,' added Polly, thinking about dead lambs. They stopped by a gate and looked back at the tumbling fields of Harrow Hill Farm.

'I wonder what we'll see if we come back here in five years' time,' pondered Matthew, taking rather a liberty, Polly thought, with her future social calendar.

'You never managed to get to the bottom of the development plans, then?' she asked.

'Not entirely. Nobody was available for comment—the usual thing. The solicitors were lying doggo. All I really had to go on was what your friend Mildred has managed to dig up. Still, it doesn't matter. I've decided to present the whole thing as an enigma. As a kind of springboard for discussion. You know, like: what's to become of the countryside? I'll have the report, and then I think I'll get three blokes in to the studio to discuss it. That farming MP, what's his name—Marcus Stone, and maybe somebody from the NFU and somebody from the Preservation of Rural England or whatever.'

'Three blokes?' asked Polly. 'Why not three women?'

'Whoops, sorry, I was using blokes in the shorthand term. Er . . . sorry. Egg on face of dogged young reporter.' He flashed her a dogged young smile. 'Of course, there will be a woman. Probably from the SPRE. They're all women, actually.'

'Well, try and get a woman farmer too.'

'Yes. OK. Promise,' said Matthew speciously. 'I did meet an excellent woman farmer once. In Leicestershire. And I suppose your Charlotte Fairfax is another.'

'Is she?' Polly was surprised, and annoyed to be reminded of Charlotte. Joe had come in very late again last night. A permanent sourness had settled on Polly's stomach, whenever she thought of Joe. It was the curdled feeling of rampant disappointment. Polly had never, in her life, willingly participated in a one-night stand. Let alone a mid-afternoon roll in the hay. Wham, bam, thank you, ma'am. 'I didn't realise Charlotte could be called a farmer. I thought her farm manager did all that.'

'Ah, but she makes the decisions,' said Matthew. 'As far as I could tell. Too bad she wouldn't be interviewed. And there's another shrinking violet.' He gestured over towards a distant patch of woodland, where Joe was busy rebuilding a stretch of wall which had collapsed. At the sight of him, Polly's stomach gave a silly lurch, and something hot flashed up her neck. She did not want to go over and bother him. Not with Matthew. But Matthew had different ambitions.

'I'd just like to go over and say goodbye,' he said. 'Have a word, you know. Pass the time of day. Yokels like that sort of thing.'

'He's not a yokel!' Polly heard herself exclaim.

'Whoops, no, sorry. Egg on face again. It's only an affectionate term I use to describe the people I work with. Mind you, they make a bloody awful mess, sometimes, of the countryside they're supposed to be looking after for us.'

'What do you mean?'

'Well, look what his folks have done to that farmhouse.'

'Just adapted it to their taste, that's all.'

'Well, some people would say that a lot of the original features had been destroyed. And what if they do sell to developers? Executive residences or bungalows or whatever all over the place. Light industrial units. Too many farmers have been doing this, recently. Flogging off good agricultural land for speculators to build on.'

'Yes, but what choice have they got?' cried Polly fiercely.

'I know, I know. It's a hopeless time for farmers. You don't have to tell me about that. I meet farmers going bust every week.'

'What's the answer, then?' demanded Polly. Matthew

had this infuriating air of criticising what everybody was doing, without offering any positive suggestions.

'Ah. What's the answer, indeed.' Matthew framed the surrounding fields with an imaginary lens. 'That's exactly how we'll present it. *Look at all this. Nature as we know and love it. Can we afford to keep it like this? And how? Do we want a landscape preserved in aspic? Do we want Disney-style theme parks? What's to become of it?* Title music, tan tan tara!'

'Singing, eh?' Joe straightened up from his walling and placed his hands on his hips. 'You must be happy in your work, mate.'

'I am, I am!' Matthew beamed. 'Coming out here—seeing all this—admiring this fantastic natural landscape. Wild country. I love it.' A small bird burst into loud song in a tree above Joe's head. He looked up into the branches and smiled. Then he turned to look at the fields, with an expert and sceptical eye.

'It's not a natural landscape, though,' Joe said. 'Farming's made it what it is. Those fields were made by farmers. And these walls. Bloody awful job they made of some of them, an' all.' He struck a part of the collapsed wall with his fist.

'Of course,' agreed Matthew. 'Of course. I just meant . . .'

'If this was natural,' Joe went on, 'it'd just be woodland. We wouldn't be able to see across the valley like this. All just woodland and scrub. Probably all sycamores and brambles.'

'Well, this woodland here feels pretty natural to me,' smiled Matthew, as the bird above their heads sang on—a warning song.

'The wood's not natural either. It's one of Charley's. Very carefully managed, Fairfaxes' woods are. No rubbish. All nicely thought out.'

Polly looked at the woods with a new eye. Although she'd been with Charley once whilst he worked, she had forgotten that all the woods around here were managed. It was curious. She took the look of the land for granted.

'It's wonderful how nature responds to being sensitively managed by man,' said Matthew. 'Or should I say woman,' he added, with a teasing smile to Polly.

'You should say woman,' affirmed Joe. 'Round here, anyway. All this woodland is Charlotte's patch. She looks after it, and does a bloody good job an' all.'

Polly felt an absurd sting of jealousy.

'Well,' said Matthew. 'I wish I could've persuaded you to say this kind of thing to camera.'

'Nah,' shrugged Joe. 'Sod it. I'm not that sort of bloke. I leave all the bullshitting to my dad. He's the West of England Champion.'

'He certainly did very well,' said Matthew. 'It's going out on the fifteenth of next month.'

'I shan't watch it, I'm afraid,' said Joe. 'I don't have time to watch the bloody telly.' And he turned back to his wall.

'Well.' Matthew felt his cue to depart. 'I'll be going, then. Thanks for everything.'

'I haven't done sod all,' commented Joe with a grin, extending a dusty hand.

'You let me shoot on your land,' said Matthew.

'Aye. Shooting rights. Eight hundred a year, that'll cost you.' They laughed, and the bird sang ever more strongly above their heads.

'Well . . .' Matthew hesitated. Would Polly walk him back across the fields? He hoped so. He had a few more sensitive things to say about Nature. He felt he hadn't performed all that well, so far. He might say something about Nature herself being female, the Earth Mother. That would redress the feminist balance a bit. Great, creating Nature. Nature's teeming womb. The bosom of Nature. Whoops! Careful! He was turning himself on.

'Goodbye,' said Polly. 'Thanks for coming down. I think I'll stay here—if I can be any help?'

Joe nodded. 'I could do with a hand, aye.'

'Goodbye, then,' said Matthew. 'I'll give you a ring. Let you know how things are going.' And with a slightly clumsy wave, he walked off. They watched him go.

'He's a bit of a prat, I'm afraid,' said Polly quietly.

'He seemed a decent enough sort of bloke, to me,' Joe observed. 'Only doing his job.'

The bird still sang above their heads. Polly looked up into the branches, seeking a glimpse of her.

'A little Jenny Wren,' Joe said, smiling. 'I felt as if we were interrupting her.'

The fierce song continued for a while, like a knife against a stone.

'The trouble with Matthew,' said Polly, 'is he would never have said anything like that.' She hesitated, trembling, not wanting to say too much. 'It's good to be in your company again.'

Joe picked up a large stone, examined it, and set it carefully into the wall. Then he looked at her—a strange, disturbing look. 'You and I have got to have a talk,' he said. 'It's time you knew.'

Polly's heart froze and she waited, dumbly, for the axe to fall. Like a lamb to the slaughter.

Chapter  Thirty-seven

'I expect you've noticed,' Joe leaned against the wall, hands on hips, and looked at her. Polly's knees felt weak. *I expect you've noticed* always led to a thunderbolt, absolutely always: a thunderbolt one had never remotely suspected. Was he secretly engaged to Charlotte? Polly tensed every muscle, prepared to be a good sport, desperate to hide her weakness, cranking herself up towards congratulation. 'I've had a lot on my mind for the last few days.'

Polly nodded. He looked keenly into her face. She hoped she was not betraying anything unfortunate. Then he peered away again, across the fields, towards the horizon, and wiped a dusty hand across his brow.

'It's Charley,' he said suddenly. 'He's not well. He's not at all well.'

Alarm bells started to ring in Polly's head. She waited, silent, her heart hammering.

'He's in hospital in Exeter,' Joe went on. 'That's why I had to go down there.'

The wren's song broke out again, further away. From the depths of the wood, a pheasant called to his mate: a choking sound, like a thick echoing cough. Wind stirred the branches above Joe's head, and patches of sunshine and shadow raced alternately across the landscape. Then came a large cloud, like someone drawing a curtain across, to shut something out. Polly felt cold.

'What is it?' she managed to say. 'What's wrong?'

'He's HIV positive,' said Joe. 'He's been more or less all right up till now, but now . . . he's started to get ill.'

Polly's whole body shrieked silently. Her knees were seized with a terrible shaking. Huge, urgent questions crowded into her brain, but she could not utter them. Joe sighed. He stared at the stones at his feet, and nudged one lightly with his foot. His face was heavy. He would not look at her.

The silence deepened. For an instant Polly glimpsed the whole thing in a single horrible flash: a doctor looking sympathetically at her, a few hieroglyphics on a medical form containing the enigma: the death sentence. A poem by William Blake rushed through her brain.

> O Rose, thou art sick!
> The invisible worm
> That flies in the night,
> In the howling storm,
>
> Has found out thy bed
> Of crimson joy;
> And his dark secret love
> Does thy life destroy.

Her parents aghast, distraught; her friends numb and helpless. A life transformed into watching and waiting, the merest shiver, the slightest sore throat, the sudden sweat in the night, a hint of terror. Why had she come here? Why had she submitted to this madness? Let herself fall in love? Fall was right, nowadays: fall into the deep dark pit. The plague-pit. She had known it was reckless, too: in the back of her mind the prudent voices of her education had protested, that warm afternoon in the barn, but she had ignored them. If not safe here, in the bosom of Nature, then where? Nowhere.

'Was he your lover, then?' she burst out suddenly, shaking all over. Joe looked astonished.

'Don't be so bloody silly,' he said, indignant but loving. 'I would never have made love to you like that if I hadn't known I was all right. We're friends, that's all.'

Tears of relief burst from Polly's eyes and her face crumpled. Joe took her in his arms, patiently, like someone comforting a child.

'Not that he didn't fancy me a bit, to be honest,' he went on. 'But I'm just not that way inclined. And sex ruins relationships, anyway.' In the midst of her relief, Polly felt a qualm. If he thought sex ruined relationships, was theirs doomed already, then?

'In fact, it was you I was worried about. All that London crap.'

'What London crap?'

'That *I don't own him* crap. Old Daniel going off to San Francisco and screwing anything that moved as far as you knew, and you turning a blind eye. That crap.'

Polly surveyed the way she and Daniel had lived, and she saw that it was indeed crap. She shuddered, and turned her face into Joe's shirt, and wept. There seemed so many things to cry about: her stupid past, her hair's-breadth scape, the fact that Joe's arms were round her again and that he was not going to die, and she was not, either. Not yet. And most of all, she cried for Charley. Because he was.

Dear, delightful Charley, with his angelic smile and teasing wit. The earth was opening its terrible mouth for him.

'He seemed so strong that day I watched him work,' she said, at last, and looked up to see Joe's eyes were also wet.

'When he first knew,' he said, 'he told me he wanted to top himself when he started to get ill. Wanted to blow his brains out. Couldn't face all that crawling about like a bloody skeleton for months. But now he's ill he feels different. He can't help hoping. New drugs, breakthroughs. You know.'

'I can imagine.'

'I want to look after him, though,' said Joe. 'He'll have to give up work soon, I expect. I've talked it over with Charlotte. She's been very good.'

'What did she say?'

'She says he can stay at the Bothy for a while. They'll get another forester but the new bloke can live at The Manor: there's a little flat at the back, above the stables. But when Charley gets bad, I want him at the farm. It's no use him being all by himself in that wood.'

'No,' agreed Polly, wondering how Mr and Mrs Swain would cope with it all.

'I've got to pack my folks off to Bournemouth,' said Joe. 'As soon as possible.'

'But if this sale goes through, won't you have to leave too?'

'Not for a while.'

'I could sell my flat,' Polly blurted out. 'And I could get a mortgage of about a hundred thousand, probably, if that would be any help.'

Joe looked amazed. 'What?'

'I want to help you. And Charley. I'll help take care of him. If I may. I'd love to. He's so . . . wonderful,' she concluded lamely.

'But what about your work?'

'A writer can work anywhere. But actually I'm not sure I want to go on with it for much longer. I want to work outdoors. I'd like to . . . to help you, here,' she concluded, nervously. 'Or wherever.'

'You tender-hearted little thing,' murmured Joe, looking gently into her tear-stained face, and wiping it with his warm fingers. 'Of course you can.'

Joe stayed to finish the wall, so Polly walked back to the farm, alone. She felt she had glimpsed some kind of future in this place. It was a strange thing for urban, street-wise Polly to long for. But at the farmhouse door she felt, beneath all the panic and uncertainty, that she was where she wanted to be. The revelations had bruised and exhausted her, however. As she reached the farmhouse door, she thought she would have a cup of tea and then spend the afternoon in bed. She'd lost a lot of sleep recently.

Mrs Swain was on the phone, and at Polly's entry she looked up and signalled.

'It's for you, dear, yes, yes, she's just come in, now: here she is.'

Polly took the phone, praying for no more crises, today.

'Polly? This is Joyce Lillicrap. I just wanted to check that you're still OK for tonight.'

'Tonight?'

'The WI talk, my dear. Catherine the Great! We're all so excited! Is everything all right?'

'Oh yes,' said Polly, as the last drops of blood left her brain, ran down the backs of her legs, and sank through the flagstones. 'Everything's quite all right, thank you.'

Chapter  Thirty-eight

There they all were, assembled in the village hall: Maisie, smiling and scratching herself in bulging denim (she had evidently redone her roots for the occasion); Mildred, polishing her glasses; Gloria, dressed in a strange striped shroud covered in childish fingermarks; many other of the village women including Elsie of the famous pies; and, surprisingly, Lady Fairfax and Charlotte, sitting rather apart from the rabble at the back. *They should really have a family pew*, thought Polly, rifling through her notes. Although notes was rather a grand term for the few berserk scribbles she had managed that afternoon.

Faced with her total ignorance of Catherine the Great, and the absence upon the Swains' bookshelves of anything remotely relevant (the nearest thing they had to Catherine the Great was *Big Farm Weekly*), Polly had panicked. She had lurked in her room and indulged in an hour's free-association about Russia. She had jotted down any word, no matter how remotely related to her subject, and had come up with the following:

KGB
Vodka
Sledges
Russian Orthodox Church
Beetroot soup (or is that Polish?)
Samovars

Birch trees
Weightlifting
Ivan the Terrible
Battleship Potemkin
Winter Palace.

It was not much on which to base a talk, but it was all Polly had. *Never mind,* she told herself, *if I'm totally ignorant about Catherine the Great, so will they be.* She was, after all, a fiction writer. As long as it sounded plausible . . .

Joyce Lillicrap rose from her seat with a polyester crackle, and turned to face her fellow members.

'We're so lucky,' she gushed, 'to have the writer Polly Partridge staying in our little community. Polly is famous of course for her wonderful TV series *Skyscrapers*, set in the financial markets, and the one I'm sure you all remember from a couple of years ago: *A Bit of Needle*, set in an East End tailor's shop. I'm sure you're all as delighted as I am that we've persuaded her to leave her research, just for one night, and come to address us here – '

'Get on with it!!' hissed a fierce-looking woman at the front, with a moustache and warts, and wearing baseball boots.

'Shush, Vera!' whispered her neighbour, a tall thin fair creature with buck teeth. Joyce Lillicrap glared at them both.

'Polly wants to talk about Catherine the Great—a heroine of hers. And I'm sure, Polly, that by the time you've finished your talk, she'll be a heroine of ours too!'

There was a scatter of slight applause as Mrs Lillicrap sat down. Polly stood up and placed her notes on the lectern. All eyes were on her: her suit, mainly. She'd decided to give them an eyeballful of Jacques LeFroq. Maybe it would distract them from any hint of hesitation, deviation or invention on her part.

She murmured a few chivalrous greetings, and then launched into her talk.

'Catherine the Great,' she declared with astonishing confidence in one inventing every word, 'was born in Murmansk in 1681. Her father was Ivan the Terrible.'

'So was mine,' growled Vera. Polly darted her a warning look. Interrupting Joyce Lillicrap was a duty. But interrupting the speaker was bad manners. Vera dropped her gaze to the floor, looking a little abashed. Polly was wearing her most chilling eyeliner.

'Ivan was hunting at Murmansk at the time,' Polly went on. 'Shooting bears. And apparently he took a fancy to the daughter of one of his beaters. His name,' she paused, momentarily at a loss for Russian nomenclature, 'was Sanilav Proushkev.'

'Bless you!' murmured Vera, but was instantly shushed by other members of the audience.

'Sanilav's daughter was called Sonya. And when Sonya gave birth to Catherine nine months later, Ivan took such a fancy to the child, he took her and her mother back to Moscow with him. I mean, St Petersburg, as it was called then. Leningrad, I mean. At this time, Moscow was little more than a village. Famous for its, er, cows.

'Well. Sonya and her baby daughter were given the best apartments in the Kremlin—sort of *la Crème de la Kremlin*, ha ha!' She laughed. Alone. 'It wasn't the Kremlin, of course, it was the Winter Palace in St Petersburg. And they spent the summers by the Black Sea. Ivan was not really much of a family man, but he was very fond of his daughter Catherine, partly because she was such a bonny child. That's why she was called Catherine the Great, you know— she was simply enormous. Even as a child. She could put away a litre of beetroot soup and a whole roast goose even at the age of ten.'

A ripple of astonishment ran through the hall. Polly warmed to her task.

228

'Yes, hard to believe, isn't it?' she affirmed, waving a piece of paper adorned only with one of her old shopping lists. 'But here is the report from the Italian ambassador who witnessed the whole thing—it's written in Latin, of course. Shall I read it?'

'Oh do,' cried Joyce Lillicrap, 'I simply love Latin, especially the Pope at Easter. Not that I'm all that high, I just adore the cadences.'

'*Catherina filia Ivanum Terribilissimum,*' intoned Polly, begining to enjoy herself, because, alas, she had nerved herself up beforehand with rather too many gin and tonics at the pub, *enormum greedum possedit. Ad unum dejeuner Catherinum, quarto trotteri porcum devorit*— That means she ate four pigs' trotters at a sitting.'

'I done better'n that last Michaelmas,' muttered Vera, reluctant to be impressed by all this specious scholarship.

'Well . . . Ivan had sons as well of course, legitimate sons by his Queen—er—Pushovska. But they were all rather sickly, and in a fit of madness Ivan had them strangled one night because one of them forgot to say "Please" when he asked for the samovar. Then he had them salted, and cast adrift on the Volga in barrels.'

A frisson of horror ran through the audience. Polly decided that more ghastliness would be in order, so gamely ploughed on.

'Then he executed his Chancellor Leonoff, had him stuffed and put on the top of the royal Christmas tree, complete with gauze wings and wand. Then he went completely manic and because the Royal Orchestra played out of tune, ordered them to be murdered with their own instruments. It took ages to do the poor chap who played the piccolo. Still . . . despite this rage, when all about him cowered, he continued to adore his fat daughter Catherine, who was by now sixteen. And since his sons were pickled and floating down the Volga in a barrel, he made her his heir.

'At length Ivan went too far, and there was a plot to assassinate him, masterminded by the mad monk Xenophobius. They poisoned him by putting hemlock in his tights!'

Here several women in the audience crossed their legs restlessly.

'He died in anguish, but he deserved it,' concluded Polly sternly. 'And Catherine was crowned Queen of all the Russians at the age of sixteen.'

Polly took them through Catherine's early career, inventing a series of early passions for her elderly advisors, and making sure Catherine took good care of her mum (that bit would appeal to the WI, surely) by installing her in her own dashka equipped with the first water-closet in Eastern Europe, all the vodka she could drink, a sledge drawn by Arctic foxes and a personal bodyguard recruited from the Secret Police.

'Of course, there were diplomatic crises galore,' Polly went on, seeking to leaven the spicy mixture with a little sober politics. 'But Catherine showed great skill in manipulating not only her own native peoples but the nations of the world. She suppressed the Kerbs, the Gherks and the Agapanths, and negotiated a peace treaty between Saveloy and Maraschino, who had been at each other's throats for centuries. The king of England even courted her.'

'Which king?' asked Joyce Lillicrap with sudden excited emphasis. Any mention of Our Royal Family was evidently meat and drink to her.

'William the—er, thing,' said Polly recklessly. 'While Mary wasn't looking. Well, Mary was ill, actually. She had the distemper. She wasn't expected to live, so William started sending these flirtatious little letters to Catherine, just on the off-chance. But Mary got better.'

'Bloody good thing an' all,' burst out Vera indignantly. 'Heartless sod.'

'Well, quite,' said Polly, and launched into a series of

military adventures Catherine had undertaken in the Baltic. After a bit of religious ferment, her audience's eyes began to glaze over and Polly judged it might be time for some more filth.

'By now Catherine was middle-aged and stouter than ever,' she cried, 'but that did not stop her enjoying life. She had an insatiable greed for young men.' Several faces in the audience lit up at this news, and Maisie muttered, 'Hear hear!'

'At the age of fifty-three,' Polly dropped her voice to a sexy whisper, 'her eye fell on the eighteen-year-old son of her cousin Count Spotnik. His name was . . . was Valery.'

'Funny name for a bloke,' observed Vera.

'Valery is a man's name in Russia,' explained Polly severely. 'Anyway, Catherine appointed Valery to be Custodian of her Wardrobe, which means basically he had to supervise her disrobing.'

A titter ran through the hall. Joyce Lillicrap fanned herself ecstatically with an envelope.

'Poor Valery did not live to see twenty,' lamented Polly, 'and it was rumoured—she had worn him out!'

Several respectable matrons groaned audibly in disappointment that the promising Valery had expired so soon.

'But Catherine was not long in mourning. Before she was sixty she had got through no less than ninety young men— the equivalent of eight cricket teams.'

'Give me Yorkshire!' cried Maisie, inspired with heroic lust.

'And she had also toyed with no less than five foreign suitors: William the er of England, the Duc du Bleary, Prince Alfonso Azda, Count Alfalfa of Romeo and the Portuguese heir Dinis the Unwieldy. She devoured them all like pigs' trotters!' cried Polly in triumph. 'And spat out the gristly bits!'

There was a cheer. She paused for a moment, enjoying the spectacle of the flushed faces below her, whose lives of rural English decorum she had inflamed, for an evening, with a glimpse of exotic debaucheries, acceptable because they had happened three hundred years ago. And they had loved it. Maybe she should take to bodice rippers after all.

'And that,' she smiled, 'concludes my talk. Are there any questions?'

At the ordeal of pronouncing a question out loud in front of their neighbours, the members of the WI quietened down and looked at their laps, each pretending she was not really there. Joyce Lillicrap began to look desperate.

'Come on, ladies!' she urged. 'Ah, Lady Fairfax.' Lady Fairfax rose, timid, slightly palpitating, festooned, as it were, with invisible cobwebs.

'I'd just like to thank Miss Partridge for her fascinating talk,' she murmured. There was a chorus of assent from the hall, though Joyce Lillicrap looked thwarted. She had composed a most elegant speech of thanks, herself, and that wretched Fairfax woman had trumped her as usual. Polly smiled gratefully at Lady Fairfax, hoping that her performance tonight had done something towards reinstalling her in the Manorial favour. Lady Fairfax had not finished, however.

'Knowing that you were coming to talk to us about Catherine the Great,' she said, 'I took the liberty of borrowing a biography of her from Sedgeworth Library.'

Polly's blood froze solid, her heart began to clank, and all her capillaries tinkled.

'And I must tell members here tonight that Miss Partridge has uncovered a staggering wealth of previously unknown material, which throws an entirely new light on what must be one of history's most distinguished women. Thank you so much.'

Lady Fairfax sat down, shooting Polly a look of meek reproach which somehow made her feel as if she was sitting in a puddle. Polly gulped, nodded, and summoned all her strength to the urgent task of preventing her head from falling off. *At least,* thought Polly, *there could never possibly ever be a more humiliating experience than this.* But she was wrong. The gods had booked her in for something even worse, the day after tomorrow.

Chapter  Thirty-nine

'Council of war at Gloria's tomorrow morning!' hissed Joyce Lillicrap as Polly, replete with tea and cake, made her excuses and shuffled towards the door of the village hall.

'Council of war?'

'The developers! Can you come?'

'Well . . . of course.'

Polly was quite keen to throw herself with renewed vigour into the campaign. Anything to distract her from tonight's debâcle. As long as she never had to meet Lady Fairfax again. The memory of the Long Dangley WI talk would make her shudder even when she was sixty-six.

'I'm sorry I couldn't get to your talk, dear,' lamented Mrs Swain as Polly gained the sanctuary of the farmhouse, 'but we got caught up in some business, see?'

'Oh, of course, it's all right, really, it's fine, there were masses of people there,' smiled Polly and ducked upstairs. Never had her own little room seemed such a haven before.

But only Lady Fairfax knew her wicked secret. All the rest of the audience had seemed quite pleased and entertained. Perhaps the awful truth would never get out. Lady Fairfax seemed a discreet sort of person. She might not inform even Charlotte of Polly's public descent into pulp fiction. Polly had her fingers crossed. She did not want Charlotte to know what a complete prat she was.

Next day, she walked up Gloria's path with a sense of foreboding. She had failed to get any hard information out of Joe about the proposed sale. Mrs Lillicrap was certainly going to put pressure on her to do something. And worst of all, there were Gloria's children to endure. It was going to be a long time till lunchtime.

Before she had time to open the door, Sky had flung it open and Terry burst out on his tricycle, banging her shins. Gloria did not appear, so Polly seized the moment, grasped both children by their collars and immobilised them for a split second by the privet bush.

'Any more of that,' she growled, 'and I'm going to bang your horrible little heads together. Geddit?'

Both children instantly set up an outraged wail. 'Mam-maaaa!' they howled, rushing in to where Gloria was struggling to clear the table of a natural disaster involving plasticine, Play-Doh, Lego people, the severed limbs of plastic dolls, a wilderness of tangled wool and a snowstorm of bits of torn paper. 'Mammaaaa! The nasty lady's come! An' she said we had horrible heads!'

Gloria gave Polly a puzzled glance, as if amazed that anyone could not see that her children had the finest heads this side of Michelangelo.

'Go out and play in the garden!' bawled Gloria. 'I told you to!'

'We *were*!' seethed Sky venomously, 'but *she* stopped us.'

'I did not stop you,' said Polly serenely. 'My shins inadvertently stopped Terry's tricycle. And if you don't learn to leave room for other people to pass you in the opposite direction, you're going to get into big trouble when you're grown up.'

'That's right!' affirmed Gloria, but with more of a wheed-ling tone. 'Now go out and play like I said. Sky can be the colonialist and Aqua and Terry can be the native peoples.'

Aqua sucked her thumb and clung to her mother's skirt. 'Don't *want* to be a native people!' she whinged. 'Sky always hits us and says we're her slaves.'

'Then you should rise up against her,' said Gloria, rather

foolishly in Polly's view. 'Ask for your independence. Throw her out.'

'But every time we try to throw her out, she hits us,' whined Aqua. 'Want to stay here—with *you*.'

'I've told you, you can't,' said Gloria in exasperation. 'Look, if you all leave us in peace for half an hour, you can all have a bag of crisps and a drink of apple juice afterwards.'

'*Not* stupid apple juice,' commanded Sky. 'Fizzy pop! And five pence each!'

'All right, all right.'

'No—ten pence,' demanded Sky, understandably encouraged.

'No! Now go! And if you don't want to play the colonial history game you can see how many different leaves you can collect for me.'

'Will you give us five pence for each one?'

'No! Now go! And put your coats on.'

Gloria slammed the door on their bickering. 'Oh dear,' she said. 'They really are so awful. They're the worst things that ever came out of my body, not counting that food poisoning I had in Turkey.'

'Never mind,' said Polly unconvincingly. 'I expect they'll grow up and leave, eventually.'

The doorbell rang, and Mrs Lillicrap and Mildred were admitted, with Aqua clinging to them. Eventually she was detached and ejected, carrying a small bag of yogurt-coated raisins thoughtfully provided by Mildred.

'Share them, Aqua!' cried Gloria. 'Remember, it's equal rights for everyone in this house!'

Except for you, you poor sod, thought Polly.

'Now, let's get down to business,' said Mrs Lillicrap. 'Don't bother with coffee, Gloria dear, I know you're very busy and time is short.' Polly silently applauded Mrs Lillicrap's evident desire to be out of the house again as soon as possible.

'Is there some further information, then?' Polly asked. 'I haven't been able to get anything out of Joe, I'm afraid. He acts as if it's none of my business, which is true, of course.'

'Mildred's friend has been nosing about. Tell us the details, Mildred.'

'Well,' Mildred took a deep breath and leaned forward. 'My friend, and she might be wrong of course, I've no way of checking what she's been able to come up with, but still, my friend says she got a quick look the other day at some detailed plans for a whole industrial estate. Car parking for a hundred and fifty cars! Access for articulated lorries—the lot.'

Polly's blood ran cold.

'We've got to stop this,' said Mrs Lillicrap. 'The trouble is, the local council here is hopeless. Simply awful people. The Tories are all free-enterprise types, do what you like, growth and investment at all costs. And the Labour people are even worse. As long as it creates jobs they don't care what happens. The Liberal Democrats are not much better. One or two of them are sensible people but that dreadful Mrs Lyon with the glasses, well frankly . . . Do you know, she wouldn't cough up for Nether Swell Church bazaar? Not even a cake!'

Incredulity and outrage were expressed.

'I did try to persuade Lady Fairfax to stand for the council,' the lament went on. 'That's what we need on our council. Some good old-fashioned paternalistic Tories. Conservation minded. We did have a Green candidate last time but quite frankly he smelt. I mean, honestly.'

Polly shook her head in despair, but a grand design was forming in the back of her mind.

Lady Fairfax. Old-fashioned Tories. Conservation minded. And Joe and Charley had praised Charlotte despite her unfortunate personal manner: praised her management of her estate. Surely . . .

'Why don't I go and talk to the Fairfaxes about the whole

thing?' said Polly suddenly. 'I mean, has anyone approached them about it?'

'I never presume to approach them,' sighed Mrs Lillicrap with pursed lips. 'Not since that council business. She sent me away with a flea in my ear. Evidently I am *persona non grata* at The Manor for some reason. The gentry are absolute experts at making one feel like a worm. But you, my dear— why, I'm sure that would be a different matter. They might listen to you.'

There was something about her tone of voice, however, that hinted she knew better and would privately be shaking her head all too soon and murmuring, ever so politely, 'I told you so.'

But Polly was struck by the charm of her own idea. What could be more natural than for the Fairfaxes to take an interest in land bordering on theirs? And surely they would want to stop a development that threatened the very nature of their environment?

'I'll go and see them tomorrow,' she said, getting up. 'I've got to go and do a bit of work now, but I'm sure the Fairfaxes could help somehow. Their objections, forcefully expressed to the Planning Committee thingy would carry a lot of weight. After all, they are the Lords of the Manor.'

'Quite right, my dear, quite right,' nodded Mrs Lillicrap.

'Oh, don't go, Pol.' Gloria looked crestfallen. She had obviously been looking forward to a heart-to-heart when she and Polly were alone together.

'Ring me when the children are asleep,' suggested Polly. 'I'm afraid I really must go now. My boss from Granada came down the other day and he was a bit disappointed that I'd managed to get so little done.'

'Oh well,' said Gloria. 'Never mind. Good luck with the Fairfaxes. Sock it to 'em.'

'Aren't we lucky,' observed Mrs Lillicrap to Gloria, 'to have someone of Polly's eloquence to plead our cause? I'm sure, my dear, if you can't sway them, nobody can. Good luck!'

Further encouragements were curtailed by the appearance through the cottage window of a garden fork and associated fragments of glass, plus an extensive stream of infantile oaths, but Polly was excused participation in the clearing up operation because she was such a very, very important person. Shamelessly exploiting her fame, she fled.

Chapter  Forty

Polly made an appointment to see Charlotte at noon the next day. *Shoot-out at High Noon*, she thought, crossing the field. Though arriving at The Manor by car might have made her feel more confident, she preferred to steal up obliquely through the fields and woods. She had discovered all sorts of paths and tracks now, and she wanted to savour the full glory of the doomed valley, to nourish her eloquence. She had to be eloquent, today. She had to convince Charlotte to take up arms. She thought a campaign might suit Charlotte quite well. She had distinct military qualities.

She would not think about her past encounters with Charlotte and Lady Fairfax. To do so would be to sink into embarrassment and despair. She had to do justice to her cause. For a moment she paused by a favourite gate, leaning on it and looking across the lower valley where golden light was flooding through the glowing domes of trees. Suddenly, a ghostly, mocking call floated across the air: cuckoo! cuckoo! It couldn't be the cuckoo this early, surely: it wasn't even halfway through April yet. But it was the cuckoo. O bird of fear. Polly wondered how long it was since she had last heard it. Not since she was a child.

'My dear, Good morning! You have a faery look, you know, as if you might vanish into the mist!'

'Sir Antony!'

'Did I startle you? Did I? Poor fowl, don't ruffle your

feathers. Good morning!' Sir Antony leaned gratefully on the gate beside her, and looked at the view.

'What do you make of it, my dear? Are you a faery of field or garden?'

'Oh—field, I think,' laughed Polly.

'Quite right! G'morning! I am myself a Meadow God. A garden's all very well in town, but here, I can't be bothered with it, except for the raspberries and sparrowgrass, of course. My wife, you know—she's been at it all morning, at her knees, poor soul, it's a religion with her, a religion. But I say, to hell with a religion that thrusts man down on his knees! Or lovely woman on hers, by God! Bring back Dionysus!'

The whole valley echoed to Sir Antony's roar. Polly had heard something very similar once at the zoo.

'All this penitence, my dear, all this sin, can't be doing with it. G'morning! As that fellow said—what's his name—Pound—not quite sound politically, but he got it right about this, by God! Phallic and ambrosial, phallic and ambrosial, my dear, if you don't mind my saying so, as I'm sure you won't, Good Morning! For you are a blackstocking of the finest kidney, I can tell.'

'The old religions?'

'The old religions, quite right, quite right, boozing and screwing and chucking hay about in a frenzy. Diving through waterfalls and what have you. The churches wouldn't be so damned empty if they could offer you that on a Sunday morning, hey? Hey? Ask any man—and any woman too, dammit, when they've felt nearest to Paradise, and they'll all tell you, they're not fools, dammit, boozing and screwing in the open fields.

'Never trust a religion that starts in a bloody garden, it's all gone downhill since the Greeks, they understood it all, the fields and woods, my dear, the fields and woods and the rivers.'

Polly was silenced. Her eyes filled with tears. Sir Antony sighed, grunted and whacked the gate with his stick.

'Good old gate!' he boomed. 'Oak! They don't make them like that any more. Damned metal. It's all gone downhill since the Iron Age, come to think of it. Good morning! I must bid you farewell, my dear. I must go and inspect my sheepies.' And he stomped off down the side of the hedge, still growling to himself like a dyspeptic old badger following the scent of ripe blackberries.

Polly sighed too. If only her dealings with the Fairfaxes could always be conducted through Sir Antony, she would have no trouble. Charlotte may think her old man had lost his marbles, but to Polly they seemed infinitely grander than Elgin's.

As she plunged down the valley and neared The Manor, the sun went in. She hesitated for a moment by the church, as she was ten minutes early. Looking up at its tower, she saw strange stone monsters rearing their ugly heads against the scudding cloud. Gargoyles. Devils. Built to terrify the ungodly, to bring them to their knees.

'Dear God,' murmured Polly, because despite agreeing with every word Sir Antony had said, she also liked the idea that there was somewhere up there a kindly old buffer—rather like Sir Antony himself, perhaps—who would wipe away the tears and gather you to his loving old bosom when you were feeling fragile. One does not feel up to diving through waterfalls all the time, after all.

'Dear God, I'm very sorry I made up all that stuff about Catherine the Great, please let me get through this meeting with Charlotte in one piece, and please, if Thou canst spare the time, show They hand in a sort of ex machina thingy and convince her that her opposition to this scheme might make all the difference. It is a very beautiful valley, after all—one of your best.'

Laughing to herself, she passed through the wrought iron gates into the garden of The Manor. This rustication had entirely destroyed her brain. Here she was, praying! Praying! She hadn't prayed since she'd played in the Under Twelves hockey against St Benedict's. But so much time had passed since then, she couldn't remember if they had won or not. Had God showed his hand? Actually, her few years of adult observation of life on the planet had almost convinced her that God had chucked it all up as a bad job and retired to Bournemouth.

'Good morning!' Charlotte showed her in. 'Would you care for a sherry? It's rather pleasant in the Orangery just now.' She led Polly to a room she had not seen before: a sunny place, filled with the most exquisite scent.

'Oh, what's that?' gasped Polly.

'Azalea thing,' replied Charlotte, indicating a large tub containing an evergreen bush covered with white flowers. 'Or a Rhody. Always get them mixed up. *Fragrantissimum*, anyway. Medium or dry?'

'Dry, please,' said Polly. Some things never changed. The sherry spread its comfortable flames down through her chest, and the delicious lemony scent of the azalea thing drifted over their heads.

'So,' said Charlotte. 'How can I help you?'

'Yes,' Polly nerved herself up. There was no need to beat about the bush. Charlotte was too busy to waste time on small talk. 'I'll come straight to the point. There's a plan— maybe you've heard about it—anyway it could change the whole nature of this area. We've got to stop it, and with your help I'm sure we can. I've come to you because people have faith in you. They know you respect tradition and simplicity and and and all those other principles, you know, country life and so on. Er.' She took another, rather more urgent, sip of sherry. Charlotte was watching her from hard little black eyes. Her lips, as usual, were pursed. Polly breathed in, taking strength from the azalea, and ploughed on.

'This is a wonderful place. You know that of course,

you've been living here for years. I'm only a newcomer. But it really is remarkably beautiful. Not just the village but the surrounding countryside. Well, much of that is due to you, too, of course. The Fairfax estates. I mean. You know. Landowners like you – ' (Did that sound offensive? Probably) 'who have a responsible attitude – ' (Did that sound patronising? Certainly). 'Well, families like yours, have made England what it is, I mean, I understand how important good husbandry is, and well . . .' She lost her drift and sank into a swamp of abandoned compliments.

Charlotte hauled her out. 'You're too kind, but just what is it exactly you want me to do?'

'Oppose this plan!' gasped Polly.

'What plan?'

'This dreadful plan—you know the Swain farm—Harrow Hill Farm – ' Out it came in a passionate blurt, nought out of ten for content and presentation. 'You may not be aware of this, but the Swains are selling up, and a friend of Mrs Lillicrap's—Mildred something—has got a friend in an estate agent's who's unearthed these development plans, they're planning to build a housing state and an industrial estate in that lovely valley! We've got to stop it, Miss Fairfax! It's criminal!'

Something strange was happening to Charlotte. Polly watched, distracted from her plea. Charlotte's nostrils curled up in a weird animal-like way. Was she going to sneeze? Have an asthma attack? Curious lines appeared on her brow. Her lips folded back . . . was she having a stroke? A seizure? And then it came. A sudden violent bellow of what must have been laughter. Polly was nonplussed. Her mouth hung open—for the first time since she was five. She waited, amazed, for the bellows to stop.

'Oh dear,' said Charlotte, as the laughter eventually shuddered to a halt. 'Forgive me. But you should never believe a word that Mildred woman says. She makes it all up, you know. Everybody knows that. Except newcomers,

I suppose. Like Lillicrap. And your friend Gloria. And of course, you. She invents stories, you see. To cause trouble. To stir things up. She's nothing but a fibber! Famous for it.'

'But . . . but . . .' Polly hesitated, 'I know the farm's being sold, because Joe told me, and – '

'What Joe obviously didn't tell you,' said Charlotte with a purposeful surge of energy, 'is that I'm buying it.'

Chapter  Forty-one

Polly became aware that her mouth was hanging open again—something that had not happened very often in Hampstead. She hastily made adjustments.

'So the scare about housing estates and factories and things was a complete red herring?'

'I'm afraid Mildred Squires is a frustrated fiction writer.'

'So is the—forgive me, I know it's none of my business but I do care about the place—is the farm going to stay as it is?'

'Hardly.' Polly felt a qualm of foreboding. 'The Swains couldn't make it pay. The way farming's going at the moment, no one could. No, things are going to have to change. Simply in order to preserve what's good about the place.'

'Yes, yes, of course. How are you—going to set about it, exactly?'

'Well,' Charlotte poured them both another sherry. Polly hadn't drunk so much sherry since those tongue-tied meetings with her tutor at university. It was powerful stuff. She was begining to feel sightly disoriented. 'What's the best way of making sure that the countryside is protected and appreciated in future?' demanded Charlotte with a rather fierce inquisitorial glare.

Polly's mind went blank, but luckily the question was a rhetorical one.

'The next generation!' declared Charlotte. 'Make them

aware of how important the environment is, and it'll be in good hands.'

Polly thought of the environment in the hands of Gloria's children, and shuddered. In thirty seconds, she reckoned, they could tear Harrow Hill Farm into little pieces, stamp on it, and drop the sticky bits into the nearest piano.

'So how exactly do you propose . . .?'

'Well, the farm will go on working much as it is, but with reduced stock levels. But we'll be introducing a leisure and education element from early next year. We reckon we can have quite a lot of it in place by next summer.'

'What will it involve exactly?'

'Well, we'll have a rare breeds section where the children can get really close to the animals: pet the lambs, that sort of thing. Then we might have shearing demonstrations throughout the summer. The wood above the farmhouse would make a perfect nature trail—there are several rare species of orchid in there.'

'And some very early violets,' observed Polly with a smile.

'Quite. The lower barn, the one at present more or less derelict, we'll convert to dormitory accommodation, with a two-bedroom flat at the end, so school parties could come and stay for a week with a couple of teachers—go on walks, that sort of thing. And of course they can have access to the estate lands as well. We're thinking of introducing deer, or if that's too problematic, falconry. A friend of mine is very hot on birds of prey.'

Polly felt a bit faint. It was very warm in the Orangery now. Also her imagination would dwell rather insistently on the spectre of hordes of ghastly children running all over Harrow Hill Farm.

'And there's the whole forestry angle, too: we can quite easily set up a woodland trail with a picnic spot or two.'

'Goodness me,' said Polly, 'you're certainly not short of ideas.'

'That's nothing,' smiled Charlotte. 'I haven't even told you about the Alternative Environmental Centre, yet.'

Polly gawped.

'There's a lot of scope in this particular tract of land, for a comprehensive alternative energy project.'

Polly's eyes glazed over.

'You've heard of the Alternative Technology Centre at Machynlleth?'

Polly shook her head. It sounded like the sort of thing she had always been very careful not to hear about. She feared it might lead, among other horrors, to hairy legs. Polly glanced down for a moment. Good God! Her legs were hairy! She must have forgotten to –

'Well, they were the pioneers, really, and they're a whole community who live there. Inspiring place, you should go there. North Wales.'

'I will,' Polly nodded obediently. She did not think she would ever be brave enough to contradict Charlotte Fairfax.

'Well,' Charlotte went on, 'we reckon we can set up a few wind generators behind the top wood, and some solar electric displays in an old stable yard we've got on the estate, and the Whiddle's just crying out for a generator.'

'The—Whiddle?'

'The river that runs along the bottom. Charley's already got a flourishing tree nursery and we've always had a comprehensive composting scheme, of course, because of Mother, so we're off to a reasonable start, I think. So you see,' she crossed her arms and looked pleased with herself, as well she might, 'no need for industrial estates, yet, I think.'

'No,' agreed Polly. 'Well, I'm flabbergasted.'

Charlotte seemed to find it satisfactory that Polly was flabbergasted. 'So when are you pushing off back to Town?' she asked, not unpleasantly.

'To tell you the truth,' said Polly, 'I don't think I'm pushing off back to Town, at all.'

248

'Oh yes, the usual thing,' observed Charlotte. 'We get quite a lot of it round here. Writers and artists and so on. They buy up the little cottages, do them up quite well on the whole, and since they tend to work from home, we welcome them, rather. If you do settle here, Miss Partridge, you'll certainly find plenty of congenial arty types scattered about.'

'I don't need arty types,' Polly smiled. 'I don't necessarily find them congenial. Too often they turn out to be drunk and self-pitying.' For a split second she was aware that this description might, at the moment, fit herself. 'In fact I think I prefer the other lot. The rest of humanity.'

'But won't you find it rather lonely down here? All your friends, and so forth, in London, I assume?'

'Not at all,' said Polly emphatically. 'I've always liked solitude.'

She rose. She needed the long walk home—home!—to digest Charlotte's news. But of course she had other, more obsequious, questions to ask.

'We were hoping to film at the farm next summer,' she said. 'Granada Television want to do a version of *Cold Comfort Farm*. Do you think that will still be possible?'

'Oh certainly,' beamed Charlotte, 'for a generous location fee, of course.'

'But the old tumbledown barns and things won't all be renovated by then?'

'I shouldn't think so,' said Charlotte. 'These things take time. Rome wasn't built in a day. Ask your people to get in touch with me. I'm sure we can come to an agreement.'

'Very well,' said Polly, slightly missing the front door and exiting, instead, into the doorpost. That sherry was certainly strong stuff. 'Thank you—well, thank you for saving the farm, I suppose.'

'It's a pleasure,' said Charlotte, 'as well as a duty. I would ask you to stay for lunch but Father's completely barking today.'

'I met him in the field,' said Polly. 'He seemed remarkably lucid to me.'

'He changes from moment to moment,' said Charlotte, 'like the weather.' Charlotte shrugged, and they parted.

Walking home, Polly experienced a strange sense of defeat. She had been marginalised, negated, more or less sent packing. There were to be no housing estates or factories in the lovely valley, but packs of shrieking children instead. And she was going to have to phone Matthew, urgently, to explain that his whole projected TV programme was based on a menopausal hallucination on Mildred's part. Her heart sank.

But it was Tony she rang first. He would have to know about the plans for the farm. They could affect the shooting schedule. And he'd have to nerve himself up to ring Charlotte and discuss dates and fees.

'It's all right, Pol,' he burbled, in the event, 'I know all about this.'

'What?'

'Charlotte told me all about it. I had lunch with her, remember? It's all OK. In fact, I wanted to thank you, Polly.'

'To thank me? What for?'

'For introducing me to Charlotte.'

'What!?'

'We got on quite well, actually. She's a very confident woman, isn't she? I like that. In fact, I invited her up here next weekend to show her round the studios and watch *Dreaming Spires* being recorded.'

'Really?' Polly could not conceal her amazement. 'She's going up to see you in Manchester, is she?'

'Yes. I thought I'd take her to that Thai restaurant, you know. She's been to the Far East.'

I bet she has, thought Polly.

'It's really put a bit of zip back into my life, you know,

meeting Charlotte.' Tony's voice could not conceal a quiver of excitement.

'Well, Tony, I'm delighted.'

'Thanks, Pol. You're a brick.'

'So I take it you can sort out all the negotiations with her without any trouble, then?' teased Polly.

'I think so. I might ask her if she'd like a weekend in New York. If we get on all right when she comes up here. You can never tell, can you? With these whirlwind things.'

'Well, Tony, all I can say is, congratulations.'

'Thanks. Er – ' Tony hesitated. 'I hear you and Daniel have split up. I'm so sorry.'

'Not at all,' soothed Polly. 'It's been on the horizon for ages.'

'Well,' concluded Tony, 'maybe you'll meet somebody down there. After all, I met Charlotte. She hasn't got any brothers, has she? That's a pity. A brother of Charlotte's might have suited you rather well.'

'I'm all right,' said Polly. 'Don't you worry about me. I'll keep in touch, Tony—so long.'

She replaced the phone, and two seconds later, Joe's Land-Rover pulled up in the yard. Polly's heart gave a ridiculous kick, and she felt as if she'd had a transfusion of Golden Syrup straight into the vein. This Love business was certainly fatally high in calories.

But she did not want to hang about downstairs to see him now: Mrs Swain was bustling round in the kitchen. It was about the time when Joe sometimes dropped in for a quick lunch, to discuss the latest disasters with his father. She would wait, and hang about hopefully in the evening. The days were getting lighter. They might even manage an evening stroll. It was no good trying to talk to him in the parlour, where they could be overheard by the senior Swains. She wanted him all to herself—even if it was only for half an hour. They had a lot to talk about.

Chapter  Forty-two

Polly was lying on her bed rereading *Cold Comfort Farm*, when there was a thump at her door: different from Mrs Swain's tentative tap. Joe's head appeared.

'Fancy a drink? I've finished early tonight.'

'Oh yes!' Polly got up immediately.

'Not yet, not yet, don't get too excited. I've got to have me bath first, splash a bit of the old aftershave about. Can't be seen down the pub in the state I'm in, with a classy piece like you.'

Polly smiled and went back to her book.

An hour later she was tucked away in a corner of The Fleece with the cleanest man she'd ever sat opposite. He smelt like the perfume department at Harrod's. But beneath it all was a smell of male skin which was the most delicious scent of all.

'Is this a date?' She smiled mischievously.

'Yeah. Only don't expect me to kiss you goodnight. I've only got as far as page two of the Kama Sutra.'

'So,' Polly lifted her glass, 'here's to Harrow Hill Farm Alternative Energy and Rare Breeds Centre.'

'Ah,' Joe sipped his beer. 'You've been talking to Charlotte. What do you make of it all, then?'

'I don't know,' Polly shrugged. 'Don't you think . . . somehow, it takes all the guts out of the farm? I mean, you're halfway to being a museum, having all these demonstrations and things. It's a bit Disney, isn't it?'

252

'I knew you'd sneer,' said Joe, with a malicious glance. 'You'd like us to be up to our ears in pigshit, and harvesting by hand with bloody scythes an' all, wouldn't you, 'cause it'd be more picturesque. You'd prefer the barns to be tumbling down, I bet. Same goes for us yokels. You'd rather we were piss-poor, probably, so we can look more like something out of a bloody painting.'

'That's not true!' cried Polly. 'Of course I don't want you to be poor.'

'Well, I'm not going to be. Charlotte wants me to be her manager, and she's offering me a bloody good whack. It'll be more cash than I've ever earned in my life, I can tell you.'

'But you won't be your own boss,' said Polly. 'You'll have lost your independence.'

'What's the point of being your own boss if you've gone bust, you turkey?' snapped Joe. 'And I'll be more independent if anything. Any time I've had enough I can say, "That's it, Charlotte, I'm buggering off at the end of the month, girl, so long." Couldn't do that with the farm round my neck, could I?'

'But she'll own it,' objected Polly, still clinging to her instinctive Hampstead dislike of the feudal system.

'You can't take it with you,' said Joe. 'Generations of them Fairfaxes in the churchyard, and what good is all their wealth to 'em now?'

'Yes, but all the same, they had jolly comfortable lives, thanks to their wealth. Unlike your ancestors, struggling night and day just to earn a crust.'

'Oh, don't give me all that commie stuff,' grumbled Joe. 'It never worked, did it? All those collective farms, everybody getting away with the minimum, riddled with corruption, a nod and a wink, useless bloody system, rotten to the core. No. Don't tell me everybody's the same. All men aren't equal. Nor all women. Some work their guts out, some just can't be bothered. You can't go on like that.'

'You always seem to know it all,' sighed Polly. 'You always treat me as if I'm stupid.'

'Well, now you *are* being stupid,' Joe leaned across the table and pressed her nose with a single finger, like someone pushing a button. 'A clever girl like you! You're the most intelligent woman I've ever met, for Christ's sake. Those programmes you wrote: *Skyscrapers*, wasn't it? And that one in the tailor's shop. Bloody marvellous, they were. I was thrilled to bits when I realised it was you who wrote them.'

'Were you really?' Polly felt pathetically pleased.

'If I seem to treat you a bit rough,' Joe lowered his voice, 'it's because you've got under my skin, see? Got under my defences. Not many people manage that. Makes me a bit uneasy.'

'Why uneasy?'

'Because I know I could get hurt.' He gave her a strange, shy little glance—rather like the ones he used to shoot her when they first met—and hid his face in his beerglass.

'But I won't hurt you!' she breathed. 'It's the very last thing in all the world that I'd dream of doing.'

'Ah, but I saw how you treated that Daniel bloke,' said Joe. 'Mind you, he was asking for it. But all the same . . .'

'Listen,' said Polly, desperate to reassure him, 'I won't treat you like that, not for a minute. I only treated him like that because he was rude about you.'

'You may like me now,' Joe mused. 'You may think I'm the bee's knees. But you'll get tired of me soon enough. I'm only a country boy, see? You're one of these sophisticates. You'll be ashamed of me when your friends come down.'

'No I won't!' creid Polly, strangely exhilarated because they seemed to be discussing some kind of future life together, even if she felt it slipping away before it had even had a chance to take shape. 'I'd be proud of you, you idiot!'

'Would you now,' he wondered, his brown eyes playing

speculatively over her. 'Would you really? I don't see it, myself.'

'Oh God,' Polly tossed her hair back off her brow in exasperation. 'At least let me buy you another drink.'

'Orange juice please, this time,' said Joe demurely. 'I'm driving.'

On her return to the table, Polly felt she wanted to turn the conversation away from this personal stalemate.

'So you're pleased with Charlotte's plans for the farm, then?' she asked, trying to keep her feelings out of her voice. She wasn't sure whether what she felt was contempt for Charlotte's Disneyfication of the countryside, or some kind of absurd jealousy that they were hatching plans which excluded her. Either way, the feelings were too ugly to let show.

'Well, what's the alternative?' asked Joe. 'It keeps the land more or less the way it ought to be—rural and undeveloped. It preserves areas of wild woodland, and the farm as it is, stays. But don't get it into your head that it could somehow go on being a working farm and only that, like it was in my dad's day. Because it can't. There's no going on farming if we can't get our prices.'

'But somehow that way of life was so perfect!' cried Polly.

'In the paintings, maybe. In the storybooks, yeah. But your pictures and your storybooks don't say anything about the sheer grind, the hard slog. Blokes so exhausted they'd fall asleep at their work, like I've done time out of mind in the lambing shed. You want to preserve something that never was, girl. You want a little glimpse of paradise. But if that's what you want, go off and write a bloody book about it. Go on—make it all up. That's your trade, after all, writing stories.'

'There's no need to sneer!'

'Blimey, keep your hair on. I'm not sneering, you turkey! I think it's marvellous. Nothing's so marvellous as a story, for Christ's sake. And another thing. My work depends on

255

so many things: the international economy, the state of nature, the weather, and it's changing all the time, changing, and a wise man changes with it, see? But you can sit down and write one of them stories and it can last for ever and ever. Somebody can pick that book up in three hundred years time and you can make 'em laugh and cry, just as if you're sittin' at the very same table with them, like you are now, with me. Whereas I'll be dead and gone and forgotten. The best I can hope for is a handsome yew tree to grow out of my bones.'

Polly was silent.

'You know,' she said after a moment, 'you're a bit of a poet, Joe. But still . . . I do think the farm is a paradise . . .'

'Specially for a child,' Joe agreed. 'So why can't these kiddies from town come for a week and enjoy theirselves? Why do you begrudge them that?'

'Oh, I don't know . . .' Polly hesitated. 'The thought of awful shrieking children running all over the place . . .'

'Not all kids are like your friend Gloria's,' observed Joe. 'She's made a pig's ear of hers all right, not that it can be easy, a girl like that on her own. I don't know what her old man's thinking of, all I can say is, he's let his kids get proper spoiled and it's his own bloody fault.'

'Gloria's got some strange ideas about child-rearing,' admitted Polly.

'But come on, you weren't a little horror like her lot, were you? Bet you were a solemn little thing. A bright little thing an' all. Did you have plaits?'

'Yes,' admitted Polly, blushing.

'Sweet! I can see you now,' Joe beamed at her, and Polly felt embarrassed but properly happy for the first time in the evening. 'With your little plaits and your satchel. Bless you. If we weren't in the pub I'd kiss your little nose for you right now.'

Polly was speechless with pleasure. The fact was, she had never been loved tenderly, as one loves a child. Not

256

since her own childhood—and even then, not much. There had been so much emphasis on good behaviour, the cuddles had been few and far between. Now her face glowed in his eyes.

'You look lovely tonight,' he whispered. 'Just wait till I get you in the back of my Land-Rover on the way home.'

Polly laughed foolishly.

'The back of your Land-Rover! 'I'd like to see you try.'

'Ha! You'll be a pushover, mate,' said Joe, draining his orange juice. And Polly knew it was true.

'The trouble is,' she admitted at length, 'I don't really know what to do with children. I've always been a bit afraid of them, I think. Being an only child. I've got no nephews or nieces or god-children or anything. They just seem to be, well, wild and awful and rather frightening.'

'What you need,' said Joe, looking directly into her eyes, 'is one of your own.'

Polly was caught on his eyes like barbed wire, for several minutes.

Out in the car park, the sky was clear. They looked up at the millions of stars.

'There's the Plough.' Joe pointed it out. 'And there's Venus.'

'Ah, Venus,' sighed Polly, half to herself. 'She's got a lot to answer for.'

Staring up at the wheeling universe she felt giddy for a moment, leaned against Joe and felt his strong arm encircle her.

'It makes me feel completely insignificant,' she murmured. 'It's as if we don't exist.'

Joe slapped her on the bum.

'Get into that Land-Rover,' he grinned, 'and on the way home we'll stop for half an hour in Water Lane and I'll convince you we exist, all right.'

257

Chapter  Forty-three

Polly tip-toed up to door of the Bothy and tapped lightly on it. She heard faint movements within.

'Charley!' she called softly. 'It's Polly!'

Her heart beat faster. She did not know quite what to expect. But when Charley opened the door, he looked almost normal. A little thinner, maybe: paler, certainly. But the smile was no less radiant, the manner no less welcoming.

'I've brought you some flowers,' said Polly, thrusting a huge bunch of daffodils and narcissi into his arms. 'And some fruit. And some books. Funny books. Clive James and Dorothy Parker.'

'Oh good!' Charley seized them gratefully. 'I love them both. Thank you so much. You are a darling.'

He reached out his hand and touched her sleeve, and Polly, consumed with a sudden desperate tenderness, threw her arms around his neck and hugged him.

'I'm sorry,' she sniffed, as the embrace dissolved, 'only I felt so—so awful when Joe told me about it all. How—how are you today?'

'Today is OK,' said Charley emphatically, and squeezed her arm. Then he turned towards the kitchen. 'Some tea? And some cake? Charlotte brought me a Lemon Drizzle cake from the WI stall.'

'Oh yes please! But—can you manage? Can I help?'

'You could arrange these flowers,' said Charley. 'I'm not

much use at flower arranging. I majored in tatting and lace-making at the Ladies' College, you know,' he giggled, and presented her with a big earthenware jar. 'Oh, and How to Fascinate a Diplomat.'

'Have you fascinated many diplomats?' asked Polly, glad to find him in such good spirits.

'I once had terribly exciting cocktails with the Cultural Attaché from Botswana.'

A strange, semi-hysterical snort of laughter burst from Polly's lips.

Charley filled the kettle and lit the Calor Gas, and carefully laid a tray for tea. He took one of the daffodils and placed it in a small vase on the tray.

'Tea for Two,' he sang suddenly, tap-dancing for a moment. 'And Two for Tea—wait a minute, I'm overdoing it, I'll have to sit down for a minute. I'm sorry.' He threw himself down on the sofa. Polly hovered anxiously. Behind them, the kettle sang. The fire crackled. Charley, who had gone ghastly white, gradually recovered his colour. Polly knelt beside the sofa and took his hand.

'Do you need anything?' she whispered.

'No, it's all right. I just must remember that my cabaret days are over. In fact,' Charley took a deep breath and sat up: Polly withdrew to a nearby chair, 'these new pills are amazing. It gives one hope, you know. I feel almost normal today.'

'You look better now. A better colour.'

Charley grinned. 'Do I? Isn't it a drag, though, being white. I've always wished I was an African. But most of all I'd like to be emerald green with jade accessories.'

'What accessories do you mean, exactly?'

Charley laughed. 'Can't say in mixed company! But the Green Man—that's what I'd like to be.'

'Well, you're the greenest man I've ever met.'

'Have you seen him carved in some of the old churches around here?'

'Who? The Green Man?'

'Yes. There's one at Nether Swell. Extraordinary, really, isn't it? A pagan divinity like him popping his naughty head up in a Christian church.'

'What's he like?'

'He's got a beard, and there are sort of branches growing out of his mouth. You can't really tell where the flesh ends and the leaves begin. It's lovely. You must get Joe to take you.'

Polly blushed. Luckily the kettle boiled and she got up to deal with it. Charley put a new log on the fire whilst she brought the tray.

'Thanks. Lovely. Who's going to be Mother?'

The question hung in the air for a moment. A teasing look played about Charley's eyes. Polly smiled.

'I don't mind being Mother if all I have to do is pour the tea.'

They settled to the teatime rituals. The cake was particularly delicious.

'Who made it?' asked Polly.

'Oh, Vera, I think. Miss Whitworth.'

'The one who wears football boots?'

'Yes. Ever so dykey, isn't she? Cooks like an angel, though.'

'I remember she came to my talk on Catherine the Great,' said Polly. 'She kept making subversive remarks.'

'Yes, that would be Vera,' smiled Charley, pursuing the last lemony crumbs around his plate.

Satisfied, and sipping their tea, they both stared into the flames. Polly felt more relaxed, now that she had understood Charley's mood. He was not morbid or depressed—or at least, did not seem to show it, if he was. Polly's heart was convulsed with sympathy for him, but he did not seem to want affection, at the moment. He seemed to want her to be brisk and witty.

'I must say,' he roused himself at length, 'I'm delighted to hear that you're going to be staying on.'

'Well, I felt the call,' Polly smiled ruefully. 'To be a shepherdess. Like Marie Antoinette.'

'You know where you'll end up,' said Charley playfully. 'On someone's mantelpiece, all in porcelain, wearing a sprigged muslin gown.'

'Sounds all right,' said Polly, helping herself to more cake, although aware that her jeans were tighter than they were wont to be.

'No really—I am glad.' Charley's voice deepened into sincerity. 'I'm so glad Joe's found someone like you. You won't let him down, will you? He's very easily hurt.'

Polly felt a great wall of tears rise in her throat. She rammed them down again, hard.

'I won't,' she faltered. 'I promise.'

'If you do, I'll come back and haunt you,' said Charley mischievously. 'I'll hurl things about and blow the smoke the wrong way down the chimney. And I'll get the black-birds to dive-bomb the windows.'

'I promise, I promise!' Polly laughed, glad he had deftly changed the tone to a light banter, though behind it lay hidden sadness beyond words.

'I think you'll do him good,' said Charley, serious again. 'And I think he'll teach you a lot, too.'

'He has already,' admitted Polly.

'He's not a bad old thing.' Charley looked at the fire again, his lip trembling slightly. 'I like to think of him being taken care of.'

'I will,' promised Polly, and the moment had a strange solemnity.

Charley stared into the fire for a few minutes in silence.

'I don't want fire, when I go,' he said suddenly. 'I want earth.'

Polly realised, with a qualm, that he was talking about cremation and burial.

'I'd like to do without a coffin, really, altogether, but I don't expect they'd allow it. Much better just to be laid in earth, naked, and let things really get cracking.'

Polly could not speak.

'And I'd like a tree planted on top of me,' he went on. 'A rowan. Because they're so romantic and graceful. And I'd be crowned with flowers in spring and filled with birds in autumn. Nibbling at my berries, greedy little devils.' He managed to make it sound flirtatious, somehow.

'So you will be the Green Man, then,' said Polly quietly. Charley looked back at her, direct and brave, dry eyed, the firelight glittering on his face and hair.

'That's what I want. See to it, please, will you, Polly?'

'I will,' Polly replied.

Chapter  Forty-four

Polly floated on her back and looked up through the
hanging plants to the white pillars of the Sanctuary. She
was back, albeit briefly, in Covent Garden. Fiona trod water
beside her, her expression of astonishment somehow
emphasised by the flakes of light thrown upwards by the
water.

'You're joking!'

'I'm not.'

'Sheep farming?'

'Why not?'

'Aren't you going to write any more, then?'

'Oh, I'll do *Cold Comfort Farm*, of course. Then I think I'll
take a few months off and see how things go. I expect I'll
still write a bit.'

Fiona shook her head in disbelief. A few drops of water
still clung to her fiery curls, making her look like an
outraged mermaid.

'And this—what's his name—Joe?'

'Yes?'

'Well, are you sure you're not being a little bit reckless,
Polly?'

'Oh yes. I mean, I'm sure I'm being reckless.' Polly
laughed, and ducked her face under water briefly—something she never used to like to do. When she surfaced
again, the water ran off her face in little rills of tickling light.
Polly laughed again. 'It's wonderful!'

'But—what's he like?'

Polly hesitated. What could she say about him? She remembered all his beauties, and best of all, his big feet and crooked nose.

'Oh he's, well, an ordinary bloke.'

'But Polly! You don't need an ordinary bloke! You'd be too deep for him! He'd never fathom you out!'

'Ah, you're wrong there,' said Polly. 'He's the one that's too deep for me.'

'But really! Surely you'd never be happy with a man who wasn't an intellectual?'

Polly smiled to herself at Fiona's Scots scepticism—a great philosophical tradition, of course.

'What I worry about,' she murmured eventually, 'is whether *I'm* intelligent enough for *him*.'

'Och, don't be daft!'

'No really.'

'What's he look like?' Fiona's voice dropped to a sensational whisper.

'Tall dark and handsome, of course! With big feet and double-jointed hands. And a crooked nose.'

'Ah!' Fiona appeared to understand. 'He's physically enthralled you! I can see it! You lucky thing! Is he all rough and primitive with you in bed?' Fiona's words echoed excitingly above the heads of other clients who were eating their lunch nearby.

'Not at all,' smiled Polly very quietly. 'He's very gentle, actually. And I've never been to bed with him yet. Not actually a real bed. It's all been, well . . . barns, and the back of the Land-Rover.'

'Ah!' Fiona pounced again. 'I see. Terribly romantic and a bit secret, eh?'

'Oh yes,' Polly hugged herself. 'A total cliché really.'

'What are his worst points?' demanded Fiona.

'Oh, that's easy,' said Polly at once. 'He's suspicious and puritanical, and it's terribly hard to get him to come out of his shell. And if I so much as looked at another man he'd probably thrash me soundly.'

'He sounds like the total opposite of Dan,' pondered Fiona. 'Are you sure this isn't just a rebound thing, Polly? And chucking everything up here, and going to live with him and help him out on the farm too . . . aren't you putting a terrible strain on the relationship? I mean, you haven't known him very long, have you?'

'Not long,' agreed Polly. 'But I don't care.'

Fiona shook her head sagely. 'Oh dear. It looks like you're madly in love.'

'Oh yes, absolutely.'

Fiona regarded her gravely. 'I'm worried about you, Polly,' she said. 'I thought you had life all worked out. And here you are turning everything upside down. Last time we were here—it's only a couple of months ago, surely—you seemed so happy with Daniel and, well, your whole life, really, I mean—I just hope, in the cold light of day, this doesn't all go horribly wrong.'

'Do you think it'll go horribly wrong, then?' asked Polly in a moment of anxiety.

'Well, it all sounds a bit too good to be true, you know. In real life, I mean. In a story, OK, you'd marry him and have honeysuckle growing up round your eaves and you'd be happy together for ever and ever. I just hope you don't wake up one day to find you've cast yourself as the female lead in the wrong story.'

'Oh well,' said Polly, striking off lazily on her back, 'if I do, you can always say I Told You So.'

'What do your parents think about it?' asked Fiona, swimming beside her.

'I'm going to see them this afternoon,' said Polly, not without a slight submarine qualm. 'I expect they'll be all right about it.'

'Are you sure?' persisted Fiona.

'Well, my mother can't really object,' Polly pointed out. 'She brought me up to be adventurous.'

'You're mad!' Kathleen Partridge's eyes flared. She turned to her husband. 'Tell her she mustn't, Gordon!'

Polly's father got his pipe out and sucked it ruminatively. He made no remark. As a scientist he was all too aware of the futility of grappling with the natural rampaging energies of volcanoes, hurricanes, earthquakes or women.

'Daddy knows I'm thirty-four, Mum,' smiled Polly. 'And I can sell my own flat if I want to.'

'Yes, but you're burning your boats, darling!' wailed Mrs Partridge, her teacake cooling, forgotten, on the dainty china plate. 'You must keep a toehold in London!'

'Why?' demanded Polly. Her carefully cultivated calm was beginning to crack.

'Well, house prices—I mean, once you've got out of London, you'll never get back!'

'Good,' said Polly. 'That suits me fine.'

'You'll regret it. I'm amazed at you, Polly. A cultured, educated girl like you. The concerts, the films, the theatre— the Peking Opera!' Her mother shrieked, snatching at straws. Although that was a metaphor she would have found particularly tactless. Straw was something Mrs Partridge would rather not think about, especially now.

'Remember how you adored the Peking Opera!'

'She could still go to the Peking Opera, Kathleen,' observed Polly's father mildly. 'Whenever they came. She could come up to town and stay with us.'

'Of course I could!' Polly was grateful for her father's timid support. 'Why are you being so silly about it? I mean, for goodness' sake, I might have been going to Peking! What if I was planning to go off and work round the other side of the world? In Sydney or something?'

'Right,' affirmed her father. 'Desmond's daughter went off to live in Peru, remember, Kathleen.'

266

'I'd probably be able to see a lot more of you, in fact,' Polly argued, aware that this was not really the point, but ploughing on. 'I'd probably want to stay whenever I was in town. It would be lovely.'

Mrs Partridge sniffed, reluctant to acknowledge the least advantage in Polly's selling her Hampstead flat and going to live on a dunghill. She broke her teacake into pieces in an absent-minded way, not looking at what she was doing.

'I'm sure I can't keep up with you,' she complained. 'Finishing with that lovely Daniel—you'll never find a better man than him, Polly, mark my words – ' Polly bit her tongue. 'And now this crazy idea! Sheep farming! I've never heard anything so ridiculous!'

'Someone's got to look after the sheep,' observed her husband mildly.

'But it doesn't have to be someone who's been to St Paul's Girls' School, Gordon! Or Oxford University!'

'But it doesn't matter if they have, surely,' he persisted. Polly sipped her tea and watched them. 'I mean, if it's what Polly wants to do, why not? If she gets fed up with it she can always come back.'

'Not if she's sold her flat she can't!'

'I shan't want to come back and live in London, anyway,' said Polly. 'I'm pretty sure of that. If I do get tired of it, I can always move on. I might like to live in a provincial town or something.'

'But there's no culture in the country!' cried Mrs Partridge. 'That's what I can't understand. A girl like you. Where would you be without your culture?'

'That's hogwash, Kathleen.' Gordon Partridge suddenly knocked out his pipe on the ashtray. His wife, startled by this sudden self-assertion on his part, stared. 'What about your sister's place? Newton Parsloe. There's the most tremendous culture going on. Concerts and dances and goodness knows what.'

'The fact is, Mum,' said Polly, 'you seem to think there's

nothing worth seeing or doing outside London. Well, I've discovered there is!'

'And we can always go down there,' her father urged. 'I bet it's lovely down there in the summer, Kathleen. I expect she could put us up, couldn't you, Polly?'

'Of course I could, Dad!' Polly cried. 'And it's the loveliest valley, and the most beautiful farmhouse. You'll love it, Mum—honestly.' Mrs Partridge shuddered.

'It's an awful thing, when you can see that your only daughter is making a big mistake,' she sighed, taking up her embroidery and shaking her head. 'Ah well. You won't get me down there in a hurry, that's all I can say.'

Chapter  Forty-five

'Grandma! Can you mend my dolly's dress, please? The popper's come off.'

'Bring it here, sweetheart.' Kathleen Partridge caressed her granddaughter's dark curls before inspecting the doll's clothes. At last here was a child with proper hair. Very different from the way Polly's lank and mousey locks had been. How she'd struggled, all those years ago, with the curlers, trying to give Polly the Shirley Temple look. But in vain. Luckily little Midge took after her father. Mrs Partridge smiled down into Midge's huge brown eyes.

'Eyes like chocolate drops, you've got, little Midge. Fetch Mummy's needlework basket for me, darling.'

Kathleen Partridge looked out of the window and down the valley. The trees tossed their full summer skirts about: it was a day of blazing sun and playful gusts of wind. The child returned with the needlework box, passing through a sunbeam.

'It's a lovely breezy day, isn't it, lovey? Grandpa's windmills will be whizzing round like nobody's business.' She threaded the needle, proud that she could still do so without glasses. Midge leaned on the arm of her grandmother's chair, her breath playing around the old woman's neck like the smell of strawberries.

'You are clever, Grandma,' she said, watching the dextrous fingers sew the new popper on. 'And you've got lovely hands.'

There was a knock at the kitchen door. Kathleen sighed, put down her sewing, and got up.

'Sometimes,' she observed to the child, 'it's worse than Piccadilly Circus round here.'

A woman stood at the door, with a young boy, a year or so older than Midge, at her side.

'Mrs Swain?' she asked. Mrs Partridge shook her head.

'My daughter's just upstairs. Midge, go and fetch Mummy.' The child ran off.

'Come in,' said Kathleen Partridge, and the woman stepped inside the kitchen.

'How lovely!' she exclaimed. 'What a perfect country kitchen. You are lucky.'

'Well, it's my daughter's kitchen really, of course. We don't actually live here, my husband and I. Just visiting. Although we're thinking of buying a little cottage in the village. My husband's got very involved with these windmills.'

'Ah—I think we may have seen him. Andrew was talking to a man up by the windmills. Weren't you, darling? A tall distinguished-looking chap, smoking a pipe?'

Kathleen looked pleased.

'I wouldn't say distinguished,' she smiled. 'Dotty, more like.' Polly appeared carrying an armful of dirty bed linen. She dumped it on the table and smiled at the newcomer. Midge hung back behind her, inspecting the boy shyly.

'Hello,' said Polly. 'I'm Mrs Swain.'

'Ah—well, we've just arrived. The party from Ashcroft School. My husband did all the bookings and things. Buckridge is the name.'

'Yes of course,' Polly smiled. 'Would you like a cup of tea?'

'Thanks, but I think I'd better get back—give Paul and Diane a hand, you know. Settling them in.'

'Twelve-year-olds, I think your husband said?'

'That's right.' Mrs Buckridge pulled a face. 'The girls are

270

all right—little women, most of them. But some of the boys are terrors. Thank God I'm not a teacher.'

'And this must be your son.'

'Yes. Andrew.'

'Hello, Andrew,' said Polly. 'This is my daughter Midge. How old are you?'

'Thixth,' said Andrew through a fetching gap in his teeth.

'I'm nearly six!' cried Midge. 'Aren't I, Mummy?'

'Well, you're six next birthday,' said Polly, rumpling her child's curls. 'But that's not for another ten months. Why don't you take Andrew and feed the hens?'

The children shot out together, leaving the door open. Stray strands of honeysuckle gallivanted in their wake.

'I'm so glad there's a child Andrew's age here,' said Mrs Buckridge.

'It'll be nice for Midge, too,' agreed Polly. 'She gets a bit lonely sometimes. Especially in winter.'

'Well, you know the remedy, love,' said her mother, biting off a thread. 'Plenty of room for another grandchild on my lap. I'm only seventy, you know. There's a few years of babysitting left in me, yet.'

Polly laughed. 'Is everything all right down at the barn?' she asked, although she was sure it was. She had seen to it herself, and enjoyed making it immaculate.

'Oh yes, thank you—lovely. Thanks for putting up that little spare bed in our room. And the flowers everywhere! It was a marvellous welcome. I just brought you the milk order.' Mrs Buckridge placed a piece of paper on the table. 'And we weren't quite sure about the cooker. I can't get the oven to come on. I'm hopeless with dials and things.'

Polly explained the mysteries of the cooker, and Mrs Buckridge jotted them down.

There was something about her attitude as she wrote: the bent head, the slope of her shoulders, which rang a faint bell in Polly's memory.

'Thank you,' said Mrs Buckridge, snapping the top back on her pen. She prepared to go.

'Excuse me,' faltered Polly, 'but—haven't we met before?'

Mrs Buckridge looked astonished.

'I don't think so. I've never been to this part of the world before.'

'Your face is so familiar . . .' Polly mused, but could not force her mind reliably back into the far-off days of BM— Before Midge. The scrupulous indexes and archives of her social network were all overgrown, now, and rusting.

Mrs Buckridge laughed in a faintly embarrassed way. She evidently didn't recognise Polly, and wanted to be gone.

'Well,' she suggested, making for the door, 'perhaps you'll remember, sometime this week. Maybe it'll come to you in the middle of the night.'

'I've got it!' Polly cried suddenly. 'I remember now! Didn't you come and interview me once, years ago? When I lived in London?'

'Interview you? Why . . .' Mrs Buckridge looked blank. She stared at Polly, but no flicker of recognition dawned in her eyes.

'You did! I'm sure it was you. You were pregnant—with Andrew, of course! You had to keep eating bananas all the time to stop yourself fainting.'

A strange, hesitant half-light crept into Mrs Buckridge's face.

'I'm Polly Partridge,' Polly went on. 'You know. I used to write for TV. *Skyscrapers. A Bit of Needle. Cold Comfort Farm.* I lived in Hampstead then.'

Lynn Smythe—for it was she—simply stared. Her jaw dropped.

'Are you really?' she faltered. 'No, that's stupid. Of course you are. Good God. I would never have recognised you. Well – ' she added hastily. 'I would never have expected to find you here.'

'No, well, quite.' Polly pushed the hair out of her eyes,

self-conscious for a moment. She glanced down at her ensemble: torn T-shirt, baggy trousers. 'And the fact is, I've got fat.'

'No, you haven't!'

'Yes I have. I've put on over a stone since I had Midge. I just can't get rid of it.'

'Never mind, dear,' said her mother, putting on the kettle. 'You know Joe likes it. He says he likes a woman cuddly. Have you met my son-in-law yet, Mrs Buckridge?'

'Not yet.'

'He's gorgeous. Well, I think so, anyway. But then, I'm biased.'

'Well,' said Lynn Smythe. 'Fancy meeting you again like this. I'm sorry I didn't recognise you. But – '

'It's all right,' said Polly. 'I've gone grey, too. You haven't changed, though. In fact, you look younger.'

Lynn Smythe gave her hair a rueful little tug.

'All out of a bottle,' she grinned. 'Well. I must be going.' She paused in the doorway. 'You've certainly found your little corner of Paradise,' she said. 'I envy you.'

'How extraordinary,' mused Polly, after she had gone. 'Meeting her again like that. After all this time.'

'What was this piece she wrote on you, dear? Was it good?'

'I never saw it,' said Polly. 'I expect she made it all up. Still, as long as it was a good read, what does it matter?'

That night, Polly undressed and examined herself in the big looking-glass in the bedroom. No wonder Lynn Smythe hadn't recognised her. She was much plumper, and almost totally grey. Her belly, stretched by pregnancy, now hung slackly, like a ball of dough. She was forty, and a mother, and she looked it.

An owl hooted outside, and wind stirred unseen leaves in the dark. She heard her husband's quiet step on the carpet behind her.

'What a pretty sight.'

His face appeared above her shoulder, and his dark hairy arms encircled her waist.

'Do you know,' pondered Polly, 'that woman—the teacher's wife—Lynn, her name is—she interviewed me when I lived in London. Just before I came here. And she didn't recognise me! Well, I suppose it's not surprising. I'm almost completely grey. It's awful.'

'Oh no, it's not.' Joe turned from their reflection and kissed her neck. 'Grey's the most beautiful colour,' he whispered, nuzzling against her earlobe. 'It's the colour of thistledown. And doves. And the mist.'

Tears came into Polly's eyes. 'You don't mind, then?'

'Mind? Daft wench. I love your grey hair. And your knock knees. And your goofy teeth.'

He clasped her naked body to his. Polly relaxed into his familiar warm strength, and felt all her anxiety float away on the rising tide of his breath.

Chapter  Forty-six

'The tree's bigger than me, now!'

Midge stood on tip-toe but the flickering leaves of the rowan had grown beyond her.

'It'll be bigger than me, next year,' said Polly, on her knees and weeding.

'Can I help you, Mummy?'

'Yes, love. These leaves are the violets, and these are the primroses. Those are weeds. And those.'

Midge weeded for a couple of minutes, and then got bored.

'It's not fair!' she moaned. 'My godfather's dead.' Polly sighed. 'Tania's godfather took her to the ice rink.'

'Charley couldn't help dying, darling.'

'But it's not fair!'

'No,' agreed Polly. 'It's not.'

'Why did he die?'

'He got ill. Some people do, sweetheart.'

'You won't die, will you?'

Midge grabbed her mother round the neck with desperate passion.

'Not unless you strangle me!'

The child laughed, then squatted down and started to make a face with pieces of gravel and earth.

'What was Charley like, Mummy?'

'You remember him, don't you?'

'I remember him on the sofa playing cards with me.

275

And upstairs in bed. Was he nice, Mummy? Did he like me?'

'He was a lovely man. And he adored you. He had a face—well, like an angel.'

'And now he *is* an angel!'

Midge's face exploded in revelation. She jumped up.

'Don't tread on the violets,' warned Polly mildly.

'But Mummy—I've just realised. It's a good job Charley's dead!'

'Why's that?'

'Well, he's with God, isn't he? And he's an angel with all the other angels. And he's my God father. So he can talk to God about me. Can't he?'

'So he can,' said Polly, marvelling at the way the child found consolations for herself among the stars and the echoes of old songs.

'So it's all right after all. I'm going to make a face like Charley. What colour was his hair, Mum?'

'Golden.'

'I'll get some of those leaves, then, for his hair.' She ran off and ransacked a nearby privet.

Maisie came into the churchyard carrying a bunch of flowers, and greeted Midge with a hug. She waved to Polly, and then, with much wheezing and straining, got down on her knees and started to arrange the blooms.

'Cor, Len, we ent arf at sixes and sevens over this holiday lark,' she confided to the grave. Midge glanced at her mother and giggled. Maisie talking to the dead was a familiar sight.

'Fred wants to go to the Wye Valley, you know how he loves all them castles and stuff, but all Bert wants to do is go down the Oval for the bleedin' Test Match. I told him straight, I said Bert if you think Fred and I are going to sit through five days of them blokes hitting balls about you've got another think coming. Mind you – '

276

Maisie leaned back on her heels for a moment and eased her fallen bra straps back up her huge arms.

' – it seems a shame reelly, to spoil his fun, I mean, it's harmless reelly, cricket, ent it? I mean, what if he was always on the booze and knocked me about? To tell you the truth, Len, I think we'll leave it till the week after. Vera did say she could do the shop for me then and I don't know why Fred's got it into his head that we've got to go on the nineteenth, but you know what he's like when he's got a bee in his bonnet. I'm at my wits' end, sometimes, trying to keep 'em both quiet, you know.

'Tell you what I fancy, though. I fancy a week in Brighton. On that nudie beach. What! Think of Bert in the buff, eh?' A peal of laughter rang out among the tombs. 'Frighten them to death, he would.

'The best holiday I ever had was when you took me to Derbyshire. Remember? Remember that petrifying well thing in—where was it—Matlock. Where all that water dripping down turned things to stone. And you said – ' Maisie keeled over sideways in another paroxysm of mirth. 'You said, "If I stuck John Thomas under that drip, how long d'ye think it would take him to turn to stone?" You are a one, Len.

'And remember them tarts we had in Bakewell? Makes me mouth water just to think of them. Christ, what tarts. Oh well. Those were the days.'

Maisie fell into a reverie, picking her nose.

'Mummy?'

'Yes?'

'Andrew's going home on Saturday isn't he?

'Yes. Never mind.'

'He lives in London.'

'I know.'

'He says there's a big bouncy castle there. In the park. Can we go?'

'One day.'

'Why not today?'

'I can't just drop everything and take you to London, darling! It's miles and miles away.'

'But I want to go to London. I've never ever been!'

'But you've been to London masses of times. Every time we go to see Grandma.'

'But that's Finchley!'

'Finchley is London. Part of London.'

'I want to go on the bouncy castle.'

'You went on the bouncy castle at Sedgeworth fête.'

'That was last year!'

'No it wasn't. It was in May. Only a couple of months ago.'

'But I want to go to London!'

'We will go,' Polly cuddled her. 'I promise. I'll take you to Harrod's.'

She wouldn't mind a nostalgic little amble through Knightsbridge. She could get her hair done, maybe buy a new outfit. Take herself in hand a bit. Lynn Smythe's slim figure and sleek dark hair had been a reproach to Polly, somehow. But a trip to the city would never restore her lost youth. Polly sighed. Now she supposed the taxis would all zoom by ignoring her, and the traffic be fierce and frightening, and herself dusty and provincial with a headache coming on.

'What's Harrod's?'

'A big shop.'

'It sounds frightening.'

Well actually, thought Polly, it is. In a way. You have to live up to Harrod's. Like everything else in London. That was what was so nice about Long Dangley. It enabled you to live down.

Maisie picked up her basket and waddled over to them. She gave Midge a toffee out of her apron pocket.

'Hello, darlin'!' She smiled. 'I see your friend Gloria's moving out, then, Polly?'

'Yes,' Polly sighed. 'She says teenagers need towns.'

'What, to wreck, like? I wouldn't put it past that Sky: she's a terror.'

Sky had burst into a furious adolescence that threatened all living creatures within half a mile. Polly was glad her own child was still young, and more or less contented to be living in the country—Nature's adventure playground.

'I don't like Sky,' said Midge. 'She gave me a Chinese burn.'

'I heard a rumour,' hinted Maisie slyly, 'that your folks was thinkin' of movin' down here.'

'Yes. They are.'

'Maybe they could buy Gloria's cottage, then.'

'They may well. They've looked at it.'

'Be nice for you, wouldn't it? Havin' your mum just down the road.'

'Yes. Lovely.'

'Tired of London, are they?'

'I think they are. Surprisingly enough.' Polly got to her feet. 'And they want to be near Midge. To watch her grow up. And of course it'll be lovely for Midge, too.'

'Yeah.'

Maisie looked at Charley's gravestone and ran a finger lovingly across the top of it, like someone sweeping crumbs off a table.

'Cruel, wasn't it?' she murmured. 'A lovely man like that, an' all. It were wonderful what you done for him, though. Looking after him like that, right to the end.'

'Oh no,' said Polly. 'It was nothing.'

Polly and Midge walked home across the fields. Her mother had borrowed the car to visit Joyce Lillicrap. They were hatching some plot to do with glee singing and the WI.

'What do you think heaven's like, Mummy?'

'I don't know,' Polly thought for a while. 'I think it must be rather like diving through waterfalls.'

'Hooray! I hope I die soon!'

A shudder engulfed Polly's soul, and she held her daughter's small hand very tight. Once love had opened you up, you were helpless. Like a chicken who dreads seeing in the moonlight the terrible flash of a fox's teeth.

They passed through a gate and out into a lane. Sir Antony Fairfax rolled towards them in a motorised wheelchair, attended by an enormous and impassive blonde girl.

'Ah! The nymphs o'the field!' cried Sir Antony. 'Give an old satyr a kiss on the cheek, you imp!'

Midge obeyed, shyly.

'My Great Dane is taking me for a walk,' observed Sir Antony. 'Good morning! We are bound for the Elysian Fields!'

They rolled off with Sir Antony talking to the hedges as he went: reproaching them for being so tall.

As Polly and Midge climbed the hill to their house, distant cries broke out in the green stillness, and echoed around them. It was the sound of children's laughter.

'They're rolling down the slope!' cried Midge. 'Can I go too, Mummy?'

Polly nodded.

The warm little hand slipped out of her grasp. A great wave of tenderness flooded up through the soles of Polly's feet, as if it came out of the earth. It surged through her and seemed to explode out of her head and encompass the birds and the clouds, the trees and the distant planets. Her daughter ran off up ahead, and vanished round a bend in the lane.

A Selected List of Fiction Available from Mandarin

While every effort is made to keep prices low, it is sometimes necessary to increase prices at short notice. Mandarin Paperbacks reserves the right to show new retail prices on covers which may differ from those previously advertised in the text or elsewhere.

The prices shown below were correct at the time of going to press.

☐	7493 0576 2	**Tandia**	Bryce Courtenay £4.99
☐	7493 0122 8	**Power of One**	Bryce Courtenay £4.99
☐	7493 0581 9	**Daddy's Girls**	Zoe Fairbairns £4.99
☐	7493 0942 3	**Silence of the Lambs**	Thomas Harris £4.99
☐	7493 0530 4	**Armalite Maiden**	Jonathan Kebbe £4.99
☐	7493 0134 1	**To Kill a Mockingbird**	Harper Lee £3.99
☐	7493 1017 0	**War in 2020**	Ralph Peters £4.99
☐	7493 0946 6	**Godfather**	Mario Puzo £4.99
☐	7493 0381 6	**Loves & Journeys of Revolving Jones**	Leslie Thomas £4.99
☐	7493 0381 6	**Rush**	Kim Wozencraft £4.99

All these books are available at your bookshop or newsagent, or can be ordered direct from the publisher. Just tick the titles you want and fill in the form below.

Mandarin Paperbacks, Cash Sales Department, PO Box 11, Falmouth, Cornwall TR10 9EN.

Please send cheque or postal order, no currency, for purchase price quoted and allow the following for postage and packing:

UK including BFPO	£1.00 for the first book, 50p for the second and 30p for each additional book ordered to a maximum charge of £3.00.
Overseas including Eire	£2 for the first book, £1.00 for the second and 50p for each additional book thereafter.

NAME (Block letters) ....

ADDRESS..

....

☐ I enclose my remittance for ....

☐ I wish to pay by Access/Visa Card Number ☐☐☐☐☐☐☐☐☐☐☐☐☐☐☐☐

Expiry Date ☐☐☐☐